*The Daughter of the Pangaran*

DAVID DIVINE

# The Daughter
of the Pangaran

LITTLE, BROWN AND COMPANY · BOSTON · TORONTO

PRINTED IN THE UNITED STATES OF AMERICA

# Contents

# Historical Note

ALEXANDER HARE was perhaps the most colourful, as he was unquestionably the most picaresque, of all the band of adventurers who accompanied Stamford Raffles to the seizure of Batavia. This novel follows precisely the salient features of his remarkable career. He did attempt singlehanded war against the Dutch. He did maintain endless quarrels subsequently with the Dutch and the Batavian Governments, the East India Company, the Cape Government, and the home Government. Through all this he developed and added to the most astonishing harem that any of the British 'nabobs' ever established, and he did transport it about the world in defiance of the new antislavery laws. He was a rumbustious character cut from the whole cloth.

The Clunies-Ross brothers were lesser figures of the time, but in their own way equally picturesque. Whaling men, they changed to other ways of sea life but retained the traditional adventurousness of their first trade. The clash at Cocos Keeling broke what had been a long and intimate relationship, and the moral attitudes developed by John Clunies-Ross in the course of the subsequent quarrels are odd reading, for he was fully implicated in everything that Hare did in Borneo and was almost equally unpopular with the Governments.

None of the authorities, who tried from time to time, was able to crush Hare and it was left to the young Scottish artisans, brought to Cocos Keeling by Ross, to accomplish what even the East India Company failed to do.

BOOK ONE

# THE SHIP

# *One*

THE WIDE, out-thrust walls of the gateway were incandescent in the blaze of the afternoon sun. From the lion's head on the eastern curve a jet of water leapt down to the circular basin, flecked with still more brilliant facets of light. Three ring-doves sat on the splashed rim of the basin, two of them close together and companionate, one apprehensive and apart. The fountain on the western wall of the gateway was blocked as usual. Only a trickle of water crept down the wall, adding to the wide virescent stain on the snow-white plaster. The monogram of the Dutch East India Company was defaced but still legible, as if the tolerant English had half decided to continue the Company's customs here at the Cape.

Beyond the gate the tunnel of the oaks began, dark, cool, and, from where the three women sat, endless. Through the screen of the oaks they could see one corner of the Governor's house. Above the oaks and beyond them rose the mountain, olive-green on its lower slopes and then sheer, austere, and unsculptured blue.

The man approached the gates as if defying them to close against him. His carriage was arrogant and angry. The sun winked on the great brass buttons above the tails of the long coat. His buff trousers had a wide, sea-flavoured air. The white froth of an elaborate stock showed above the collar of the coat. The hat was unduly curled and its angle too was arrogant.

He walked in fury.

The three women watched him. The central one of the three was enormous. The arms that rested on the supports of the great stink-wood chair on which she sat were like legs of the fat-tailed Cape sheep; her breasts like Kaffir melons. Her body ballooned in enormous, uncontrolled curves, but her head was small and her features improbably delicate.

She said: 'I've never seen him so angry.'

The elder of the other two—the third was only a girl—said: 'The Governor has sent for him. Perhaps it is to tell him to go.'

The fat woman disregarded her. 'I've never seen him so angry,' she repeated. 'There will be a battle.' She quivered pleasurably with anticipation.

'Lord Charles will not fight.' The other woman's voice had a rasp in it. 'He cannot forget to be an aristocrat. Five times now he has told him to go.'

'With this one it is necessary to do more than tell him.' The fat one strained her neck as far as it would go, following the progress of the man.

'Why should he go now?' asked the girl. 'He has been here six years—'

'Seven,' the fat woman interrupted. 'He came first in eighteen-nineteen, the year before the settlers.'

The second woman said viciously: 'Because the scandal has grown beyond bounds. So long as it was the Malay and the Chinese women only it might not have mattered, but last month there was the Zulu girl that the Portuguese brought down from the Natal coast and . . .' She hesitated.

The fat woman demanded: 'And what?'

'This is in secret.' She made an enormous play around the words, giving them significance. 'My husband would be rightly furious. Yesterday there was an affair with the Indiaman that came in from China—something to do with a young girl, a child, a Malay child. I do not know all of it. It is, in fact, for that that the Governor has sent for him.'

The girl said, her senses pleasantly titillated: 'He is a monstrous man.'

The fat woman said majestically: 'At least he is a man. He is . . .' She paused, searching for the just comparison: 'He is more than a man. He is a—kudu bull.' She sighed, thinking at once of her shrivelled, dusty husband.

The other two contemplated the comparison. The shadow was about to swallow him, but the breadth of the shoulders was still apparent under the well-cut blue coat—enormous shoulders and a wide, deep chest were like the powerful forequarters of a kudu bull, and the arrogant-held head like the arrogance of a kudu, and the great upper body easing away to the well-proportioned hips like the fine sculptured withers of a great male antelope, splendidly, exquisitely, proportioned to speed and movement and to the virile purpose of existence.

'Ai-i-ah, he is a man,' the fat woman repeated. And the shadow swallowed him up.

The secretary bowed formally. 'Mr. Alexander Hare, my Lord.'

Behind the great desk with its asymetrical islands of paper the Governor sketched out the movement of rising without actually lifting himself from his chair. He did not hold out his hand. 'Ah, Hare!' he murmured.

Hare walked with boldness into the room and stood, rocking gently on the balls of his feet. 'Excellency, sir.' He made the greeting as abbreviated as Somerset's gesture of rising. 'You sent for me.'

The Governor looked at him with a glint of humour in his big, hooded eyes. 'Sit down, sit down! I sent for you, yes. You are a much-travelled man.'

The approach was so improbable that Hare, in the act of centring himself on the cool, wide rattan seat of his selected chair, looked up under his luxuriant eyebrows.

'It has occurred to me,' the Governor went on suavely, 'that as a man who knows so much of the world you must be growing tired of our poor colony; that, in fact, you might wish to move to some climate more'—he looked up at the splendid crystal chandelier—'more adjusted to your way of living.'

Hare settled himself with a thump in the chair. Lord Charles ordinarily was devious in his approach. He enjoyed the circumlocutions of diplomacy; he played them as other men play chess, savouring his moves. This was only another of a series of interviews that stretched back almost through his governorate, far more than the five that the women had agreed upon. Always he had led up to them with talk of the harvest or the vintage or the trouble with the American sailors or the stiff-neckedness of the remaining Dutch officials. The Governor would begin a topic and pursue it, outlining its main elements, exploring its side issues, and only at the end of some slight tributary issue would come suddenly to the matter in hand. There was always a logic in his approach, but it was not always discernible until the critical moment of challenge. In the past Hare had enjoyed the method; he believed that he could anticipate the moves, he believed that he understood the workings of the Governor's mind. The crudity of this approach surprised him. It was possible, of course, that the Governor had heard something already of the affair of the Malay child, the pirate's daughter.

He accepted the challenge. 'I find it intolerably arduous to arrive at a conclusion, Excellency. I have been embarked six months now, but I find it difficult to tear myself away from the Cape of Good Hope—your Cape of Good Hope, Excellency. It is one of the world's exquisite places. I would not have sold my small property had I not been offered so vast a profit. Even now, if I could find another that suited me, I might . . .' He let the words trail away.

The Governor smiled. His smile was almost benign: Hare knew that it was wholly false, a diplomatic smile. 'Your perceptions are acute. It is a place of rare beauty, but I would have thought it a shade cold for your'—he spread one hand palm upwards on the polished desk—'for your

exotic requirements, at least'—the smile now was almost conspiratorial—
'at least in the winter.'

Hare lifted his head challengingly. 'I have learnt to live with the cold.'
And it was plain that he was not referring to a climatic cold.

'But your household . . .' said the Governor.

'My household has acquired a resistance to cold.' Hare's voice was
only obstinate now.

The Governor sketched with one hand a series of curves in the air
that might have been Eastern domes or women's breasts. 'Your tastes
are oriental, Mr. Hare. I would have thought they might have flourished
better in the East than in our crisp African air.'

Hare abandoned the fencing, knowing as he did so that he was aban-
doning it too early, but moved by a rising anger. 'The missionaries have
been carrying tales to you.'

The Governor put the tips of his fingers together. He was exuding
paternalism. 'It is true that the Moravians brought me a complaint, but
that was four months ago. The child from Genadendal—I spoke of that
the last time I saw you. No, it was the time before.'

'And I satisfied you, my Lord.'

'You satisfied me.'

'Who else has complained?'

Like a kingfisher stabbing at the water in an instant reaction to a half-
seen opportunity the Governor pounced: 'Everybody has complained,
Mr. Hare. The Catholics have complained as well as the Moravians, the
Wesleyans as well as the Catholics.'

Hare's eyes glinted uneasily, for it was common knowledge that the
Governor disliked the Wesleyans and that he should use them thus was
intimidating.

'My own chaplain has complained to me.' Somerset paused, contemplating the inward curves of this joke, knowing that Hare himself knew,
as he did, the vagaries of the chaplain, his secret self-indulgences.

Defensively Hare said: 'I held the *Hippomenes* here so that I could
live aboard her and away from these complaints.'

'They call the *Hippomenes* the *Seraglio* now,' said the Governor,
pouncing again. 'You should have realized that you could hide yourself better in a town than in the open bay. They see your ship when they
walk along the Strand of an evening in the cool. They speculate upon
what happens on board her. They see her with every movement they
make into town or out of it. She is an entity, Mr. Hare, a closed con-
tainer of something that they regard as sinful—something that they believe is not under the law.'

'And you?'

'I know that it is lawful, Mr. Hare. You have papers to prove it, I have seen them—papers signed by Sir Stamford Raffles, by the magistrates at Bencoolen. But what is lawful and proper in Sumatra, Mr. Hare, may be lawful but improper at the Cape of Good Hope. You would be wise to sail, Mr. Hare. Six months is a long time to lie at anchor. There is a story of one of our ships, one of the King's ships, that stayed so long in Spithead that she grounded on her own beef-bones, Mr. Hare.'

'I protest, sir!' Hare half raised himself on the chair. 'I protest! I have my rights as a citizen.'

'Sir Stamford would have been better able to protect you in those rights than I have been,' said the Governor slowly. 'I am told that the new colony of Singapore is flourishing exceedingly. The climate'—for the first time he allowed himself to look with a cynical directness at Hare —'the atmosphere would have suited your—ah—establishment better.'

'Tom Raffles has returned to England,' Hare answered sourly.

'I am aware of that'—the Governor continued to look at him—'but I am informed that his memory lingers.'

'And if I refuse to go?' Hare's anger overrode his discretion.

The Governor looked at him benignly. 'I have, of course, no means of compelling you. As you say, you have your rights and your papers. At the same time we should, I think, say good-bye at this interview.'

Hare looked at him puzzled, faintly startled.

'I am myself returning to England'—the Governor bowed gently, as if expecting a burst of applause—'on leave. I understand that official approval will arrive with the next monthly mail.' Hare thought he detected a menace in the tone. 'I shall be succeeded as Acting Governor by General Bourke.' Somerset tapped the desk with the tips of his fingers as if the name evoked a certain response. 'General Bourke, as you are aware, has injected a splendid state of discipline into the Army here. It is his ambition, I understand, to inject a discipline into our somewhat lax community.' He put his head on one side. 'He has secured his discipline by making examples of delinquents. I myself would hate to be one of General Bourke's examples.' His tone now was man to man, almost bonhomous. 'So would you, Mr. Hare—so would you.'

He rose in his chair. This time there was no half-measure about his rising. He stood erect. 'Possibly General Bourke might consider it necessary to act in the matter of a Malay child of which some insubstantial rumour reached me this morning.'

'Governor, if you think——' Hare's voice filled with bluster and then stopped cleanly as if he had become aware of its uselessness.

'If you were prepared to remain by yourself'—the Governor watched him speculatively—'without your . . .' He hesitated, as if apologetically, and then said: '. . . harem, no doubt General Bourke . . .'

Hare disregarded the offensive word as if he had not heard it. He muttered almost sadly: 'I could not abandon my chattels, my fiddle-faddle. Whether wise or no, I am in the habit of considering them necessary.'

He came out of the dark tunnel of the oaks into the space between the curved walls of the gateway and became abruptly three-dimensional in the bright afternoon sun.

The girl saw him first. She said: 'He is raging.'

At once the other two turned. Hare came towards them, his face dark with fury.

The fat woman stared acutely. 'He has been told to go. Ha!'

'It is the child.' The second woman's intonation was virtuous. 'The Malay child. This was too much at last.'

The girl asked with a hint of excitement: 'Where did she come from?'

'I do not know—from the east somewhere. She was taken from a prau after a fight. My husband knew no more than that.'

Hare was almost parallel with them. He turned sharply to where they sat on the high stoep, framed in the delicate iron railing with its brass finials. He lifted his hat with the jerkiness of an automaton and made a leg. 'Madame du Plessis,' he said harshly, addressing the fat woman. Even as he spoke he looked sidewise at the girl and his eye was speculative. 'Good day.' He made a grating sound like a farewell, and turned at once.

'Now, well!' exclaimed Madame du Plessis.

The second woman said: 'A terrible man, a terrible man!'

'But a man!' Madame du Plessis returned to her first assertion. 'Forty women—Malay, Chinese, coloured, Zulu—heaven knows. And even after a fight with the Governor he can look at a young girl . . .'

The girl said defensively: 'He spoke to all of us.'

'Me, I am too fat.' A soft laugh heaved itself down the enormous curves. 'You'—Madame du Plessis turned to the second woman—'are too scrawny.' Her small head turned round to the girl in its odd, disembodied way. 'You still have youth.' She paused, thinking back. 'It is youth he searches for—always.'

The girl said: 'He is not old.'

'Forty-nine,' murmured the fat woman abstractedly, as if it were of no importance. 'No, it is not youth he searches for—it is the quality of youth. I do not know why. He was in Portugal first: it might be that it was something that happened there. Afterwards he went to Calcutta. There were stories at Calcutta. Afterwards again he went to Malacca.

He had three girls first, then five. He was wealthy, he traded in pepper, and gem stones that the Bugis brought, and spices. There was no scandal. He had a great house, he entertained.' She lifted up an enormous arm, making a gesture that expressed an almost regal welcome.

'Sir Stamford Raffles met him there, or it may be that he met him in Calcutta—I do not know, my husband has not told me—but he went with him to Java.' She paused, savouring the memory of all the anger and the calumny that the expedition to Java had awakened in the Dutch. 'It was Sir Stamford who sent him to Borneo. In Portugal he was a clerk. In Calcutta he was a secretary. In Malacca he was a merchant of wealth. At Banjermasin he was a king; he made war, he judged, he hanged. And because the Sultan knew of his needs he gave him girls and more girls and yet more girls.'

The angry figure of Hare had disappeared from the line of her vision down the Heerengracht. She shifted from one buttock to the other, but could no longer see him. She said: 'He is a man. He has lived.'

# *Two*

THE GIRL watched the flames with an absorbed and silent concentration. One tongue crept up the left breast of the waistcoat, adding for a moment to the brilliance of its bright silk flowers, and then transmuting them into a dark parody of splendour; the other ate at the curve of the pocket, and after a minute a little shower of coins fell out and hit the wooden floor of the cabin with small metallic sounds. She noted the sounds with grave satisfaction.

The flames ate their way higher. The silk shirt caught the contagion of fire and exploded with a soft, menacing upward rush of light. Her skin was beautiful in the light; it acquired subtle tones of gold, a translucence under its even brown. There were highlights on her small, slim shoulders, and the immature breasts were given an illusory fullness.

She knelt in complete patience, watching the flames ascend until they licked at the deckhead of the cabin and the white paint began to burn.

The flames lit the white lettering on the sea-chest below the clothing. The name 'Alexander Hare' stood out scrolled and baroque and assertive. It conveyed nothing to the girl except as a symbol of power.

There was very little smoke yet, but she knew that in a moment the cabin would fill with it. Carefully, almost with a sense of ritual, she poured the last of the whale oil from the base of the lamp over the high boots and over a pair of nankeen breeches that had fallen down when she started the fire, and watched while the fire discovered them.

The heat began to beat against her, but she ignored it. A drop of oil trickled from the base of the lamp on to her finger and she wiped it delicately on her sarong. At last, with the smoke coming lower and lower and the flames furious, she permitted herself a smile of satisfaction and, rising in one lithe movement to her feet, began to scream.

The women came first. She heard the bare feet outside the cabin door and the twittering, agitated Malay voices. She thought she could distinguish a Chinese woman by a different, a more metallic, tone. Then she heard booted feet on the deck above, running, and a white man's voice, an English voice. 'Bloody cabin's afire!' She could not understand the words, but the note of indignant surprise was unmistakable.

The crackle of the flames was loud now, the smoke stung at her eyes and clutched at her throat. She began to beat the panels of the door with her fists. Now and then she paused to scream.

The mate broke down the door. It was intensely dramatic. She noted every detail with the same grave satisfaction with which she had watched the falling coins, then she precipitated herself into his arms. The women screamed at her; men came running with buckets of water; the narrow alleyway became a chaos of noise and moving bodies, swearing, and shouting, and smoke.

The women pulled her down with them. They were huddled against the bulkhead at the far end of the alleyway. They said: 'Why did you do it?' repeating the question over and over again as if by monotonous iteration they could compel her to speak.

For a while she resisted them. Then she said breathlessly, speaking as if she were frightened: 'The lamp—I did not know—I have not seen such things. It was hot, it burnt my hands.'

She held them up and the women chorused: 'Her hands. It burnt her hands.'

'I dropped it,' she went on, lying easily and fluently, 'when it fell. The fire . . .' She made an uprushing gesture with her hands.

One of the older women said: 'She comes from the pirate boats. She would not know of such things.'

'I do not know,' she agreed humbly, filled with contempt for the women.

The mate drove them out on to the deck. He was still swearing but he found time enough to demand: 'How did it happen?'

The one woman who had enough English to understand him answered: 'The lamp. It burned her hands. She dropped it.'

'Bloody little fool!' He stared at her distastefully. 'Shouldn't've bin locked in his cabin alone.'

'It was the Tuan's order,' said the woman.

'Get that blasted pump going!' The mate turned to harry the men. There was no need for the fire pump—he knew it and the men knew it; the fire was under control already. But he would be blamed for it in the end and there was a certain degree of consolation in taking it out of the men now.

The girl knew that the fire was under control too. It had served its purpose of getting her out of the locked cabin, but she had hoped that the ship might burn. She moved slowly and carefully away from the other women and stood at the rail, trying to calculate the distance to the shore of the bay, wondering if she could swim so far, wondering if there were sharks.

The mate saw her. He bellowed at the women: 'Watch that damn' girl! She's goin' to make a bolt for it.'

The women got hold of her, took her into their circle again. They spoke at her rather than to her. 'She is the pirate's daughter. Naturally she would try to escape. She is the daughter of the Pangaran Illtu. It would be proper for her to try to escape.'

The oldest of them broke up the slowly forming chorus of admiration. 'None the less, the Tuan said that he would take her to his bed tonight.'

The mate knew enough Malay to understand what she was saying. He looked at her sardonically. 'Not in that bed—not now.' Then he turned and went back to the cabin where the fire was almost out.

Hare walked heavily down the jetty and men looked curiously at him as he passed: Malay fishermen from the seine-boats, sailors from the East Indiamen, townspeople from the waterfront houses, for the jetty at sunset was a meeting place. It was clear that the news had reached it.

The choleric anger of the early afternoon had ebbed to a black, deep fury. Already he had arranged for the fresh water to go off to the ship. The clearance papers would be ready by nine o'clock; he had bribed the clerks in the port captain's office. He had drawn the last of his ready money from the bank. The fresh provisions should have gone off already: the sheep, the fowls, the vegetables, and the flour.

He looked out to the ship. She lay etched with almost intolerable clarity against the stillness. The water was glass calm, pale in the first twilight like sun-bleached mother-of-pearl. The ship was hard and dark and black in it like an irritant on its perfection. Scattered about her was a small flotilla of shore boats. People on the end of the pier were looking out towards her. Hare remembered the Governor's words: 'They see your ship when they walk along the Strand of an evening in the cool.' Aloud he said bitterly: 'The *Seraglio*.'

A small dark turbaned figure in a faded sarong came up the jetty to meet him. He crouched so low that he gave the impression of kneeling. 'Tuan, Tuan, there was a fire,' he said. 'We saw the smoke. There was shouting.'

Hare looked out over the flowered turban on the man's head. The shore boats were lying well clear of her. There was no smoke. 'She is not on fire now.'

It was a statement but the man chose to answer it as a question. 'I do not know.'

'Why did you not go to her?'

'I would not have dared,' answered the man, cringing. 'I was told to wait for the Tuan. I waited.' He straightened himself, and suddenly, in justification, said: 'There were shore boats.'

Hare stalked past him and went down the steps. The men in the boat put out the oars, thudding wood against wood. The serang gave a melodious cry, somebody pushed the bow out and the boat began to move across the water.

At once, by the magic of movement, the town diminished, and by a counter-magic the mountain increased behind it. Where before it had been a blue wall it was a rampart now, the bastion of an enormous fortress, clean-cut along the parapet, squared at the ends, dwarfing to a total insignificance the green-black bastions of the Castle of Good Hope on the inner curve of the bay.

Hare's mind was confused with mingled streams of thought. It was as if with one lobe of his brain he was occupied with the indignity of the interview in the Governor's room and with the other of the prospect of new adventure. He thought: It is not possible for him to understand me. No one who has not lived in the East can understand my necessities —not all of those even who have lived in the East. I should have told him. But he was aware that he could not have told him, aware that he had gone to the meeting full of aggressive intention to justify himself and that he had offered no justification, aware of failure. His inner tensions were more occupied with his own failure than with Somerset's success. The Governor had outplayed him.

'I should have told him of the Treasury's delays,' he said to himself. 'I should have told him of John's letter.'

He ruminated for a minute or two over the intricacies of the East India Company, of the Treasury in London, of the injustice. He had had no compensation for the loss of the Moloeko grant; he had still to be paid for the services of the ships in Borneo. He should have told the Governor of van der Wahl: van der Wahl was the root of the trouble, the origin of all disaster, the scoundrel. And even as he ran over his grievances he knew that he had told them all to Somerset before. In a different way, with different emphasis, he had told them all, and none of them, he knew now, had been accepted. Somerset had played with him. Without warning, Hare was immensely humiliated, a flood of shame spreading over the blackness of his anger.

The boat moved on through the pearl water, and over to the right of it the earth shadow crept up against the afterglow, exquisitely blue against its fading rose. The serang was giving the boatmen the stroke now in a soft-stressed song in a dialect that only Hare half understood. The mountain grew still greater with the earth shadow, looming enormous in the fading sky.

Roach, the mate, met him at the top of the ladder. His blunt face was aggrieved. He judged everything personally. 'We've been on fire. It's out now, but I thought one time that it might 'a' been serious.'

Impatiently Hare demanded: 'Where was it?'

'In your cabin.' Roach's head was turned away from him, only his eyes flickered towards Hare's face.

'My cabin—how?'

'The girl dropped the lamp.'

'What girl? What imbecility is this?'

Roach pointed wordlessly to the group of women under the fo'c'sle. The girl stood in the middle of them. Two of them were holding her arms as if they still feared that she would leap overboard to swim in to the shore. She stood submissively, slender, her head bowed.

Hare had not seen her before. She had been brought from the Indiaman at night. It was not a transaction for the open daylight, and he had slept the night ashore. Now in the middle of the restless shimmer of the group of women she was a focal point; her small body seemed to acquire stature from it. She was quite still. There was no need for the hands on her arms. From where he stood Hare believed that she was trembling.

He called out in Malay: 'Let her go! Let her come to me.'

The women set up a bawling at once: 'She will go . . . She will leap from the rail . . . She will . . . She will kill herself!'

'Be still! Let her come to me.'

Roach watched him curiously.

The girl stood motionless for an instant after the women took their hands from her. Then she moved forward. She walked aristocratically, almost with an air of authority. She carried her small body with pride, but her head was still bowed and submissive, her chin down to the hollow of her throat.

'There was a fire.' Hare became conscious of her eyes looking up at him, half hidden by the fringe of smooth black hair.

'It was the lamp,' she explained patiently. 'I do not know about such things. It burned my hands and I let it fall.' She made no attempt to express regret or to excuse herself beyond the plain statement of fact.

He watched her gravely. 'Let me see your hands.'

She held them out palm upward. She had long, delicate, tapering fingers. The palms and the inside of the fingers were a pale shell-pink in contrast to the golden-brown of their backs. Across the palm of the right one and across the base of two of the fingers were blisters and a score of small new burns. He was not to know that she had held the lamp deliberately, closing her eyes and her mind to the pain of it so that if it were necessary she might have evidence of proof.

He bawled over her head to the women: 'Fools! Her hand is burnt. See that it is dressed. Take her below!'

Roach looked after her questioningly, but he said nothing.

'Where is Ross?' demanded Hare, bringing an end to the scene.

'Captain went ashore when the boat come with your note,' replied Roach. 'We need four hands. Said he would come off with them by dark.'

'And Mr. Downie?'

'Dunno. Hasn't been aboard since they brought the girl last night.'

'Take the boat and find him!' ordered Hare with a flat anger. 'Search the taverns along the waterfront first and go inshore after if you have to.' He lunged his face forward suddenly, his neck lowered between his shoulders so that he looked like a crouched vulture. 'See that you don't get drunk yourself! We sail at sunrise.'

# Three

THE SHIP was full of noises: feet overhead, and the thud of heavy objects let down at a run from the tackle on the yard-arm, and boats bumping alongside, and men shouting, and hatch covers being dropped on the deck, and canvas drawn swishing across it with a sound like a squall in summer-parched reeds.

The women sat in the half-gloom of the lanterns, divided into small groups. Children swarmed between the groups, moving incessantly. Babies cried and were instantly silenced with the breast. The girl decided wearily that this was how they divided naturally, the coalescence of friendships and special relationships. She wondered what group would try to absorb her into it, would try to use her.

They knew that the ship would sail. They knew that the captain was ashore searching for men for the crew. They knew that the man Downie would come back drunk. They knew everything. The only thing they did not know was whom the Tuan would choose for this night and where he would sleep with her, his own cabin being burnt. They came back to this again and again as if it were the magnetic force that pulled at their irresolute and unreliable compass needles. From time to time they talked of the girl openly, without hushing their voices. They were shocked, not because she had burnt the cabin, but because she had not greeted the Tuan with a proper submissiveness, had spoken to him directly and without the honorifics that they used themselves as a badge of subjection.

The door opened and the small brown man who had spoken to her earlier in the day, before she was taken to the cabin, staggered by her with an enormous pan of rice. He sidled past her as he went back to the door and murmured: 'We sail at sunrise.' She knew that already, but before she could question him further he was gone.

Where would they sail? This was the thing that mattered. The *Iphigenia*, the ship that had brought her to the Cape, had sailed south-west, away from the islands—her islands. This was a ship like the *Iphigenia*, it too would sail west. The few words of English that she had acquired on the long passage across the Indian Ocean were not enough to help her here. She could not ask the white men where the new ship would go. The women knew nothing of the ways of the sea; already she had dismissed them contemptuously in her mind. Only this little man with the rice had offered help, and his words were a warning. She had to escape—to escape before sunrise.

She searched the long, low room with her eyes again. Hare had had the partitions between the four cabins on the port side of the ship torn down to make one long room for the younger women. All the doors save one were blocked. There were four small scuttles in the side of the ship, too small even for her slender body. The only possible route of escape she had marked and assessed long since. Over the top of the inner bulkhead at one end there was a space where the skylight trunk came down. To reach it she would have to pass through the women, to pass the gauntlet of their suspicious eyes.

She thought: They will sleep. But she knew that they would not sleep until Hare came. They would squat there in an uneasy rivalry of anticipation.

Another man came in with a pannikin of curry. They called to her to come and eat, and she went. She was unashamedly hungry.

There was no moon, but the brilliance of the stars was enough to underline the secrecy of the night. Over beyond the Amsterdam battery the loom of the new lighthouse at Green Point, the pride of the Cape, rose and fell like a slow-beating heart. There were lights along the waterfront and lights climbing the curve of the Lion's Rump, and a sprinkling of lights beyond the Castle and about the jetty.

The boat approaching the ship had a light in her bows. She moved erratically like an angry insect on a pond. They could hear voices from her and once shouting. Hare watched grimly. It came alongside with a ragged stroke and bumped. Voices shouted up from it, and Hare bellowed down, suddenly beside himself with rage: 'Bring him up in a rope's end, then!' And he heard Roach laugh, low and derisively.

They hauled the man Downie up the side of the ship, scraping him, and stood him on his feet and held him while they unknotted the loop under his armpits. When they took the support away he collapsed in the scuppers and lay there, snoring.

Hare bellowed down from the poop rail: 'Throw a bucket of water over him!'

The little brown men on the deck, moving in and out of the light of the lanterns like night creatures, entered into the spirit of the thing. They dropped a bucket joyously to the water at the end of its line. At once the water shivered into a multitude of green and luminescent sparks. They hauled it up—it held quivering facets of phosphorescence—and flung it at the crumpled body of Downie. He gasped only, he made no move.

'Another!' ordered Hare abruptly.

The fourth bucket roused him. He began to crawl away on all fours, the men shouting with laughter.

The mate came up to Hare on the poop deck. 'Found him seventh place I tried.' Roach spoke truculently. He himself was not drunk, but it was clear that he had taken liquor. He looked contemptuously down at the man who was standing now, shivering, against the bulkhead. 'Wouldn't 'a' done any harm to leave him, my opinion.'

Hare said furiously: 'Mind your business!' He needed Downie, he was suddenly aware how much he needed Downie. Downie pimped for him, settled the larger troubles of the women for him, toadied to him. He could not now do without him. 'Get below, God damn you!' And then, almost without altering his inflexion, he said to the mate: 'The sheep will be coming off any time. Make sure that the pens are secure!'

'I know,' Roach answered him belligerently. 'We came through them on the jetty. Wanted to make love to them, he did.' He spat over the side in a large, easy contempt. Then he turned and went down the ladder. Over his shoulder he said: 'Captain's got his four hands.' And as he went along the deck, he added derisively: 'Waiting for them to say goodbye to their girls.' He side-stepped a rough-tied bale of fodder as it dropped from the whip, and went forward, whistling.

Later the same small man came in for the rice dish and the pannikin that had held the curry. The girl watched him, but this time he said nothing. He was not supposed to speak in the cabin. Only, as he closed the door, he paused for an instant, looking at her with enormous, lustrous eyes.

Much later the women began to go to sleep. They had after all despaired of Hare's coming. They slept tangled together, some on the bunks, most of them on cloths on the floor. They were of all ages, the youngest perhaps a year older than herself, the oldest—she could not guess—not very old. The senior wives, the women who ruled the household, were not here. They were in another cabin. They no longer even hoped for the attentions of the master and took refuge in authority and spitefulness.

When most of the women were asleep, and only two or three talked at lengthening intervals, the girl got suddenly to her feet. Unhurriedly, as if secure in the knowledge that no one could touch her, she walked to the door to see if she had properly interpreted the look in the man's eyes. It was, as she had believed it would be, open. She let herself out into the alleyway while the women who were still awake whispered uneasily to one another, and slipped through the outer door to the deck.

The waist of the ship, hung with lanterns, was almost as light as the cabin had been. Men moved on it a-rhythmically, throwing enormous, whirling shadows as they moved across the light of the lanterns. Beyond the main deck they were sending up a new foretopsail. The great lashed anaconda of the canvas was swaying up in helpless curves. Closer at hand the sheep were coming inboard, petulant and complaining. Men were shouting everywhere, their bare feet thudding on the deck. The mate was calling up the foremast and voices answered him, as it were, out of the sky.

The Tuan—she was sure it was the Tuan—was walking back and forth across the poop with heavily booted feet. She could sense the anger in his footfalls. She shrank against the corner of the break of the poop and the high, scrolled fairing-piece at the side of the ship, merging in the shadow of the ladder and the broken light of the lamps through the rigging. Her sarong was dark, a cloth of purples and browns and dull greens that flowed into and seemed to increase the shadows.

She was sure no one had seen her, and yet, a long while afterwards, the little man slipped past her. He carried a bucket of rubbish to empty over the side. He leant over the bulwark with an engrained caution to see if the water was clear of shore boats below. Then he lifted the bucket to the edge of the rail and threw its contents out. Fish swam into the floating rubbish at once from vertiginous depths, trailing spear-shafts of phosphorescence behind them. Only after he had watched them for a full minute did he turn and say, his voice like a gusty sigh: 'We sail towards the sunrise.'

She did not answer him. She absorbed the softness of his words, try-ing to evaluate them. He spoke a dialect of Malay that was all but foreign to her. On her father's prau she had spoken either the Illanun tongue or the Malay of the Orang Laut. It was essential to know whether he meant towards sunrise or towards *the* sunrise. She waited with a curious, un-childish patience, like a pile of drifted leaves in the corner under the poop, while, over her head, Hare's boots stamped out his fury with the Governor and himself.

The man came again at last. He had another bucket.

'To the east?' she asked, as soon as he had rested the edge of it on the rail.

'Timor,' he said, 'to the east—to the sunrise.'

'Then,' she whispered despairingly, as if appalled at her error, 'it would have been wrong to burn the ship.'

'Ya, Allah. . . .'

# *Four*

THE MOUNTAIN flooded with an improbable, antique pink, the delicate colour of the interior of a sea-shell—a colour altogether wrong for something so substantial, so warlike.

The wind rose with the sun, as Hare had said it would. The *Hippomenes* had already come to her anchor. The clicking of the pawls had accelerated now. The capstan shanty grew faster, lighter in tone as the work lightened. They broke out the anchor. Men swarmed up the foremast. The new foretopsail fell away from the jack-stay in stiff folds and creases. It looked staringly white above the weathered foresail as that in turn was sheeted home. The ship's head swung to the wind ruffle that spread in dark blue corrugations over the water, and she began to head softly out of the bay. The high houses on the slopes of Table Mountain began to glisten white as the sun reached them in the middle of the tangle of young oak and vines and up-thrusting pine.

Half the women had come on deck to watch the sailing. They seemed unable to take in the fact of departure. They looked about the ship vaguely, huddled together in a knot like the sheep in the pens.

The girl looked from them to the sheep contemptuously and back again. Once she went to the rail and stared out over the bay. Nobody attempted to stop her now. Either they accepted that she no longer intended escape or they had forgotten her in the excitement of sailing.

Once the main topsail was sheeted home the ship steadied on course, and the girl looked up the centre line to the high-reaching bowsprit and then calculatingly at the red sun over the mountains of the Hottentot's Holland. The ship was heading north-west. It would have to go west to clear the bay, but the north in it woke doubt in her. She had put the idea of escape aside in that moment of whispering in the night shadow. Now it was too late to escape. Even if she tried to swim they would only lower a boat and retake her. If this man was wrong about the ship's intention it was now too late for anything. It might be necessary to kill him if only to restore her self-respect. He was hovering outside the galley door at this moment, waiting for the early food. She watched him sombrely. He was an insignificant person, a Bajau, she judged, a small fisherman who had taken to seafaring.

As if he had divined her anger, he came aft. This time he carried coffee. She drifted towards the poop ladder and as he came up to her he said: 'There are rocks. She will go north for a little and then come round. The rest is God's will.'

She relaxed softly, released of her fears. The morning air was crisp, exquisitely clean, sea-smelling. She felt something of the immense exhilaration of other morning departures with her father, remembering the motion as the prau laid over to other dawn winds, and the singing and the laughter.

There was no laughter on the *Hippomenes*. Roach was cursing the men as they catted the anchor. Behind them the dawn wind freshened, and the buildings along the shore began to shift in relation to the slopes of the hill beyond. They could see clear to the tower of the Green Point light now, but the light was out, snuffed at sunrise.

The dawn wind failed them eight miles off shore. They lay becalmed in an increasing heat. Even the gulls were too languid to flight in this dead air; they lay in small, snow-white clusters on water that was as lack-lustre as the blind eye of a cat.

The captain busied himself with the ship's log on the wheel-box. The gnarled Irishman at the wheel—one of the new hands picked up the night before—rested his hands listlessly on the spokes, steadying the wheel only when the movement of the swell tugged irresolutely at the rudder. The captain wrote slowly, with apparent labour, yet the script that came away from his pen had a fine copperplate quality about it. He used to say that it was the one thing that he had learned in his brief schooling. He filled in the ship's name at the head of the new page: '*Hippomenes*'. He filled in his own name, flushing a little, as always, with pride: 'Robert Clunies-Ross, Master'. Port of departure: 'Cape Town, Cape of Good Hope'. Then for a little while he waited, staring at the word 'toward', the word that was the ultimate expression of the humility of the seaman, the word that acknowledged that beginnings were with men but that endings were with God.

At length he said coolly: 'Mr. Hare, sir!'

Hare, pacing up and down athwartships, grunted.

Ross said with a questioning inflexion: 'Toward . . . ?'

Hare grunted again.

Ross repeated the word, stressing the inflexion.

'Toward? Toward where?' Hare exploded irritably.

'Yes, Mr. Hare'—Ross's voice was still low, faintly threaded with amusement—'toward where?' The emphasis betrayed the flat Orkney Island burr that ordinarily had vanished from his voice, overlaid as it was with accents and modulations from half the world.

Hare abandoned his introspection. 'What d'you mean "toward where"?'

'I am entering the log. "Left Cape Town, took departure Green Point light toward . . ."?'

It was old matter this, discussed often over drink after dinner in the cuddy during the long wait at anchor, discussed before Hare had brought his people aboard the *Hippomenes,* discussed ashore in taverns, in waits on the jetty. Where would he go? Where would he take his 'chattels'?

Hare resumed his walk. At the far side of the ship he croaked: 'The Andamans.'

Ross held his pen poised, not beginning to write. When Hare had come level with him again he said: 'The new slavery laws, Mr. Hare— you have remembered them? The Andaman Islands are British. They are under the Bengal Government. Your position with the Bengal Government . . .'

Hare looked at him stormily. 'A pack of fools,' he snapped. 'Pusillanimous fools! Eleven months and there is yet no reply to my last memorial. They will pay for my losses at Banjermasin or there is no justice in Governments! I told Somerset that. I told him that I was a prisoner of policy.' He knew that he had not told Somerset. He knew that he had meant to use this as his defence and that Somerset had outplayed him. 'He would not listen,' he muttered angrily.

Ross nodded. All this he had heard before. He had helped to pen earlier memorials. It was Hare's contention that he had been ignored in the terms of the treaty that handed back Java to the Dutch. He claimed vast compensation. The number of his memorials was already a legend in the East.

Ross said, trying to bring things back to practicality: 'None the less, the Bengal Government would give you no peace in the Andamans. The world is changing towards the institution of slavery, Mr. Hare.'

This too had been said before. Ordinarily Hare exploded in passion, but now he was drained, filled instead with self-pity. 'My people are not slaves, Captain Ross.' The use of Ross's rank was an indication of acute displeasure. 'They were a present from the Sultan of Banjermasin, a present in accordance with the custom of the time and the place. Tom Raffles approved of my proceedings. I have the Java Government *Gazette* issued under his hand. "Mr. Hare was hailed throughout His Highness's dominions as the deliverer of that once powerful kingdom." '

Hare straightened himself. He seemed to fill out as if the memory of that time had flooded back to restore him to his glories. The note of self-pity went out of his voice. 'I pacified Borneo. I took peace to the island and I maintained it. And that cold aristocrat at the Cape'—he looked angrily over at the serrated western flank of the mountain— 'what does he know of the East? No one who has not lived in the East can judge me. No one who has not lived there has the knowledge with which to judge. I was the law in Moloeko. I made the law in Banjer-masin.' His indignation was real now; it had none of the falsity of his self-pity. He was remembering what he had been, remembering triumphs. 'Political pro-consuls! Younger sons! He was given his task only be-cause of the votes his family holds. A mean-spirited man, sir, a mean-spirited man! What can he know of my necessities?' He glowered at Ross.

'Yet,' the captain persisted, 'the tide is rising against slavery. He has to retreat before it or he is lost himself. He's no Canute.'

'They are *not* slaves! I freed them in Bencoolen before I sailed for the Cape. I have the papers to prove it. It was done with the consent and agreement of Tom Raffles.'

Ross nodded, his face half averted from Hare, his eye cynical. 'But do *they* know it?'

'They know,' replied Hare magistrally, 'that they are my family, my people. That is enough for them. I must have a place that is off the shipping routes. I need peace for them. I do not choose to have a place where they will be exposed to men coming ashore after months at sea, men from the whalers.' His voice took on a sudden spiteful note and his eyes fixed on Ross. Ross had begun his sea life on a whaler with his brother. 'The Andamans are off the shipping routes.'

The captain ignored the thrust. 'There remains the Government.'

'There are Governments that do not care in these matters—the Amer-icans, for example.'

Ross looked up at the flaccid sails as if he were instantly plotting a new course. 'Southern America? North? There are the Portuguese colonies.'

'I was at Lisbon.' Hare's mind flicked back thirty years, concentrating momentarily on memories of corruption and intrigue, but he formu-lated no objection in words.

Ross tried a new line, deliberately goading the older man. 'Batavia, then?'

'It would be inappropriate until the matter of my memorial is settled,' replied Hare with dignity. He began to walk backwards and forwards.

Ross examined the point of his pen. The ink had dried on it, and he took out a knife and sharpened it with the delicate precision of a big man labouring at a minute task.

After a long while Hare came to rest again. 'An island—an island outside the authority of Governments, an island without people.' He was momentarily inspired with enthusiasm for the idea. 'The Maldives, Chagos, the Seychelles.' His mind ran swiftly over the names, savouring them, testing them out. One by one he rejected them without explanation. 'Christmas Island!' he exclaimed at last, and, harking back with the curious verbal pertinacity that he sometimes displayed: 'Toward Christmas Island, Captain Ross—toward Christmas Island!'

Without comment Ross dipped his pen in the ink and began to inscribe the name 'Christmas Island' in his meticulous script.

The calm endured. At noon they still hung indeterminately in a sea that to the westward merged without distinguishing mark, without horizon, into the sky. The gulls still formed little groups that changed their density and their shape from time to time but remained elegantly without purpose where the last of the ship's offal had floated finally out of their reach into the depths.

They ate on deck. Four of the women served Hare and Ross with twittering solicitude, while Roach watched them with a face blank of all expression and yet radiating disapproval. From time to time he stopped watching them for long enough to walk to the taffrail and throw over a chip from a store that he kept in his pockets. The chips showed no indication of movement.

They sat on after the meal was complete, a bottle of Constantia between them. The women squatted about Hare's chair, silent and watching him. Hare was curiously light-hearted, and Ross wondered if it were because he had made up his mind at last as to a destination. For six months he had debated difficulties. It was strange that he had never mentioned Christmas Island before. The captain wondered if this was because he had always held it in the back of his mind, not to be brought out unless his memorial failed or until some other event forced a decision.

Ross himself had sailed close in to Christmas Island but had not landed. 'About a thousand feet high,' he said. 'Fairly steep most of it but there's a little bit of a cove to the north.' And then after a time, in answer to a question: 'Yes, covered with trees, jungle—palms. Ought to be plenty of water.'

Hare seemed satisfied. He asked no more questions; instead he held his glass up in the sunlight and made a slight murmur of approval. 'I hope we have more of this on board.'

'Two hogsheads,' answered Ross abruptly. He felt that he had not had adequate appreciation of his efforts in getting the ship to sea at half a day's notice. He had known, of course, that it would happen like this and had held his supplies for such an occasion. The fresh water had been topped up twice a week. If it had not been for the extra hands he could have got clear by midnight. There had been no wind at midnight but he would have been prepared to tow her out. He would have been prepared for anything to put an end to the intolerable waiting—six months swinging round his anchors, unsnarling cables, six months facing out the north-wester (twice he had thought they were going to lose the ship) and then the south-easter when the season turned, coming down off the face of the mountain like a pampero off the Plate. He would have done anything to get clear. Lately he had not often gone ashore; they talked too much there, they asked too many barbed questions. The women ashore no longer liked the ship. He had no place for a town where the women did not like him. He emptied his glass.

Ross said: 'I must work out a course for Christmas Island.'

'As you would go for the Straits of Sunda.'

'Sunda Strait . . .' Ross savoured the smell of the narrow gut between the islands, spiced wind coming off the mountain sides, heavy mud smell—rank, sweet, like the smell of a brothel—from the mangrove swamps, the gateway to the farthest East.

When Hare woke there was still no wind, but the ship's head pointed out to the open sea; some whim of the current had altered her heading. The gulls trailed abeam of her. Nothing marked the passage of time, for even the shadows had altered with the swinging and had no relativity. Hare lay as he had slept. Only his eyes opened, searching out indolently as if he were trying to discover in the haze the separation of earth and sky.

The four women were still clustered at his feet. They were awake, watching him.

He said after an interval: 'Bring me the girl!'

Abbott, the second mate, on watch, lifted his head sharply, as if he were startled at the voice.

The ship rolled very slowly, a swell was making up from the south, somewhere a block banged against a mast, there were creaking noises and the dry rustle of ropes over wood. Apart from these, the ship slept as Hare had slept, noiseless and purposeless.

The girl came up the starboard ladder and walked across the deck, slowly and with an almost unnatural dignity.

Abbott, watching her, thought: She is not like the others, she has been accustomed to ships.

She met the movement of the deck in the roll subconsciously, as if she were a part of the ship. She stood before Hare, offering no salutation, silent, watchful, and very straight. Her small body glistened in the harsh afternoon sun. Her sarong was wound neatly and firmly, but it made hardly more than a crease in the skin of her belly. Clearly her flesh was firm, there was no fat on her. It had the lithe firmness of a leopard; perhaps it had the same illusive softness. Her arms and her shoulders were slender, exquisitely proportioned, and her neck was moulded out of them with an evident pride. She held her head with a poised and expectant wariness. Her face was softer than her body, its lines less firmly modelled. The mouth was young. The nose, more delicately cut, narrower than was ordinary amongst the women of the islands, was still not fully determined. Only the eyes offered a speculative entry to her reality. Now they were hooded, but they gave to the soft contours of the face an improbable, unchildlike beauty.

Hare watched them for a long minute, trying to penetrate them. She gave him back the stare, showing no emotion either of apprehension or of anticipation. His eyes dropped to the small childish breasts, suddenly greedy. 'Who are you?' he asked, using the Malay that he spoke habitually with the women.

'I am the daughter of the Pangaran Illtu.' She spoke with an exact economy of tone, loud enough for him and the women to hear, hardly loud enough for the second mate. Her voice was modulated, without a quiver.

'Of the Pangaran I have heard,' said Hare gravely. 'You have a name?'

'I am called Plandok.' She offered him the exact information that he asked for, neither hesitating nor elaborating it.

'How did you come to be aboard the *Iphigenia?*'

'We sought to take her,' the girl answered evenly. 'We lay in wait for her off the islands.'

'You sought to take an Indiaman?' Hare's voice rose sceptically.

'We had knowledge,' she said coldly, reacting for the first time to his tone. 'She had many sick. We would have taken her had Yussef of Brunei not lost his heart.'

'Yussef of Brunei?'

'A dog!' commented the girl coolly, and spat on the deck.

Hare began to sit up in his chair, the indolence drained out of him, as if he were fascinated by this adult attitude of mind. 'And then?'

'She had men enough to man the guns on her port side. Our mast was broken. Before the rowers could get way on she rammed us. Even then we might have conquered her, but the breaking of the oars destroyed many of us.' Her voice was quite passionless.

'And your father . . . ?' With an odd accession of respect Hare hesitated before he said: 'The Pangaran was killed?'

'He was not killed,' she replied firmly. 'He was knocked into the water as the ships hit. He lives.'

'How far were you out at sea?'

'Eight miles, ten miles perhaps—it is nothing! He was a great swimmer; he could live in the water.'

'Maybe he could at that,' Hare murmured to himself. 'And you?'

'I would have swum with him but I was pinned by a broken plank. They could not have taken me otherwise.' For the first time the small head lifted back on the neck in an intimation of arrogance.

Hare considered her version of the story as against the version that he had heard from the captain of the *Iphigenia*. According to the captain of the *Iphigenia* he had fought a prolonged engagement, a battle against overwhelming odds—had by his own virtue destroyed a pirate fleet. He had hanged three survivors for a proof of it and he had the girl. Hare placed the two accounts parallel in his mind: he thought that the girl told the truth. As to her father, there was no answer to that; there were sharks in those waters. 'They found you and they took you aboard the *Iphigenia*? You were their captive?'

Sombrely she agreed: 'I was their captive.'

'Now,' he said, 'you are mine.'

She stared him straight in the eyes, and he lifted his own from her body and answered her look. 'I am the Pangaran's daughter,' she said softly, but with a controlled fierceness.

'None the less, you are mine.'

'I am my own and I am the daughter of the Pangaran.'

'Who is dead,' said Hare cruelly.

'Who is alive'—the girl's voice was almost insolent now—'and who will find me, and who will judge according to the treatment that I have received.'

It was so palpably a threat that Hare flung himself back in the chair and laughed. Plandok remained facing him, but her eyes looked out over his shoulder towards the land, as if she were judging the distance, as if she still contemplated an intention of escape.

Abbott, watching her, recognized her fanatic courage. It was implicit in the whip-taut stance of her body, in the poise of her head, in the instant alertness of her eyes. He was suddenly certain in himself that if

Hare made a movement towards her she would be over the side and into the water before anyone could stop her.

Three of the women laughed with Hare, but the fourth looked frightened at the girl.

It took a long time for his laughter to abate. When it subsided finally Hare leant forward, staring at her. 'You set fire to my cabin.'

Instead of answering him she said, making for the first time a small gesture towards the bows of the ship: 'Do we go west?'

'West?' he repeated, puzzled.

'Do we go'—she groped at the unaccustomed name—'to England?'

He laughed again, shortly this time. 'No, we go east—south first and then east.'

As frankly as she had admitted it to the little Bajau, she said to Hare: 'It was wrong, then, to try to burn the ship.'

Again he leant forward, studying her gravely, as if he felt for the first time the real shock of her personality. 'By God, you're a wild-cat!' he said in English.

Abbott, looking at her, thought that the comparison was inadequate: a young leopard was closer to the mark. 'I wouldn't tangle with that one in the dark,' he said to himself, watching Hare's face.

But Hare said only: 'You will be tamed.'

'I am the Pangaran's daughter,' she said again obliquely. It was at once a warning, a statement of identity and an expression of personality. She stood looking at him, grave and controlled, her hooded eyes speculative.

The old Malay at the wheel spoke, his voice liquid and soft, almost caressing, and Abbott jerked his head away from the little scene with reluctance. The man pointed inshore. On the water was a dark flaw, a wind ruffle. The surface inside this area had turned abruptly from a pallid, nacreous uncertainty to ultramarine.

Abbott took two steps to the skylight and, bending down, shouted: 'Captain, sir! Wind's coming away from the south-east.' Then, without waiting for more than a grunted acknowledgement, he went to the rail. 'Both watches!' he shouted down. 'Both watches! Jump to it. Look alive! Wind's coming.'

Hare, without turning, demanded: 'From the south-east?'

'Aye-aye, sir, from the south-east.'

# Five

ROACH CAME up the ladder in the darkness with the sureness of long habit.

Abbott said: 'You're early.'

'First night at sea,' answered the mate self-derisively. 'He reckoned it would be light enough at the change of watches.' Both men looked doubtfully across the darkness of the water. 'What happened this afternoon,' Roach asked softly, and added: 'here?'

'The girl . . . ?'

'The girl.'

'She defied him,' said Abbott, thinking over the words gravely. 'She stood there, four foot of nothing, and she defied him. She's a cool one!' And then for no particular reason: 'She knows ships.'

'That won't help her with him.' Roach was surprised at the sorrowfulness in his voice. They were silent for a moment or two. He looked up into the sails, accustoming his eyes to the darkness.

'What's a Pangaran?' Abbott asked.

'You never been East?' Without waiting for the other's answer, Roach explained: 'It's the name they give to the sons of the sultans, Java-way. It would be a title—duke or something, prince perhaps.'

'Then,' said Abbott slowly, 'she's a princess.'

'Her?'

'She said: "I am the daughter of the Pangaran." '

'The Pangaran who? There should've been a name. She wouldn't say it without the name.'

'There was a name,' agreed Abbott softly, searching his mind. 'Illtu—Illtu, she said, the quartermaster told me.'

'The devil she did! The Pangaran Illtu?' Roach slapped his thigh sharply as if he were overcome with inner laughter. 'The Pangaran Illtu! She's not a princess, then.'

'Why?'

'He's not a prince either, he's a bloody pirate. Damn my eyes, he's the man who burnt the *Lady Hastings!* He captured the *Seringapatam*—you wouldn't know her, she was a country ship. There were others. He's a

black devil. They called him the Pangaran after he captured a prau with
the two sons of the Sultan of Surakarta. He cut their throats at the end.
That was about all there was to cut then. That was before this girl was
born—must've been. They haven't forgotten it round the China Sea,
though. They frighten children with his name.' He mused over this for
an instant. 'Frighten themselves too. He's from the north—Balanini
maybe. No, he stays out longer than that; he'll be Illanun.'

'She said Illanun.'

'They've got a hide-out up the coast of Borneo, somewhere up above
Labuan. His daughter, you say?' He whistled softly and long.

'She said he would come for her.'

'Ha!' Again the mate slapped his thigh. 'She said that, did she?'

'She outfaced him. He let her go after that. Would he be misgiving?'

'No.' Roach spoke decisively. 'No, he's got no fear in him. You mis-
judge him if you think that.' He considered this and went on: 'He could
lick any man in this ship, old as he is, except maybe the captain.' And a
little late he added quaintly: 'And me, that is.'

Abbott stiffened and let it pass. 'I don't know about him except what
I've seen in the two weeks I've been aboard.'

'You'll hear a lot of him East.' Roach assembled his judgements carefully. 'They don't love him much.'

'Because of the women?'

'Because of the women,' agreed Roach quietly, 'but that's not more
than the half of it. He was with Raffles at Java. The Dutch don't like
Raffles, lots of others don't either. Raffles sent him to Banjermasin
—that was when the captain's brother took up with him. Little brig he
had called the *Olivia;* sweet as a nut, she was. Lost her captain at Cou-
pang and captain's brother took over.'

'John Ross?'

'That's him—brother John. Mate of a whaler, he was, and he took up
with Hare runnin' convicts across from Java to work his plantations.
Sultan, he'd given him a piece of land big as Kent, more perhaps, and
then when we had to give Borneo back to the Dutch he was out of it.
Lost a lot.'

'And Ross?'

'He was left behind to hold on to what he could. He had his own war
against the Dutch. Built batteries across the river from Tabico. I tell
you it was a kingdom! He had his rights. Fitted out the *Olivia* and two
other ships as gunboats.'

'Did they fight?'

'No.' Roach shook his head as if he were still disappointed. 'He
hoisted the Union Jack; Dutch, they wouldn't fire on it. Whole thing

went to pieces. Afterwards they took some convicts back to Java. That was when I joined up with the captain.'

'Rum,' commented Abbott, 'rum.'

'It was rum all right,' agreed Roach. 'Damn my eyes, it was rum! Hare's been trying to get the Government to pay him for what he lost ever after. By his reckoning he's a rich man with what's owing to him. Maybe he is—I don't know.'

'And he won't be affrightened of the girl's father?'

'Not him,' replied Roach equably. 'You've listened. You don't think he would care, do you?'

'No, I wouldn't. Is she with him?'

'She's here.' Roach's tone was full of irony. 'Been here all the time.'

'Where?' Abbott looked sharply round.

'In the corner between the locker and the rail.'

Abbott took three steps forward and looked down. He could see in the shadows a more solid shadow. It made no move. 'By God, she is!' he admitted reluctantly, as if angry at the reflection on his watchfulness. He did not attempt to approach the girl closer, but after a little he added: 'It's against his orders. He's told them not to come to the poop. There is supposed to be a watch on the door.'

'This one makes her own orders, I'm thinking,' said Roach, not far removed from laughter.

Abbott turned and went aft to the skylight and, crouching low, squinted under it to look at the clock. 'Wants five minutes,' he muttered and, straightening himself, asked: 'What will happen?' It was obvious that he referred to the girl, not to the business of the ship.

'He has the black girl tonight, the Zulu girl.' Roach smacked his lips reflectively. 'Black velvet! I could do with a bit myself. She'll last him for another ten days or so. You can't ever tell, but she's a lively one. Then he will send for *her*.' He nodded in the darkness towards the still shadow.

'Will she go?'

'She'll have to,' replied Roach dispassionately.

'Will she submit?'

'What else can she do?' Roach shrugged. 'She'll like it maybe. You've never been East, you don't know the ways. She's old enough—big enough, old enough. They don't think like we do.'

'I don't know,' Abbott muttered. 'I watched her yesterday. I watched her face him—out-face him. I don't know.'

He spoke to the spare hand, and the double shock of the ship's bell shattered the night silence. Men moved about the deck like shadows and from the fo'c'sle the watch below came stumbling out. As if it had waited on the bell, the dawn began to show itself in the hardening of the eastern horizon.

The captain came up the poop ladder, grumbling.

The long, low room was foetid, full of woman smells and child smells. The heat increased every day now as they came up from the low latitudes. They still carried the trade winds, but the water here in the Indian Ocean no longer cooled them.

The three old women sat together, their position slightly crescentic. 'Timah, the oldest of the wives, the autocrat, sat in the centre. Mei Ying, the Hakka woman, sat a little in advance of her to the left. The third woman was the Kling. She was gaunt and hard-featured, and she coughed softly but incessantly. It was believed that she was Hare's spy. Otherwise there was no explanation for the fact that Hare kept her. She was known always as 'the Kling woman', as if she had never had a name of her own. The three had come from their own quarters to sit, as it were, in judgement. The other women had crowded into the after-end of the range of gutted cabins.

Plandok sat cross-legged, with her hands in her lap and her back against a rib of the ship. She sat wholly motionless, her skin polished and delicate and shining. She might have been a sculpture, a concrete symbol of disdain. She sat in profile, not looking at the three old women.

'Timah said: 'In two days at the most he will surely send for you.' Plandok made no move. 'He grows tired of her.'

There was no sign of the Zulu girl in the room. It was obvious that the old woman referred to her. Still Plandok made no acknowledgement.

'Hear,' said the Chinese woman softly, 'he will send for you.'

'I do not choose to go.' She spoke for the first time, quietly, gravely, without altering her pose or turning even her eyes towards the women.

There was a small gasp of shock from the after-end of the space. The old woman's voice took on a note of warning. 'You will go.'

'I do not choose to go,' said the girl again.

'Then,' said Mei Ying, 'you will be taken.'

'Who,' asked the girl dangerously, 'will take me?'

The Kling woman spoke for the first time, her voice even. 'The man Downie.'

'Ha!' said the girl scornfully.

'None the less, you will go or you will be taken'—the old woman 'Timah spoke as if delivering sentence—'and he will lie with you and it will be accomplished as he desires. It is the adat.'

The girl said, and there was neither impertinence nor fear in her voice:

'It is not my adat. My customs are other than these. Hear ye!' Again her head turned to the other women, ignoring the old wives. 'I will tell you'—her voice altered in pitch and in character, it took on with a surprising exactitude the high singsong of a story-teller—'I will tell you a hikayat.' She meant the long, involved biographical stories of the bazaars and of quiet afternoons in the praus. 'Listen to me, O ye women!'

The character of the room changed subtly, as her voice had changed. It ceased to be a hall of judgement; it became a place of listening, a place of story-telling. Those at the far end of the room moved, relaxed. They all faced her now, as if the momentary fears that she had inspired in them had been forgotten.

'Upon my father's ship there was a young man. He was tall, and his skin was coloured like gold so that it shone in the sunlight, and his back was strong. His eyes'—already she had established an almost hypnotic *rapport* with the younger women—'his eyes were like the eyes of a sea eagle.'

'Ah!' breathed a woman's voice deep in the crowd, and somebody repeated the words: '. . . like a sea eagle.'

'He fought well with the parang and with the saif; he was a warrior. We took the ship, my father and I'—she gave herself equal status with an impressive naturalness—'to wait for the Bugis's fleet and we were a long time from the land, for the winds failed and the fleet did not come, and we waited alone, my father's ship and two others. The men were a long time from women.'

'Ai-e-e-e!' A voice of sympathy came out of the crowd.

'And he touched me.' The girl used a word that had implicit sexual connotations, not stressing it, but again a gasp ran through the younger women.

She waited a long time before she spoke again, while the room grew almost intolerable with tension.

'My father asked him why he did this thing, and he said: "Oh, Pangaran, we have been a long time at sea and I had a desire for thy daughter. I would take her for my wife." '

She waited for the little explosion of admiration, mingled with astonishment, at the young man's audacity to subside. Then she went on, her voice unemotional and soft: 'My father said: "Touching the matter of thy aspirations, there is nothing that I need to say, for thou art a dead man already; but for what thou hast done there are certain punishments prescribed." '

A little shudder of fear ran across the women like wind on the strings of an instrument. Again she waited patiently for absolute stillness. When it had come she said: 'So they bound him in accordance with the custom of the praus and they made a line fast to his parts according to that custom.'

This time the shudder that passed through them was accentuated by little moans. Enough of the women knew the nature of that terrible punishment of the pirates.

'When they had put him in the sea they made fast the end of the line, and my father ordered them to let the sails fill.' She paused, projecting her mind back to that quiet morning.

Compulsively the youngest Chinese girl, Kam Ho, demanded: 'And the young man?'

Plandok shrugged her shoulders delicately. It was the first movement that she had made except with her eyes. 'I do not know. When they hauled in the line the knot was still fast but there was nothing there.'

Above the sweep of horrified exclamations the voice of the old woman 'Timah said with irrelevant compassion: 'Allah alone is merciful.' And among the younger women the voices took refuge in the mechanized assurances of religion: 'The One God . . . The Sole . . . The Existing . . . The Perfection.' But the names of God became lost in a chorus of 'Ai-e-e-e!'

The girl sat through it imperturbably. She did not even consider it necessary to reiterate her conviction that her father would find her in the end.

# Six

THE ENORMOUS stink-wood chair was too large for the cabin. It dwarfed the simple painted furniture. Its rich, splendidly proportioned black curves were slashed through with yellow streaks. It was an alien thing in that place, but the fine split rattan of the seat and the back, delicately woven in the Cape style, made it cool and comfortable. Hare sat in it in many ways: sometimes as a throne, as the seat of a magistrate, or as the seat of a father. Today he was relaxed. He wore a light coat of tussore silk and silk trousers. His shirt was open down almost to his navel and the great pad of hair on his chest showed like a displaced beard. He lay back in the chair and contemplated a new-filled glass.

Downie sat himself back in his own chair. He had, as always, the air of a small, apprehensive animal—like a fox perhaps. His too bright eyes peered out over their lower lids in a perpetual watchfulness. His own glass was only half filled.

Hare said: 'It would not do to be in a place where ships call frequently, ships that I am unable to control. It would unsettle the women. I require peace.' He sat up and stared almost menacingly at Downie, as if he suspected him of attempting to disturb his peace. 'For five years now, for more than five years, I have had to fight against intolerance and prejudice. I could have been peaceful at the Cape of Good Hope.' The name seemed to remind him of his wine and he drank, sipping it carefully, savouring the full-bodied redness. 'I am by nature peaceful.'

The other man murmured softly: 'Quite, quite.'

Before the repetition was complete Hare swept on. 'I offer no hurt to any man. I wish only for the privacy of my own circle. All the reports of Christmas Island agree with my wishes. It will be better than the Andamans.'

The bright black eyes watched him. There was a dance of malice in them. 'Christmas Island has no inhabitants.' Downie offered the statement as if it were new.

'It is that that recommends it to me more than any other thing. I need a place that I can plant myself, a place in which I can expand. I could have built a kingdom at Moloeko. A kingdom—no less! But I will

be satisfied to build a place of peacefulness where I can create a society
out of my own family, my people.'

Downie allowed his look to become faintly sardonic. Hare was not
more drunk than he was ordinarily at this time of the afternoon; he was
mellow only, surrendering himself to the perfection of dreams. Aloud
Downie said: 'You had better send the daughter of the Pangaran on
with the ship when she leaves us then.'

Hare put down his empty glass angrily. 'Why?' he demanded.

'The women are terrified of her.' Downie did not answer the question
directly. 'They believe that her father will come for her. She has told
them stories of what he has done to men.'

'What men?'

'Men—I don't know. Men he has captured, I suppose—tortures,
brutalities. He is a bloody-minded man, Mr. Hare, sir. Bloody-minded.'

'Have you heard of an Illanun fleet that came through the Sunda
Straits ever?' Hare had recovered his temper.

'I have heard of them in the Bay of Bengal.' James Downie's manner
took on an unaccustomed and careful honesty. 'They have passed
Penang before now. I have heard of them up towards Rangoon.'

'Keeping close against the coast!' snorted Hare contemptuously. 'They
would not face the open ocean.'

Downie made no reply; he omitted even a shrug of the shoulders.

'They do not navigate: they use known winds, they travel tried
courses. Christmas Island lies more than two hundred miles to the southward of Java Head. They would not dare!' Again he allowed himself
to be a little angry. 'You do not know these men, James Downie. I know
them. I destroyed the pirates about Banjermasin.' An echo of what was
almost magnificence came into his voice. 'What I have done once I can
do again. It is time to make an end. Send the girl to me!'

'Do you wish Fatimah or the Kling woman . . . ?'

'Alone,' Hare answered royally. 'Send her to me alone!'

Downie, half humorous, half apprehensive, got up from his seat and
went to the door. As he opened it he hesitated, and then, his voice hardly
more than a malicious whisper, said: 'And if she will not come?'

'Bring her!'

He looked for her first on the poop deck. She had defied the order
against it so often that it had established itself as a custom. But she was
not on the deck. He made his way to the door of the long, foetid
women's room. She was sitting in the place that she had secured as hers
by the right of her ascendancy over the women, her back against the
rib, still and self-communing.

He called to her in Malay: 'The Tuan wants you.'

The word he used implied needs almost more than wants, and from the women the inevitable muttered chorus went up: 'He has sent for her! He has sent for her!'

'And if I do not go?' The calculated insolence of the voice cut crisply across the softer pattern of the other voices.

Uneasily Downie straightened himself. His hesitation was brief but the girl measured it before he answered: 'His orders are that I was then to bring you.'

She sat watching him with her enormous, fawnlike eyes. At last, when the silence was about to break of its own weight, she said: 'It is not . . .' She paused briefly, searching until she found a Malay word that had something of the implications of the English word 'meet', and then, giving it due emphasis, continued: 'It is not meet that I should be touched by such as you. Therefore I will go.' And she rose to her feet and walked calmly out of the room.

Behind her the air filled with excitement, a cross-babble of voices that drowned out even Downie's barked 'Shut up, for Christ's sake!' Awkward and defeated, he turned and followed her.

She walked down the narrow alleyway, out through the door into the waist and across the deck. The women and children sitting out there under the awning (for in the tropics the air was still and hot) turned and stared at her, and the whisper 'The Tuan has sent for her!' sighed across the ship. Women came peering out of the door behind her to stand and watch the straight, lithe back as she walked quietly across to the other door. She passed into the alley on the starboard side which led to Hare's big stern cabin and, erect and self-contained, went in through its doorway.

Downie, almost trotting to make up the lost time of his surprise, came in behind her and was greeted with a bellowed 'Get the hell out!' from Hare, and, as he went: 'And shut that damned door!'

As if to make apparent that his choler was directed only against Downie, the big man smiled at the girl. There was a surprising gentleness in his smile.

She stood in front of him, her hands at her sides, graceful and apparently quite relaxed, and said, quietly but, as always, without the honorifics: 'You have sent for me.'

He looked at her almost anxiously as if, as indeed was the case, he were puzzled. 'It is time that I sent for you. You have been of my household'—the word did not mean precisely 'harem' but it implied it—'long enough to know my custom. It is time that you came to me.' She stood quite silent, watching him. 'You understand me?'

Surprisingly she answered in English: 'Yes.'

'Ha!' He looked at her with a new interest. 'You have learnt enough English?'

She nodded.

'Then you will know that it is time to end this foolishness. You are mine, and the women will have told you all that it is needful for you to know. I will be gentle with you.' For the first time she focused properly on him, for improbably there was a complete sincerity in his voice. 'We will be friends, you and I. Come closer!'

He could not read her face. There was no play of emotion either over her mouth or in her eyes, but she stepped forward until she stood within reach of him as he sat stretched out in the great chair. To him it seemed that she moved obediently, and he smiled again. Yet even behind his smile there was a delicate, evanescent shadow of doubt.

His eyes accepted the rich colour of her skin, the dark overtones of her shoulders, the faint golden lines under the small breasts, the softer shadows of the throat. He could even see a pulse beat in her throat under the fragility of the skin. It beat slowly; she was, he thought, unfrightened. He put up his hand and stroked her, first on the smoothness of the upper arm and then across the small, bare chest, feeling the softness of her breasts with the back of his fingers, not fondling them, but none the less caressing. She stood quite calm, not giving the impression that she was enduring it against her will, not giving, in fact, any impression at all. He was totally baffled.

He found himself thinking that his fears had been unnecessary, that she would have come to him earlier if he had been firmer, that she had already surrendered in her own mind; and at last his hand, moving down across the silken smoothness of her flat stomach, stretched forward suddenly to the point where the sarong was tucked in. His finger found the recurve of it and, with the smile on his lips again, still quite gentle, he jerked at it and the sarong fell away.

He had a momentary vision of her nakedness, its childishness, its immaturity. But in the very moment of the vision he saw her arm flex, her hand flash, and instantly and with a sense of outrage he was aware of the needle-sharp point of a kris immediately under the cartilage that joined the first of the floating ribs to the breast-bone—and he was aware of fear. He was afraid because he knew that it was precisely the point, the classic point, of the murderous upward thrust of the Illanuns, the point that was vital with the shortest penetration of the weapon.

Even as the knowledge brought fear to him, so it brought at the same time a cold logic. He knew that if he moved, if he attempted to snatch at her arm, the point would drive upwards. Her strength was more than adequate; her speed of movement, her reaction time, much swifter than his own. He could snatch her arm, his superior strength could tear it away—break it, if necessary—but long before he could do that the thin, weaving point of the kris would be three inches into his body, and he knew that he would die.

He sat frozen as a man sits frozen in front of the swaying head and baleful eyes of a cobra. The point of the weapon had penetrated in the first stab but he was sure it was not deep. The small pain of it he disregarded utterly.

He waited for a long time. The girl was not watching his face; she was watching his right hand, knowing that if he moved he must move first with that. It was evident that she was remembering a careful schooling carefully attended.

He could not reach her with his eyes but only with his voice. None the less, when he spoke there was nothing craven in his tone. 'There was no need for this between you and me.'

The kris remained steady—he could tell that by the fact that there was no alteration in the pain. Her body was touching him in parts, mainly against his thigh. He could feel no tremor in it.

She waited for a long time before she answered, and for the first time he perceived emotion in her. 'There *was* need. Otherwise you could not have known of what I have determined.'

Almost dispassionately he considered the significance of her choice between the words 'could' and 'would'.

She went on: 'I am little. Moreover, I am a woman. Other women do not do these things, but I am the daughter of the Pangaran.'

Again she stood still, and, unable to bear the locked stiffness of his muscles, he shifted his position slightly. In an instant response he felt the point dig in a fraction. It was no more than a fraction, it was nothing more than a warning—but it was one that he could in no way disregard. 'Take it away,' he said. 'I will not harm you.'

She made no effort at parley, she did not even question his statement. In one movement she drew away and stood facing him, holding the dagger in her right hand.

He looked at it, marvelling. It was very small, the smallest kris that he had ever seen—delicate, beautiful, an exquisite piece of the weapon-maker's art. The damascening of its blade was deeply eroded. It was polished to an intense brightness so that it looked like a silver flame with its waving traditional line. At the end of it a smear of blood caught the light through the scuttles and glowed like a ruby. She had worn it in a

sheath bound tightly to the inside of her thigh, guarding it carefully
from the inquisitive eyes of the women when she bathed. He let his eyes
drop from it down to the front of his own body and he saw a spreading
stain of blood on the silk shirt and quite clearly a small hole in the middle where the point had gone through. Almost stupidly he said again:
'There was no need for that.'

And she answered once more: 'There was need.'

She seemed quite unconscious of her nakedness or wholly in disregard of it. His eyes moved with what seemed to be a volition of their
own over the delicate curves of her body. She watched them, balanced
like an athlete, waiting for a move. At length his eyes came back, fascinated, to the kris.

At once she said: 'It is possible for you to take it from me. My
strength is small, also you have many men. But it will not serve you, for
there are other knives. It is possible for you to lie on me, this too because I am small and my strength is small. But there will come a time
when you will sleep—it is the custom of men to sleep after they have
achieved that which they desire—and then I will find another knife and I
will kill you.'

More than anything else the absolute lack of emphasis that she put
on the final sentence convinced Hare. He said hurriedly, too hurriedly:
'You need have no fear.' And then, quite unpredictably, he laughed.
This was the first time that he had been utterly defied, this was the first
woman who had utterly defied him. Woman: he looked at her again, the
slenderness of her, the smallness of her, realizing the steel-like character-
istic of her spirit, the induration of her nerve. 'You have no need for
fear,' he repeated. 'We can be friends, you and I.'

She considered this gravely for a long minute and then, with a quick
movement, she slipped the dagger back into its sheath.

As her hand came away from it, his eyes took in the beauty of the
hilt. It was of bone of a golden colour and, though it followed the traditional line, it was intricately and exquisitely carved in the shape of a
small animal. He asked involuntarily: 'What is it?'

'It is the mouse-deer. It is Plandok. My father called me Plandok
always, though it was not the name that I was first given. When I was
a child my nurse was a woman of the Sea Dyaks, for my mother died
within the month. She told me the stories of the mouse-deer.' For the first
time a smile flickered over her grave face. 'There are many stories of the
mouse-deer. Because I too was small and cunning, my father called me
Plandok.'

Hare smiled back at her, his face gentle. 'It is fitting.'

Stooping down, she picked up her sarong and wound it round her body. 'Now I will go.'

'You will tell the Kling woman to give you a new sarong—silk, with brightness in it.'

'That I will like.' A note almost of childishness came into her voice. She bowed to him gravely, and he reflected that it was the first sign of respect that she had ever shown, but it was respect—it puzzled him to recognize it—to an equal.

As she went down the alleyway she heard him calling for 'Timah.

When she stepped out on to the main deck there was a little gasp of surprise, of incredulity even. Then at once everybody was still. They could hear Hare's voice bellowing for 'Timah now, and then the querulous voice of the old woman as she shuffled down the alleyway. The silence became absolute. Even the two mates on the poop became involved in it. The ship was motionless, the sails hung limp in the calm. Everything conspired to produce a high, dramatic tension.

Across the tension came an appalled shriek from 'Timah, a shriek that was her instinctive reaction to the blood on Hare's shirt. It was followed by lamentations and by Hare's voice, cursing and boisterous above the woman's. Mei Ying, the Chinese wife, ran in and her voice joined 'Timah's. They heard the Kling woman's voice contribute and Hare shouting them down. His words were indistinguishable but the exasperated fury of his pitch shivered across the silence.

Only Plandok herself was unmoved. She turned and climbed the ladder on to the poop and walked across it. Her movement was neither arrogant nor humble, but wholly natural. She came as far as the wheelbox, lifted herself up on to it, and sat there, looking at Abbott. She said pleasantly, if a little obviously: 'There is no wind.'

Roach demanded: 'What the hell goes on down there?'

'It is nothing,' she replied cheerfully, so cheerfully that both men turned to stare unbelievingly at her. 'He bleeds a little but that is all.'

Her voice carried in the silence, and there was a quick, deep-breathed chorus of 'Wah!'

Abbott asked urgently: 'What did she say?'

'She said he is bleeding a bit.'

'Who? Hare?'

'Who else? I don't know what she means.'

'Should we go down?'

'Listen to him! Listen to him! Don't be a God-damned fool!' Roach turned questioningly to the girl, but she did not choose to explain further. Neither of the two mates was anxious to ask her more.

She sat swinging her legs for a minute or so before she asked: 'Will we reach the island tomorrow?'

'If there is a wind,' Abbott replied.

'And the wind is with Allah,' the girl finished quickly.

The women who had been sitting under the awning were on their feet now. A small knot of them climbed halfway up the port ladder and were staring across at her. Roach heard a voice say 'She has stabbed him!' and another voice say 'She has killed him!' And a chorus of voices said: 'He is not dead. Listen! Listen!' And then all audibility was lost in a babble of comment and excitement and speculation.

Again Roach translated for Abbott's benefit. 'They seem to think she stabbed him.'

'Done something, judging by his bellowing, but she couldn't have stabbed him. She looks as innocent as . . .' Abbott paused, searching for a just comparison: 'As innocent as a man's sister might do.'

'I don't know about innocence,' said Roach evenly. 'They've got different ideas about it in the East. I bet she's got a kris hidden somewhere about her.'

'Where?' asked Abbott, as if defending his concept of innocence.

'Where d'you think, you fool?' Then, turning, Roach went to the head of the starboard ladder.

Downie was about to come up it. He looked up at the mate, his eyes wild. 'She stuck a kris in him!' he exclaimed agitatedly. 'Stuck a kris in his ribs!' And then: 'By God! Something happened—I don't know what. She stuck it in him all right.'

'Does he want her secured?' asked Roach.

'He says not to touch her, not to do anything. He says—he says she is to have a new sarong, something with bright colours.' He spread his hands over the rails of the ladder in a gesture of despair. 'I don't understand anything,' and then very softly added: 'any more.'

Plandok sat on, swinging her legs. Abbott thought that she looked happy for the first time since he had known her.

Roach also watched her for a little. He thought: By God, she's cool! He still could not understand what had happened, but there was an aura of danger about her.

He looked beyond her to the women clustered around Downie. Plandok had once compared them to sheep. They were like sheep. Perhaps it was necessarily like this with the women of a harem. They seemed to have only one mind between them, with all individuality eliminated by enforced congregation. They seemed to move with a single purpose, wanting the same things at the same time, thinking the same thoughts.

Shrewdly he estimated that their joint personality was established at the level of its lowest individual. Perhaps this too was an inexorable law of harems. Without Hare they were lost. This was the real reason for the present panic. This also must be a law of harems.

# Seven

ROACH LEANT over the rail of the poop, looking down through the gap in the awning where the starboard ladder came up. The girl was sitting with her back against the timbers of the bulwark. Except when she sat on the wheel-box, she seemed to gravitate by instinct to a position where her back was protected against attack. Now she sat fronted by a semicircle of the children, ten or twelve of them perhaps, who squatted, animated and bubbling, on the deck. Her words were punctuated by little shrill ripples of laughter or by groans of fear and exclamations of derision.

Abbott, at the mate's elbow, said: 'It's good to hear her playing like a child.'

'Ah!' Roach grunted speculatively and stooped low to catch her words. Clearly she was telling a story.

'And when he saw him the tiger was afraid and withdrew to the back of the hut and crouched there, shivering. And the giant entered and turned over the jars and took the fish and ate them.'

'Wah!' breathed the children with awe.

'Thus the pig had failed and the bear had failed and the tiger had failed.

'And the mouse-deer looked at the pig and said: "I am small and you are great, but it has availed you nothing." And he looked at the bear and said: "I am small but you are greater than the pig, and it has availed you nothing." And he looked at the tiger and said: "I am small but you are the greatest of all. Your voice is like thunder and your claws are sharper than anything in the world, but it has availed you nothing. I am Plandok, the mouse-deer. I will stay at the hut and make an end of this giant. . . ." '

'Ah!' said Roach again. 'The mouse-deer! Now what's she trying?'

'What d'you mean?' asked Abbott.

'She's telling them one o' the Plandok stories. Plandok's the Malay for the mouse-deer—and it's her name too. The mouse-deer's the smallest thing in the jungle just about, and the Malays reckon it's the cleverest—always comes out on top. I wonder . . .'

'. . . and Plandok went into the hut and lay down on the floor and tied a bandage round his head and lay there, waiting. And after a little he heard the earth shaking under the feet of the giant.'

'Wah!' exclaimed the children.

'And the earth shook and the trees shook and the hut shook. And the giant came to the doorway and he shouted: "Give me the fish!"'

'And the mouse-deer groaned.

'The giant roared: "Who is there? Who is groaning?"

'And the mouse-deer said: "It is I only—Plandok, the mouse-deer."

'The giant thrust through the door, and when his eyes became accustomed to the light in the hut, he asked: "Why is your head bandaged?"

'And the mouse-deer answered: "It is the stink of the fish. Can you not smell it yourself? It has poisoned my head so that it aches."

'The giant sniffed and said: "My head aches too."

'And the mouse-deer said: "Lie down. I will bandage it."

'The giant lay down upon the floor of the hut and Plandok took a great length of cloth and wrapped it about his head and made fast the ends of it to pegs in the floor of the hut that he had driven into the ground below. And then he said: "I have a pain in my ankles also from the poison. Do not you have a pain in your ankles?"

'The giant moved his feet and said: "Yes, I have a pain in my ankles. Bandage them then for me too."

'And Plandok bandaged his ankles and fastened the ends of the bandages to other pegs in the floor. And then he said: "Do not your legs ache?"

'The giant flexed the muscles in his legs and said: "They ache also."

'And Plandok bandaged them in their turn and fastened the ends of the cloth to the pegs in the ground. Afterwards he straightened himself and took the bandage off his own head.

'Then the giant took fright suddenly and began to strain at the bandages, and said: "What have you done to me?"

'Plandok laughed.'

Instantly, in comradeship, the children laughed with Plandok.

'The giant roared with anger.'

The children murmured in chorus: 'Wah!'

'Plandok said: "Lie still, giant, or I will take a peg and drive it through your temples and you will die." And the giant lay still.'

'Ai-e-e-e!' An exclamation of delicious apprehension spread through the children.

The girl was silent for a long while, and one of the boys prompted: 'Then?'

'Then the pig and the bear and the tiger came back from the fishing, and Plandok stood at the door of the hut and they said: "The giant has not been?"

'Plandok answered: "The giant has been."

'They said: "He has taken the fish?"

'Plandok answered: "He has not taken the fish. The fish is there and the giant is there. Do with him what you will."'

There was a deep murmur of approbation, and the same boy repeated: 'And then?'

'They killed him,' said the girl with simple finality.

'Wah!' exclaimed the children.

She stood up, and the little semicircle broke like quicksilver and scattered, excited and laughing, across the deck.

Roach straightened himself and walked back to Abbott. 'Always on top. She was tellin' them the one about how Plandok talked the giant into letting himself be tied up.'

Abbott looked at him curiously. 'What's the harm in that?'

'No harm,' answered Roach shortly, 'but what's she up to? Reckon she's tryin' to get the children on her side.'

'Why?'

Roach disregarded him.

A voice from the mast-head called suddenly in Malay, and Roach said: 'Land!' and called back. The voice floated down again, melodiously hiding its excitement. He reached out for the long glass and hoisted himself up into the ratlines.

Before he had settled himself the girl was past him and already pointing.

Below them the deck buzzed into an activity of interest. The captain came up the ladder. Downie came up a little after him. The women and the children in the waist went to the port bulwarks and stared uncomprehendingly into the distance.

Roach shut the glass with a series of swift clicks and dropped down to the deck again. He said to Ross: 'Captain, sir, Christmas Island. Bearing nor'-nor'-west.'

'Good,' said Ross. 'Keep her as she goes.'

The girl came to them, smiling, clearly happy. 'It is an island with mountains. Of this I am glad. I have too long been without my mountain.'

'Your mountain?' asked Ross curiously.

'The great mountain,' explained the girl soberly, 'Kinabalu.'

'These are less than Kinabalu.' Roach was gentle.

'No matter, they are mountains.'

The Irishman in the chains bellowed: 'Thirty fath'm 'n' no bottom.'
Ross called back: 'Right! Keep it going.'

They stared up at the overhang of the cliffs. In the late afternoon light
they were dark and shadowy, but at the south point a blowhole took the
water of the ocean swell and drove it up in a crystal fountain that caught
the sun beyond the cliffs and blazed for an instant and died, and rose
and blazed again. The east side of the island was all in shadow, and
clouds of sea-birds swept out of the shadow, caught the sun, shone bright
for a moment against the blue of the sky, and dived back into the shadow
as if they were diving into a pool. The air was full of their screaming. It
rose above the noise of the breakers against the rocks. Everywhere the
breakers rolled in and splashed and made long rolls of silver against the
foot of the rocks.

Hare stood beside Ross, his eyes straining in the effort to assure himself
of a landing place.

There was no landing place.

The wind was west of north. This was the lee side, but everywhere the
water broke in a purposeless, boiling anger. They passed up the cliffs,
heading away a little at times as the flaws hit them, and, like a punctua-
tion of their passage, the cry came back to them over and over again:
'Thirty fath'm 'n' no bottom.'

Off Low Point, the easternmost point of the island, the wind freshened. They went past it fast but the tiny cove was filled, like all the rest,
with broken water.

Clear of the point they hauled up to the north. Through the long glass
they could see a waterfall and another stream beyond it, but there was
still no landing place. Above the cliffs the land rose steeply to the northern hill. It was not a mountain, but it had, with the sunset low behind it,
a certain splendour. Trees flagged its summit and grew thick and tumbled
on its slopes. Out of the trees came now a vast flight of pigeons, first like a
grey haze against the darkness of the green, and then, as with the gulls,
flashing into the last of the sunlight, but flashing more splendidly, thousands upon thousands of them, catching the light simultaneously as they
wheeled, diminishing and increasing it with the movements of their wings.

The girl watched it all entranced. Her eyes were shining, her lips
parted. To Abbott she was the very essence of innocence—until he again
remembered the kris. He watched her, almost ignoring the miracle of the
pigeons.

The ship drove on, with the Irishman's voice, weary and disillusioned
now: 'Thirty fath'm 'n' no bottom.'

Ross took a bearing on the point. 'Mr. Hare, sir, we stand off and on till
morning?'

'Bring her about!' ordered Hare, ignoring the suggestion. 'We will look into the landing place.'

'Won't be any good,' said Ross abruptly, while Roach watched his face. 'With this wind there will be the devil and all of a sea across the reef. Leave it till morning. Maybe the wind will change.'

'Bring her about!' repeated Hare shortly.

'It will be dark before we can get abeam of it,' said the captain stubbornly. 'If the wind falls light with the sunset we shall be embayed between there and the north-west point.'

Hare turned with sudden anger. He seemed to expand to twice his size. It was not that he became inflated but merely that anger exaggerated the stature of the man. 'It is my desire that you shall bring her about, Captain Ross. The wind will hold enough for our purposes.'

Ross shrugged his shoulders. 'As you wish'.

They went past the mouth of the cove in the last of the light. It was silver and grey and purple: silver where the surf broke in a continuous line across the curve of it, grey where the beach lifted in the twilight, purple where the shadowed woods rose.

'Even when the wind fell light two days ago, wasn't a hope of a landin'.' Roach frowned at the white necklace of surf.

'There's a curse on the island,' suggested Ross sceptically.

Roach looked at him, brooding. 'How long is he goin' to keep us thrashin' back and forth here?'

'Till he gets tired. His mind don't work the ordinary ways. Any sign of a break yet?'

Roach was holding the long glass up against the rigging, steadying it against the mouth of the little cove. 'Not a break. Worse than yesterday. Do we go on for a week? Ten days? A month?'

'Ask him!' snapped Ross. He walked over to the far side of the deck where Hare leant morosely against the rail, with Downie standing in front of him yielding, always a little awkwardly, to the scend of the ship. 'No sign of a break,' Ross reported, his manner cold. Hare only grunted. The captain waited for a moment and tried again. 'You will always have this trouble with the wind in the north. Half the year nothing will land. You will have to reckon on being cut off. Supposing a ship came with stuff that you needed badly?'

'She would wait,' replied Hare belligerently.

'If she was your ship—not otherwise. You have got to reckon on that.'

'It is a good island,' said Hare, obviously adhering to a line of thought.

'It's a good island,' agreed Ross patiently, 'but it's a damned bad

landing. A ship would be in danger any time with a shift of the wind—
and there is the surf to get through.'

'Food, water, fish, timber—there's all that you need there.'

'Not all.' Ross contradicted him openly. 'Not all. And anything you
would want from outside could hang up on the wind for a month on
end. Five days we've been here now and there hasn't been a let-up—not
a ghost of a let-up.'

'Heave her to,' Hare ordered without animation. 'We will take the
boat in again.'

'We'll heave to clear of the north point,' said Ross with what was
almost open rebellion. 'I will not risk the ship again.'

It was more than an hour before they got the longboat alongside.
They had towed her for the five days in which they had waited for the
surf to die.

Hare said: 'I go with her.' And, looking past the first two men, added:
'I will take the second mate.'

They sailed her to the mouth of the cove, the second mate at the tiller.
She handled well for a ship's boat, but the course was easy. As they approached, the palm trees acquired solidity and stood out against the
deep green shadow of their background. The forest trees on the slope
became sculptural and magnificent. The rocks took on a solidity and a
roundness. Even the spray altered: it was no longer a tumbling line of
snow; it separated into individual crests, into upcurving shapes and
down-falling cascades; as they came into the mouth of the cove—sail
dropped and the oars out—it shattered into individual diamonds, immensely gay. None the less, there was no break to them. Where Abbott
knew the gap in the threatening reef to be there was only a later breaking, a less urgent brilliance, and athwart it ran cross-waves from the
edges of the reefs, and eddies, and vicious, jerking seas.

For a long time Hare watched them, his eyes hooded and brooding.
When he spoke at last his voice was angry and low and determined.
'Give way all together. Hold her bows on the dead tree beyond the three
big rocks.' He pointed.

Abbott accepted the mark instantly and at the same time said in a
voice of protest: 'You are taking her through!'

The men had already picked up the stroke and the boat was heading
for the gap. They had been lying only fifteen yards beyond the breakers,
backing water and holding their position. Now they were into the surf
almost before they were aware of what they were doing. The bows of the
boat lifted and fell with a thud as the water broke under them. Spray
came inboard. Then they could see, towering over them, the curling
crest of a wave. The stern rose with it. No water came aboard, but

they drove with the force of it into the centre of the channel. Instantly the boat was hit by a wave from the reef on the starboard hand. As the bows swung away a wave from the port-hand reef caught her. She flung up, heeled, steadied, and was hit again and again and again. And then suddenly they were in the water. One moment they were wet but upright and the next moment they were floundering, all of them—the six oarsmen, the bowman, Abbott and Hare.

Even while he threshed in the bubble-charged water Abbott thought: He will land on his God-damned island all right. He came to the surface and found the boat floating upright but completely waterlogged alongside him. The five Malays of the crew were already hanging on to the sides of her. They were shouting, full of laughter. One of the Irishmen was there, the other was invisible.

Hare had risen from the water five yards away, blowing and furious with himself. As Abbott watched him, he heaved up humorously like a walrus and dived. He came up much closer to the port-hand reef but he had the second Irishman in his grip. He held the man's head in the air, and a quirk of the water took them in towards the fanged coral. Abbott shouted, and one of the Malays, swimming like a fish, headed over towards them.

Hare showed no sign of having heard the shouts. He seemed cool and completely in control of himself. He judged the distance of the fangs of the reef and the strength of the eddy. Pulling the half-conscious man with him, he moved to take advantage of the swirl. It left them, as the run of a sea passed, and again they surged towards the coral, and again Hare, wary and collected, waited for an outward swirl of the water.

Abbott called to the bowman: 'Get in!' The bowman was light, hardly more than a boy. 'Find something! See if you can move the water.'

The Malay understood his gestures, not his words. He slithered over the bows, and the boat dipped and came back again.

Once more Abbott turned. Hare was almost on the coral now, but he still had the Irishman by the shoulders, he still fought, he was still calm. The Malay had reached him; the second mate heard him shout words that he could not understand. For one last moment Hare waited, and then, with another outward surge of the water, he won away from the rocks, the Malay helping on the other side.

After a long time they reached the boat.

Hare's greeting was: 'God damn it! Haven't you got her clear yet? You've had time to dry her out by now.'

Another of the Malays wriggled over the side like an eel. With two of them bailing, the boat rose in the water. The half-drowned Irishman hung gasping to the stern. In a little the boat was floating high enough for a third man to climb in. Two oars had been salvaged. They got her far enough clear to haul the Irishman in, and one by one the rest of them clambered aboard. The sail and the mast were gone. The boat crept out slowly, like a tired water-beetle.

Hours after, it seemed, Ross brought the ship in to meet them. Hare went up the ladder, heavy and tired.

Ross, waiting for him at the side, looked down at the longboat and asked: 'What happened?'

Ignoring the question, Hare said: 'Work out a course for the Cocos Keeling.'

Hare and Ross had gone below to take up the unending argument over the future. Roach leant over the poop rail, watching the man coiling down. Abbott stood to the side of the man at the wheel, watching the compass as the ship settled on the new course. Only Plandok, standing close to the wheel-box, still stared at the diminishing perspective of the island.

When she spoke it was hardly above a whisper, yet it had an urgency in it that reached Roach across half the width of the ship. 'Where we go now?'

Abbott, still watching the compass, answered: 'West.'

'Where?'

This time there was a fierceness in the whisper so that Abbott looked up, puzzled. 'To the Cocos Keeling.' Then, realizing that this would of itself convey nothing to the girl, he added: 'Another island.'

'England?' The whisper had the same urgency.

He answered, almost irritated now: 'Not England, another island. Two days from here—three perhaps.'

She said in Malay, and the naked desperation in her voice made Roach turn from the rail: 'I must go east! I must go east!' Her whole body was taut, gathered as if ready for a spring.

Roach called: 'Watch her, mister! If she gets at the wheel she'll have the sticks out o' the ship.' He strode across to the girl. 'Below!' he said harshly, and then in Malay: 'We're going to another island—an atoll—to look at it. After that, I don't know.'

The girl relaxed, her shoulders drooped. She turned wordlessly and walked to the ladder.

Roach, watching her, said quietly to Abbott: 'What the devil is she mulling over in her mind now?'

# BOOK TWO

# THE ISLAND

# Eight

THE GANNET flew slowly, so high that it was brilliant in the light of the sun that had not yet reached the ship. Beyond it they could already see a second and then a group of three.

Ross said: 'We're pointing too much to the north'ard. Bring her to port a bit, Mr. Roach. We'll raise the land in a little over an hour. Put a man in the crosstrees!' He walked over to the ladder indifferently.

Astern of them the sun came up. Suddenly there were hundreds of birds. They slipped through the diving squadrons.

The full day came and the horizon ahead grew hard and distinct. The line of the palm trees was like a bar of malachite when they sighted it, pencil-thin and clear.

The women in the waist clustered along the port rail, talking volubly. 'Timah, the head wife, and the Kling woman were on the poop. Plandok was apart from the other women, engulfed in a surge of children.

Abbott had the watch now. He looked down at her fondly. He was sure that she was becoming a child again, lapsing back from the harsh necessity of having to defend—sentimentally he thought of it as 'her honour'. Hare had left her alone after they had abandoned hope of landing on Christmas Island.

The children jockeyed for position close to her. When the boys climbed on to the rail she pulled them back; she answered questions; she responded to them. But he noted that she did not smile and he was sorry: she had not smiled, he thought, since they had set course away from Christmas Island. The women had left her alone too. They seemed to hover in their attitude towards her in a mixture of apprehension and uncertainty. He thought that they could not understand her.

It was possible to see the breaks between the palm trees now. They had no chart of the islands, nothing more than a rough pencilled outline that Ross had found among his papers—the sort of thing that ships' masters acquired from other masters in the course of quiet conversation over wine—but Abbott was sure that the first break must be the gap between the northernmost islet and the islet that covered the anchorage.

Pencilled against this was the name 'Direction'. He did not know who had given it that name or what it signified. They could see only the windward islands yet and only the northernmost of those. He knew that the lagoon stretched far down to the southward.

Hare came up the ladder and stood staring at the green lines of the palms. After a minute he called to the two women, and they turned submissively and went down the ladder to the waist.

Abbott crossed over to him. 'We can see between the northern islands now, sir. From the drawing the channel lies a thought closer to the port-hand islet.'

'Direction Island,' announced Hare brusquely, as if determined to accept no compromise. He barked the name so loudly that Abbott moved back a pace. He looked up at the sails as if to judge the wind.

Abbott said helpfully: 'It's falling light, sir.'

'That I can see,' retorted Hare fiercely. 'Call me when you can see the surf!'

He went down the ladder, grunting and irascible, and barked at the scatter of children that ran to meet him.

All through the forenoon watch the palm trees grew. From a bar of malachite they became a rampart, a cliff of jade. The higher crests developed out of a fretted raggedness to individuality, to shape, to solidity, and under them at last the eternal white of the reef edge began to play across the blue of the ocean. It lacked half an hour before the change of watches. Abbott called Ross and then Hare.

The captain came on deck briskly, measured the distances with his eye, assessed the weight of the wind and the set of sails in one quick, comprehensive glance, and ordered: 'Get the longboat ready for lowering. Mr. Roach will go in with her ahead of us, but I want two men in the crosstrees—two good men who can tell a coral head from a patch of weed. See to it!'

Abbott went down to the waist. As he passed the girl she said to him in English: 'This is th'island?' She ran the definite article and the noun together but her English was already acquiring clarity.

'Yes, this is it. This is Cocos.'

Almost contemptuously she said: 'A flat island!' And he remembered poignantly her heart-cry for Kinabalu.

Farther down the deck the Chinese girl, who also spoke English, asked him: 'What hurts her now?'

'The islands are flat. She was used to a mountain.'

'Mountain or flat country, it is all the same,' said the Chinese girl philosophically. 'At least the palm trees are beautiful.'

They crept in very slowly under the fore and main topsails. Well before they reached the shoal water the longboat was ahead of them, crawling like a beetle. The wind died with the noonday sun, but there was enough left for the ship to ghost silently in, the noise of the surf on the reefs rising from a thin, tenuous thread of sound to a harsh vibration that permeated everything in the ship and in their beings.

The colour of the water changed abruptly from the ultramarine of the depths to the first pale blues of the coral mass. The blues changed almost as abruptly to a dark green, and then, as they turned to port to make the anchorage inside Direction, it became suddenly, overwhelmingly, aquamarine. Abbott had never seen a transition such as this. There was no substance in the water, they floated in the green of the sunlight reflected from the bottom. The boat ahead of them also floated in light. The lead, as it was swung ahead of the boat, splashed and sent out great concentric ripples that did no more than vary the gemstone quality of the water. Abbott, in the eyes of the ship, watched with a sense of wonder.

The girl was a little behind him. Once or twice he glanced at her. She was staring with her inevitable unchildlike stillness at the inward shore, utterly peaceful inside the protective roaring of the reef. The children had not followed her up here to the fo'c'sle—the mate had frightened them away.

Behind him Abbott heard the captain's voice shouting the orders to clew up the topsails. The ship glided on, as if once in the embrace of the atoll it no longer required the motive power of the wind. The soundings from the longboat came back, always diminishing. Twice the men shouted from the crosstrees, but no helm orders followed. The passage was wide enough. The ship had all but lost way now.

Abbott waited, flexed and tense, for the word, and presently he heard the captain's voice: 'Let go, mister!' And he repeated the order to the bosun.

The anchor went away with a rush of sound and a violent tremor through the deck. The splash as it hit the water changed the nature of the sound and the quality of the surface, producing two enormous sets of ripples that rushed out from the stem and caught up with the longboat and surrounded it before they disappeared.

The mate, standing in the stern-sheets of the longboat with the tiller between his legs, half turned, called something, and the longboat began to come round.

The ship gathered an almost imperceptible sternway, swinging a little away from the anchor. Abbott could see the bottom now. The flukes had not bitten into the sand but lay flat. He held up one arm to indicate the line as the cable began to grow. The ship drifted farther and farther, and he saw the anchor come upright and one fluke begin to bite into the sand.

From far behind him he heard Ross shout at last: 'Hold that, mister!' And the men began to bit the cable. Ross himself came forward to the fo'c'sle.

Abbott said: 'I think it will hold.'

Shortly Ross answered him: 'It had better! I want an anchor watch all the time we lie here—at any rate until we know what the wind is going to do. See to it!' He turned and looked at Plandok. 'Has she said anything?'

'Nothing. I think she was pleased to come to land.'

'Don't think!' snapped Ross, and went aft to talk to the mate as he came up the ladder from the longboat.

The speed with which the girl moved was fantastic. At one moment she was standing silent and withdrawn on the deck. The next instant her body was flashing down towards the water in a faint and intensely graceful curve. She made hardly a splash as she took the water, but from her a brilliance of bubbles leaped back to the surface. A long way after it her sarong came floating up, weaving and twisting as if it had a life of its own. From the height of the fo'c'sle head Abbott could see the brown body, delicate and attenuated in the water, acquiring added colour in the richness of the green light as she lost the impetus of the dive and began to swim under water.

There was no need for him to shout. The women had done that for him, a violent, agitated chorus. Abbott began, ridiculously, to tug at his boots.

The girl broke surface a long way clear of the ship and began to swim strongly towards the crescent of the beach.

Roach, talking to Ross, said brusquely: 'The little devil! Shall I take the longboat after her?'

Hare, leaning over the rail above them, ordered: 'Let her swim! She'll come to no harm.'

'Sharks?' questioned Roach, and, catching sight of Abbott out of the corner of his eyes, shouted: 'Don't be a fool!'

Hare said: 'We've seen none. She swims like a fish.'

Sheepishly Abbott began to pull on his boots again.

The women kept up their chorus until Hare came down the ladder into the waist and strode through them, bellowing. He mounted the fo'c'sle ladder and stood beside Abbott. 'You should not have let her go.'

'I couldn't have stopped her. No one could have stopped her. She moved'—almost poetically he found a simile—'she moved like a bird.'

Already the girl was halfway in to the shallows. She swam rhythmically, leaving behind her a continuous pattern of ripples and eddies and small, bright patches of foam. Anxiously Abbott scanned the water for the fin of a shark. Nothing showed. Behind the dark of her small body the aquamarine grew polished and perfect again.

They saw her reach the shallows and lift herself swiftly from the water. For a moment she stood still. Then she began to splash in to the beach.

At the very edge of the water she halted, looking over the sand. There were no footmarks on it—no human footmarks. There were tracks where turtle had dragged themselves ashore. There were the erratic and intricate patterns of the movement of land crabs. There were bird footprints, and worm marks, and the whorled arabesques of moving shells. There was no mark of man. All this she took in in a brief questing sweep of the head. She saw the tidemark with its raffle of flotsam. She saw the clean drifted sand beyond that. And she began to walk up the beach, quite straight, quite naked, quite unselfconscious, not turning to look back at the ship or even to question if there were pursuit.

It was very hot on the beach. The glare was intense after the comparative coolness of the sea lights. The heat of the sun struck down and upwards at the same time. She walked in it encompassed in a physical glow of happiness, and the tracks of her feet, close together and firm and steady, went straight from the water's edge to the edge of the shade.

The nearest palms sprawled outwards, hanging over the sand, the crests of some of them reaching out over the water. They made a patterned shadow at first, long feathers of darkness on the whiteness of the sand that grew and solidified into patches of shade, flecked here and there with small roundels of light.

Then even the sunlight failed, and she stalked into an enchanting and perfect coolness. There was a thick litter of palm trash between the boles but the trees rose from it columnar and soaring. As she reached the first of them, a pair of fairy terns, like delicate, aerial familiars of the place, swept out to meet her, lifted in mock fright upwards, swirled through the palm fronds, and came down again, their wings silent as moths' wings, their dance ethereal as the mating play of butterflies.

She looked up at them, and for the first time in many months she laughed.

The terns followed her as she walked, picking her way through the debris of the fallen fronds and the rotting coconuts, brushing through

young trees, avoiding fallen and mouldering trunks; but always heading
to the east, as if she were drawn by a lodestone. She made no attempt to
measure distance; she was not aware of time. She moved in a cool
shade that for this imperishable moment was hers alone. She had escaped
from Hare, she had escaped from man's world.

She knew that there was nothing for her beyond the brief quarter-mile
of the heart of the island. On the other side, beyond the palm trees, there
would be another beach and the flat of the coral reef, and beyond the
reef the secure prison of the surf. But it was necessary for her spirit that
she should discover these things for herself alone and by herself alone.

She walked steadily, neither hurrying nor irritated by the devious path
that was forced on her by the trash and by the occasional ironwood
trees and scrub bushes that struggled between the palms. The white birds
flitted through the shade behind and above and beyond her, always
wholly and perfectly silent, watching her with their black eyes.

After a long time she saw a light between the boles, light that was
banded in zones: a long streak of blue that was the clear sky, a turquoise zone that was the haze beyond the sea, an ultramarine that was
the sea, and then the blinding white of the surf, and under it green and
white and shadow mingled. Nothing that she knew compared with it.
She could only see the ineffable perfection of the beauty towards which
she moved.

She came at last to the edge of the palms. The beach here had a different character. Coral boulders lay across it and smaller, rounded
stones. The water in the shallows over the slabbed coral of the reefs was
of a green so pallid that it was hardly visible until at last, with the
deeper pools, it acquired colour and texture, and farther on, with the
live coral and the shell-fish, acquired in succession beauty and form. Tiny
wavelets from the surf edge ran across it. It had a life and a liveliness.
Small wading birds darted with erratic zigzag movements about it.
Gulls cruised along the surf edge. The very character of the air was different—fresh and salty, the air of the ocean.

Instead of ending in the peace of the lagoon, here it ended in tumult.
The surf broke in a gusty majesty of sound and of brilliance. It was not
high, for the wind that had brought them ghosting into the anchorage
was not now strong enough to lift even the palm fronds. The ocean
swell made it, a movement regular as breathing, but a regularity broken
dramatically by the fanged palisade of the reef. It rose, it broke, it tossed
up the diamonds of its spray, and it fell away, sucking and roaring, into
deep hollows that filled at once again with the succession of its fellows.
The same hot sun shone down on it but it shone on a different splendour.

She stood at the edge of the shadow and stared out towards the east, towards an absolute and illimitable emptiness, and behind her the terns wove their patterns in and out towards the palms, as if they were afraid to come out into the naked sun.

After a little she wept.

# Nine

THE ENCHANTMENT had gone out of the island. She walked through the palms conscious of bird droppings and the sour smell of rotted fish. Flies rose and followed her. The leaf trash acquired the appearance of dirt. Nor was the place any longer hers alone: she saw carved on the palm stems letters, writing in the English tongue, and beyond the lettered trees pools that had been dug for wells in a clearing and lay now stagnant and covered with a green scum on which bird feathers rested incongruously.

Finally, as she came towards her landing place, she heard voices, Hare's booming authoritatively among them. With a shiver of dismal apprehension she thought: They are seeking me.

Hare strode through the clearing with an immense authority. The indecisions of the ship seemed to have dropped away from him, with the weakness and vacillation of the departure from the Cape. Once again he was a pioneer.

He said: 'Here we will build the bangsals. We can cut a clear path through to the beach in an hour. There will be no need to uproot the seedlings in the other clearing.'

He called to Abbott: 'Make a mark here for the beginning of the village!'

And he watched as Abbott, awkward with the long parang, sliced a blaze on the trunk of a palm. He measured his paces from it up the clearing, and the men, grasping his intention at once, began to hack away the undergrowth, to clear the piles of trash, to cut the path. He marked off hut site after hut site, naming them as he did so with finality. He knew precisely what he wished to do, the exact shape of the village that he proposed to build. Abbott was astonished at the expansion of the man. Halfway down the clearing Hare shouted: 'You will find pits dug for the water beyond the clearing—that way, I think.'

Abbott took three of the men, wondering. The pits were there; old, silted in, stagnant, but, none the less, there. He set his men to work to clear them out and went back to Hare. A palm tree crashing down almost involved him. He leapt aside, swearing, and came on.

Hare said: 'You'll learn to mind out for yourself, mister. Take these three and clear the path through to the beach!'

His voice was elated. He was on top of his world. The islands were bigger than he had thought that they would be; wide enough to live on, and there was a whole range of them to the southward. He was sure that there would be a water balance in the delicate equipose of fresh on salt, water that moved up and down with the tides but stayed always drinkable. Someone—the captain's brother, he was sure—had planted seedlings. There were bananas and citrus fruits and young breadfruit and papaya. The beach was an admirable landing place; the width of the island sheltered it from the north-east trades, the width of the lagoon sheltered it from the south-west. There was sea-food and fish, oysters and turtle, land crabs and coconuts. There was pandanus palm for the thatching and ironwood for timber. There was everything that a man might need. There was space. There was peace.

He called to Abbott, halfway down the path to the beach and hacking away for dear life: 'This place will do. I am not greedy. I seek no more for a kingdom. This is itself a kingdom.'

Plandok saw him through the screen of the palm trunks, striding about with magnificent gestures. He looked more than life-size. Humanly, childishly even, she giggled, and without further thought walked straight into the clearing.

The Malays saw her first. They saw and acknowledged her nakedness and discreetly turned their eyes away. Abbott, facing her as Hare's bulk moved out of his line of vision, saw her and gasped. He saw only her immaturity.

Hare wheeled round at the gasp, following with a pioneer's wariness the line of Abbott's eyes. In turn he saw her. He saw only the hilt of the kris, the polished ivory smoothness of its carving, the long, flat outline of its threat under the bandage of silk around her thigh. He called furiously: 'Cover your nakedness!'

She stood with her eyes alight in acknowledgement of the mischief she had done. 'The water took my new sarong,' she answered him directly.

Abbott, inspired by the quality of the vernal innocence that he believed he saw, stripped off his shirt, gathered it in his hands, and, walking up to her, put it over her head. She fumbled a little for the unaccustomed armholes and he felt the soft vigour of her flesh beneath his hands. Then she found the sleeves and the shirt fell, ludicrous and enveloping, about her. She stood quite still, her arms flaccid, her hands not reaching the opening of the cuffs. She allowed her shoulders to droop a little, her head to bow. To Abbott she was wrapped in an immeasurable pathos.

Even Hare for a moment was taken in, and then suddenly his enormous frame began to shake and he laughed outright. 'You look like a hantu.'

She seemed to realize by intuition that the word meant ghost and, lifting her ludicrous arms, she flapped them mournfully.

Hare laughed again. Then he said over his laughter: 'It is manifest that thou art Plandok.' And the girl laughed with him.

She settled herself in the stern-sheets of the boat, clear of the tiller and out of the way of the stroke oar. Abbott recognized again how much she knew of the ways of boats. She waited until they were clear of the immediate shallows. Then she stretched over and took a piece of cord from a box of oddments in the stern-sheets. Straightening her body, she passed it round her waist. It went round twice, gathering in the shirt, and she tied it competently. Then she rolled up the sleeves in turn and settled them. At once the absurdity disappeared. The dress became rational; the long shirt covered her completely and, gathered in by the cord, restored the slimness of her line.

She looked up at him with a face innocent of everything, even of inquisitiveness, and asked in English: 'When the ship go?'

He jumped as he always did when she used English. 'I don't know. Four days—five days, perhaps. When we've finished unloading.'

She disregarded the latter part of the explanation. What she needed was the information as to the number of days. She waited for a while before she asked: 'The ship go England?' To the last word she gave an enormous significance.

Abbott shook his head. 'No, east. We go east to Singapore.'

'Ah!' she said softly, the word almost a sigh.

After a little she moved and accidentally, he was sure, her body came in contact with his leg. He could feel the softness of it and its lithe vigour. She seemed to rest against him. He thought: She is trustful.

After a long silence she looked up at him, her eyes liquid and enormous. 'I come with *you?*' There was just enough emphasis on the personal pronoun to make it clear to him that the request had a personal significance.

He put his hand on her shoulder in what was meant to be a fatherly pat and that by some alchemy of the girl's nature seemed to change itself into a caress. 'He says that you are to stay on the island with——' He was going to say 'with him' but altered it hurriedly to 'with the others'.

Gently, as if she had not understood the words, she repeated: 'I go with *you.*'

Ross lay almost on his shoulder blades in the chair that Hare used ordinarily. Roach had his shirt off. Abbott had not yet put a fresh shirt on. The atmosphere of the cabin was relaxed, as if a weight had been lifted from each of the three men individually.

Ross held up his glass and squinted through the white of the geneva. 'And he is going to sleep ashore tonight?'

Abbott nodded. 'He wants the Chinese girl and Mei Ying, and there's a list of bedding and cooking-pots and the Lord alone knows.' He fished the paper out of his pocket.

'He has settled on the first clearing?'

Abbott nodded again. 'It's the best. The seedlings in the other clearing are coming up. We found initials on a palm tree: "J.C.R." and the date "December, 1825".'

The captain said: 'John Clunies-Ross, my brother. He must have called here on his way back. December . . . we'll have crossed him on the passage. There's no saying how long he stayed.'

'Long enough to plant bananas and a lot of other stuff. We're to get the stores clear in five days.'

'How the hell does he think we're going to do that if he's got half the hands ashore?'

'He said you were to keep as many as you needed. . . .'

'And if I do,' grumbled Ross, 'he will scream like a wounded tiger. When does he want the women ashore?'

'In the morning,' Abbott replied, 'to make atap for the roofs. They come off again each night till the huts are ready.'

'I'll be glad to be shot of 'em,' said Ross thoughtfully. He yawned and drank. 'I'm tired of being captain of a floating bawdyhouse.'

Roach looked up at him quickly and grinned. 'It's a bit late to be having scruples. If he's goin' to stay ashore . . .' He left the sentence unfinished.

Ross cut across his words. 'You leave the Cape girls alone!'

'Ha!' Roach lifted his glass and looked mockingly over it.

Abbott fumbled in his pocket for a second paper. 'He's made a list.' He held the paper up.

Ross said: 'You mean the ones who stay?'

Abbott passed the paper across to the captain. 'Forty altogether, apart from himself.'

'And the rest?'

'They go on with the ship. We're to put them ashore in Singapore.'

Ross said soberly: 'I'll have the manumission papers before I'll sail with one of them aboard. I will not risk a prosecution for slave-trading under the Act. By God, I'll not!'

Abbott asked awkwardly: 'What about the girl?'

All three men knew at once which girl he meant.

Ross, running his eye down the paper, said: 'She's on the list.'

'She is on the list,' agreed Abbott. 'She wishes to go with us.'

'How do you know?'

'She asked me,' Abbott answered stubbornly.

'You will be careful about her,' Ross ordered acidly. 'I'll not cross Hare's bows more than I have to. Keep clear of her!'

Abbott said hurriedly, too hurriedly: 'She is a child. She does not like this . . .' He waved a wide hand that included everything of the ship. 'She wants to go back to her father. By God, she looked like a waif in my shirt!'

'A waif with a knife between her legs.' Ross's voice grew still more acrid.

'She is a child,' Abbott persisted with a surprising firmness.

The Kling woman looked beyond her, as if communing with unseen faces far past her shoulder. 'You have shamed us all.' Her voice was harsh. The girl regarded her indifferently. 'It is not enough that you fled from the ship, but that when you were recaptured you were naked.'

The girl smiled gently. 'I was not recaptured.' Her voice was so soft that it was not possible to accuse her of insolence. 'I walked into the clearing that they prepare for the kampong. I was naked because the water took my sarong'—she leant forward suddenly—'and my nakedness is a matter for myself—alone.'

'It is a matter for the Tuan Běsar.'

'That is between him and me. He laughed.' She paused and considered the matter. 'He laughed with me. Is it your wish that I should go back and tell him that you will not give me my sarong again?'

Reluctantly the Kling woman pushed the folded cloth over the floor. 'It is here, but it does not resolve the shame.'

The girl rested her chin on her hand. 'All of you'—she included all the listening women without bothering to collect them with her eyes—'all of you go naked with the Tuan. If there is shame in me there is shame also in you, all of you. You call yourselves his wives but you are not his wives. The Koran says that a man may have four wives, but the Tuan Běsar is not of the faith. He is a Christian: a Christian has but one wife. You are slaves, the slaves of his body—nothing more.'

The Kling woman darted her head forward with a look of blind vindictiveness.

'You go naked knowing that you are slaves. That is the shame. I go naked because it is my will, and I will go naked when it is my will and not because the Tuan Bĕsar requires it.'

She rose to her feet and peeled off the second mate's shirt, making of the lithe, simple movements a calculated insolence. For a long moment she stood stripped, knowing that every woman's eye was fixed on the kris with its ivory hilt. Then, slowly and deliberately, she arranged the bright sarong round her waist and tucked it in. Stooping, she gathered the shirt and went to the door.

'*Tid'apa.*' The traditional Malay phrase could mean that the matter was of no importance or it could mean that it was no business of theirs. Her manner made it sound like a rebuke.

At sunset the shirt was dry again. She had ironed it with the iron that the old woman 'Timah kept for the Tuan's shirts alone. Neatly folded now and glistening, she carried it to Abbott on the quarter-deck. Her eyes were starry. She emanated an air of happiness. But when she spoke her voice had overtones of pleading. She held the shirt on the flats of her outstretched hands.

Every line of her body submissive, she spoke in Malay. 'To have worn it is too great an honour. Now I have made it fresh for the Tuan. Be pleased to accept my thanks.'

The serang, standing close to Abbott, translated.

Abbott said awkwardly: 'It is nothing. I was glad to do it.' He took the shirt, his hands touching hers—by accident, he thought. A small thrill that he could not properly understand ran through him with the contact.

The girl said: 'It was a great thing. You saved me from shame.'

Again the serang translated, and Abbott said hurriedly: 'There was no shame.'

As the serang translated back to her the girl thought: He is a fool but he is a kind fool. She bowed, supple and graceful, and whispered in English: 'I will go with the Tuan Abbott.' She pronounced his name 'Abba', following the custom of the women.

# Ten

HARE HAD decided to make the final landing ceremonious. The kampong was complete now. It had taken eleven days against the five of his first estimate, but that, of course, was inevitable.

The long main clearing ran deep into the heart of the island. A straight path ran through it from the beach. The big house, Hare's house—it was no more than a long, high roof supported on the truncated uprights of palm trees—was on the eastern side of the path. Before it and beyond it were store-houses, and sheds for the simple presses that he had brought for the manufacture of oil from the coconuts.

There were houses for the five married men. Their wives were to live with them again now—they were no longer segregated as they had been to protect them from the crew of the ship. There was another hut for the unmarried men. The three old wives had a hut to themselves. Next to it was a long hut for the younger women and beyond that a hut for the children; they were opposite Hare's own quarters. Downie had a hut near the beach, away from the rest. The kampong was Western in lay-out, incongruous in the shadow of the palms; yet it was cool and easy to keep clean, and for the time, Roach believed, it would serve.

He watched the procession ironically. The children came first, crowned with little white scented flowers, and the young girls next. Plandok walked in the centre of them between the two half-coloured girls from the Cape and the youngest of the Chinese girls. She walked with an air of ease and acceptance. Roach thought that it had an element of exaggeration. Behind her walked the black girl by herself, and then the older women with babies, and, last of all, the three old wives—'Timah, Mei Ying, and the Kling woman.

Between the huts the gamelan played. Hare had always kept enough men to make an orchestra. The plaintive, nostalgic music wandered through the soaring boles of the palms.

Hare sat on the big chair that had been brought ashore at last, watching his 'fiddle-faddle' with the air of a Roman emperor at a village festival. His aura was benign and bountiful. The children greeted him as the gay, fanciful little procession reached the chair. They made the traditional salutations and Hare accepted them easily.

Roach, watching with a sceptic eye, was convinced that he was quite genuine in his acceptance, that he thought that the salutations were his due and by his acceptance of them he was conferring a real and meaningful favour. The bigger girls made their salutations in turn, and Roach realized with a quick tingle of delight that Plandok was no longer with them. Somehow in the excitement she had slipped away. He wondered what plot she was hatching now, what mischief.

The young women made their bows. The older women followed them. 'Timah passed last of all before Hare's chair, salaamed, and moved to sit on the woven matting by his side.

And then, as Hare turned to speak to the old woman, Plandok walked softly to the chair. The laughter and the talk hushed. As if by a single impulse the eyes of the group turned towards her. She fell gracefully to her knees and stretched forward in an elaborate prostration.

Her voice came up to them clear and distinct and innocent of mockery, and yet the whole thing was a mockery as she said: '*Susuhunan, oh susuhunan!*' There was a quick catch of breath in the ranks of the women. Without lifting her head, the girl went on in a monstrous parody of the flowered greetings to the Emperor of Java—the Object of Adoration. Somewhere she had acquired a complete knowledge of the honorifics. Now, without exaggeration, she made the simple ceremony and Hare himself appear ridiculous.

Roach watched Hare growing red with anger and unable to do anything without making himself look even more ridiculous. Over his shoulder he said softly to Abbott: 'If she was my daughter she'd have her bottom smacked so hard she wouldn't sit for a fortnight.'

Hare rose suddenly from the chair, his face almost purple. 'Enough! Enough!'

The girl rose to her knees, checked herself, bent forward just enough still to look humble, and gazed at him with enormous, liquid eyes.

In the shadow of the trees a man sniggered.

Abbott had said: 'Not the last boat, but the one before the last. The last they will search for a certainty.'

She crouched under a layer of canvas and sacking that was going back to the ship. The boat was afloat already, held steady by two of the Irish hands. They knew about her; that too had been arranged. She had seen Hare less than two minutes before and had accepted a tongue-lashing meekly. She was certain that no search would be made for her, quite certain. It was unlikely that any search would be made before dawn.

Everybody was full and sleepy with the food and the liquor. The long festivity of the First Day had gone on all through the moonlit darkness. Her head was ringing with the rhythm of the gamelan, her eyes were tired.

Through the night the frightened birds had kept up a canopy of beating wings above the palms, their voices raucous over the music of the gamelan. They were silent now. This was the silence before the dawn, the silence before the gannets began their morning flight. It was time that the boat went out. The tension grew in her. From the low moon there was enough light for her to see under the canvas and make out the dim side of the boat. She was lying under the second thwart on the starboard side, as still as the oars that lay on the thwarts above her, motionless, fragile, a shadow among the shadows.

The hands plucked her out from under the canvas before she had time to get at the kris. They wrapped her in the canvas, rolling her in it like a cocoon to keep her still and impotent. They seemed to know precisely where she was. Someone must have betrayed her; one of the Irishmen, she was sure—the tall, cadaverous one. She could not think why he would have betrayed her, there was no reason for it except that he might be thinking of reward. She was carried to the shore between the two men.

Hare was waiting on the beach. He looked down at her mockingly, her face visible and furious in the moonlight. 'You would have done better to have swum, but even then I would have searched the ship for you. You did not think that I would let you go thus easily? There is still much between you and me.' He spoke to her as he would have spoken to an adult.

She watched him with her eyes hostile, recognizing that words were useless.

'Bring her!' he said at last, and stalked ahead towards the path.

In a sense it was a parody of the procession that she had parodied. This time there were no flowers and no songs and no music. They dumped her in front of Hare's doorway. The low moon made no light in the clearing but there was light enough in the sky above to make the outlines of the place distinct. She could see with her furious eyes the roof ridge of the hut of the elder wives and beyond it the hut of the young women and beyond that still the hut of the children, and over the other side the hut of the oil press and the store-house. She sought them out as if it could somehow help her impotence.

Hare came out of the doorway. He carried a whip in his hand. She had seen him beat the Zulu girl with it before. He beat her now. The first slash of it stung through the canvas in which she was wrapped.

The pain was unimportant. What mattered was the assault on her identity. She writhed desperately, her arms held close to her sides by the wrapping of the canvas, and the lash came down again and again and again. Each time her anger grew. She was infused with it. It permeated every area of her body. It was composed of humiliation and an awareness of ridicule, shame, and an intention of revenge. She moved after each blow, hardly aware of the physical contact of the lash, aware only of the diminishment of her dignity. She made no sound, no overt acknowledgement of what was happening. Twice she brought her knees under her and attempted a convulsive movement towards where Hare stood, cold and oddly impassive. Each time he moved backwards far enough and the whip descended again and again.

She could not see faces in the darkness, but she was aware of eyes. The women ringed her somewhere in invisibility, watching her and rejoicing in her degradation.

Hare stopped beating her at last with no more preamble than he had begun. He tossed the whip behind him back into the hut and stood looking down at her, sombre and tall and powerful. And while her right hand clutched frantically on the hilt of the kris under the pinning folds of the canvas he said: 'Take her to the children's hut!'

Men drifted out from under the darkness of the eaves and picked her up. The hands were impersonal on her. They carried her to the children's hut. The door was opened and she was dumped unceremoniously inside in a tangle of childish limbs and bodies. Then the door was shut again, and the chain pulled round it and the padlock locked. She lay quite still, listening to the small, sharp, metallic noises.

Then she heard Hare call out sarcastically: 'Sleep well!'

The children unwrapped her, fumbling in the darkness. They made little liquid, cooing noises. They patted her arms, her legs, her head. They made a space on the mats for her and half lifted, half pushed her to it. They were full of pity and solicitude. It was like a whispering of sympathy.

In the darkness of the hut it was impossible to know who ministered to her, except when she could recognize the whispered voices. It did not matter. They had all known that she would try to escape. They had not known the plan but only that she believed that she would sail with the ship. They waited for her to cry, but she lay quite still on the matting, and for a long time they sat around her, some of them touching her to comfort her, some keeping away, afraid to have to share in her sorrow.

The song came to them as they sat. It was very far off, deep, a song of men's voices, slow and rhythmical—the anchor shanty as the *Hippomenes* got under way. Now and then, as the drift of the night wind came in to them, they could hear even the clicking of the pawls beating out a rhythm to the singing.

Then the song ceased, and they heard shouting and wood banging against wood, and faintly, almost indistinguishable under the sea-birds' crying, the squeak of the halliards in the unoiled blocks. Another song came, a quicker shanty as the topsails went up, and then a third song that grew faint in the distance.

In the absolute darkness of the hut Plandok turned on her side. Even then she did not weep.

# Eleven

THE LIGHT in the hut was soft and gentle. No sun reached it so early in the morning. The dawn clamour of the birds was silent, the gannets long since gone on their outward flight.

The children sat in two little groups, oddly intertwined, each group centred about one of the two oldest of them, two small, gentle pyramids of different coloured limbs—pale gold with the Chinese children, dark with the Indian blood, darkest of all with the younger of the two Cape girls.

It was she who spoke first. Her name was 'Mina, the diminutive of Philomena, and she was round, soft-looking, sly. She said, certain at last that Plandok was awake: 'The ship is gone. What will you do now?'

Plandok turned her head a little and studied her. She could, of course, frighten her into silence without trouble, but she wanted the children on her side. Coolly she answered: 'I will wait.'

'He will beat you again!' The girl 'Mina brought the talk swiftly to Hare.

'He will not beat me again. Such talk is foolish.'

'And if he sends for you?'

Plandok had her opportunity. 'I will go'—she put her hand down with a quick movement to the inside of her thigh—'as I went before.' She allowed the words to be full of menace. 'I will not again be wrapped in folds of cloth.'

A delighted shiver ran through the other group.

S'pia, the centre of it, said softly: 'But if the ship never comes back?'

Plandok sat herself up and stretched luxuriously. The canvas had protected her; there was no pain from the beating. 'It will come back or, if it does not, there will be other ships. Three have been here already; you have seen the names, I myself have shown them to you. More will come.'

S'pia said: 'But Abba has gone.'

There was a little murmur through the children.

Reinforced by it, 'Mina asked boldly: 'You love Abba?'

'No.' Plandok smiled a smile of an odd, communicable wickedness. 'I did not love him. I allowed him to grow to love me so that I could use him. But he was a fool, he was not worth love. I should have swum out to the ship.'

There was a flutter of admiration through the children.

S'pia said: 'It was the Kling woman who betrayed you. The Irishman told her—the one she slept with in the ship.'

'Tid'apa.' Plandok's slim shoulders made a little upward shrug. 'It is no matter. The plan itself was folly. It was his plan—Abba's.'

'And now there is neither ship nor lover!' S'pia was incurably romantic.

'He was not my lover. I have no lover, nor will I have a lover until I choose. I am myself alone. I do not need a lover. I am the daughter of the Pangaran.' The children swayed away from her in a proper recognition of respectful terror. 'I am not a slave.' She looked at S'pia with her eyes narrowing. 'You are his slave.'

The girl had a beautiful head. Her neck and shoulders were brilliantly moulded. Her hair had strong red lights in it. She held herself with a certain pride. 'I am his slave. It is our adat and . . .'

'And when he sends for you, you will go.'

'I will go,' S'pia answered without emotion in her voice.

'Would you not rather go to a man that you love?'

Cornered, the girl answered reluctantly: 'There is here no man to love.'

'Ha!' exclaimed Plandok derisively.

The children seemed to weave themselves closer in as if in need of protection against her contempt.

'It is the adat,' said two voices simultaneously, seeking refuge in tradition.

'Other ships will come,' Plandok repeated, 'and other men with them. What can he do to you?'

'Beat us,' said five of the voices simultaneously.

The Cape girl looked at her faintly puzzled. 'You are sure that other ships will come, but you do not know. They may not come ever. No men have lived in this place before.'

'They will come,' asserted Plandok simply. 'I have arranged it.'

Again the gasp of respect ran through the children. It was the measure of her ascendancy over them that they would believe even this.

'Mina alone asked: 'How?'

'I knew that it would not be easy for me to escape. Therefore I spoke to the men. I told them that at Singapura they should say in talk upon the other ships and on the waterfront and in the eating places that the daughter of the Pangaran was upon an island at such and such a place and desired that her father should come to her.'

'I do not know where Singapura is,' said 'Mina stubbornly. 'How shall that help you?'

'They will talk,' replied Plandok patiently, as if explaining obvious truths to a witless one. 'They will talk to the people of the water. They will talk to the Bugis and the Bugis will carry the word. There is nowhere in the islands where the Bugis do not go. My father will hear of it, for he will capture a ship and someone will save his life by telling him that I am alive.' She was silent while they watched her with wide, enormous eyes. 'It cannot fail,' she said positively and, standing up, began to rearrange the bright sarong. She had already offset much of her loss of prestige.

The drink had given Downie courage. The jackal was become the wolf. He slumped at ease in his chair.

Hare had called him to celebrate. 'We are on our own now. Drink to it!'

The women waited respectfully in the distance, uncomprehending, anxious only to serve the evening meal when Hare called for it.

Hare said: 'Damned French ideas—the noble savage! They don't know these people as we know them.'

Obliquely Downie said: 'All the same, you should have sent her on with the ship.'

Hare looked at him balefully. 'Do you assert that I cannot handle a child?'

Downie waved his glass in a parody of salutation. 'There is nothing you cannot handle, but that one is a trouble-maker. She terrifies the women.'

'Good!' returned Hare obscurely. 'They will be the more docile. There is nothing she can do to them.'

'Two things,' said Downie portentously, putting down his glass and holding up two fingers, 'two things.' He bent one of his fingers over. 'Her father——'

'Her father is dead!' Hare broke across his words.

'They do not know it.'

'And there is no way she can communicate with him.'

'There is a way,' replied Downie craftily. 'You do not know everything that happens. I make it my business to know. There is a way.' He put his feet up on the table.

Hare stretched out and kicked them with sudden anger. 'How?' he roared at him.

'She told the Malays on the ship to spread the word at Singapore, to tell the Bugis that the daughter of the Pangaran was here.'

'How do you know this?' demanded Hare harshly.

'She told it to the children this morning'—for the first time Downie's voice was quite simple—'and the children told me.'

'The Pangaran is dead,' said Hare with finality. He pounced. 'Your second point, sir?'

Downie moved finger and thumb to his index finger and bent it slowly over. 'She has the aspect of murder.' His voice was thick now. 'With that kris she must kill. The women know this.'

Hare began to laugh. 'She will not kill. It is a threat only. In a little she will come to me of herself. In the meantime she has spirit; she has more spirit than all these put together.' He waved his hand to indicate the women sitting silently at the far end of the great hut. 'With her we will not grow dull on this island.' He leaned right forward and glared at Downie. 'You will have nothing to do with her. You understand this? You have your own women.' His eyes clouded and became brutal. 'If you touch her I will have you tied to a tree and flogged by the men. You understand?'

Downie emptied his glass before he answered. 'I have my own women and I would not relish a knife in my ribs. I will leave her alone.'

'Drink!' ordered Hare drunkenly. 'No one spies on us here. We are our own masters. This is no longer the Cape with missionaries, and the Anti-Slavery League, and the Governor who is too good to live. Drink!'

The Kling woman said: 'He sleeps like a pig.'

There was a little ripple of unease among the other women. They were afraid of Downie, not physically, but because of his circuitous mind and because of the meanness of his revenges. They watched him for a while in silence.

Kam Ho, the Chinese girl, asked doubtfully: 'Where has the Tuan Běsar gone?'

'To seek the daughter of the Pangaran.' She made the name seem like a vituperation. She spat largely and eyed the great red-stained pool of betel juice. 'She is a witch.'

'Timah said: 'She is not a witch, she is a wilful child. She should be beaten again.'

The Kling woman answered harshly: 'He should have sent her with the ship.'

A voice said: 'There will be no peace until she goes.'

'Therefore,' nodded the Kling woman, 'we must make a plan.'

Imperceptibly three of the younger wives edged away from her.

The Kling woman said scornfully: 'You are afraid. What are you afraid of?'

'Timah, contemplating the pattern of the mat on which she sat, murmured: 'They are afraid of the kris, they are afraid of that pig there, they are afraid of the Tuan Bĕsar, they are afraid of the Pangaran. These things are enough for fear.'

'She is one child,' returned the Kling woman angrily.

Kam Ho looked up hurriedly. 'You said yourself she is a witch and of that too I am afraid. She has told me to withhold myself from the Tuan Bĕsar. She says that we are slaves and fools to give ourselves to him.'

'That she has told me too,' said another voice.

'And me also.'

'This is all foolishness,' said 'Timah. 'We cannot withhold ourselves, those of us that he still wants. It is the adat. We have been happy in the past.'

'And yet'—the Chinese girl's voice was eager—'I would have liked a young man.'

'What can a young man do that he cannot?' demanded the Kling woman contemptuously. 'His back is still strong. It is this child who has put these thoughts in your head. This is a place of peace. We could be happy here again. Therefore,' she repeated, 'we must make a plan.'

'But how?' asked Kam Ho.

Hare walked down the path with a ponderous dignity. He was drunk, but still had total control of himself. The women's guess was right: he was looking for Plandok. The voices of the children had been noisiest from the northern side of the island. They were silent now but he knew that they were still there. They would be with Plandok; they followed her, accepting her leadership.

He heard her voice before he reached the edge of the screen of young palms on the sea beach above the constant murmur of the surf. It rose and fell in the singsong of the village story-teller. She would be telling another of the Plandok stories, he thought. She had an inexhaustible supply of them. He went quietly to the edge of the screen and looked out. The beach was in shade, the sun so low that the shallows and even the edge of the reef were dark in the shadow of the palms. The girl was seated on a coral boulder, cross-legged on a pad of leaves. The children sat below her with upturned faces. They followed the intricate, delicate movements of her hands with a rapt attention. She was telling the story of Plandok in the pit.

'And then'—she laughed, her eyes shining—'the deer stood upon the back of the pig and Plandok stood upon the back of the deer, and from there he could leap easily to the rim of the pit. And so he leapt, and easily, to the rim of the pit. And so he leapt and left the others in the pit behind him. And they were angry, and with their feet they dug against the sides of the pit until the earth came down, and they dug and they dug and they dug till they were weary and their hooves were sore and bleeding. But at last they pulled enough earth down to scramble over the rim and on to the ground again, and they pursued Plandok. All through the night they followed in the tracks that he had made, and at dawn he heard them coming and he climbed into a great tree where hung a wild bees' nest.'

She broke off suddenly. 'Look!' Her voice quivered with excitement. 'They come.'

At once the children turned away, the enchantment broken. They stared out to sea, following her pointing finger. Far away like white specks in the low sunlight they could see the gannets coming back to roost. They stood watching them with an intensity of anticipation that Hare could not understand. He watched them in his turn, swaying slightly on his feet, fascinated.

After a long minute in which the birds came closer and closer so that they were winged specks now and very clear against the pale light of the east, the girl said abruptly: 'Look!'

Instantly they turned to her: the degree of ascendancy that she had attained was incredible. She was holding her hand up, pointing high, and Hare, slightly impeded by the palm fronds, looked up into the sky where she pointed.

The sky was full of frigate birds wheeling on long black pinions, superb and graceful, making wide arabesques against the turquoise. The gulls came in. They were so close now that they could be seen as gulls. They flew slowly, gorged, flapping their wings to sustain the enormous weight of fish that they carried in their crops.

The girl had risen to her feet. She stood on the pad of palm fronds, poised as if ready to take off in flight herself, and, once again, she flung up her arm. 'Now!' she cried.

As though she commanded the evening ambush, streams of frigate birds dived on the leaders of the gannets. In an instant there was a turmoil in the air. The white birds swung off to left or to right or dived away from the raid, but always the thin-winged, exquisite precision of the frigate birds forced them to the moment of despair. The crops expelled the undigested fish. Now and then it could be seen flashing in the sunlight, and the frigate birds, turning in miracles of elegance, swooped in and took it as it fell.

The girl stood clapping her hands and laughing, her face turned up and eager.

Hare, watching her from the screen of the trees, thought: She is like a frigate bird herself; and then, grinning ruefully, but she is also like Plandok. At last he turned and walked back along the path. As he went he thought: Is it possible to have an utterly ruthless child? As he reached the big hut he answered himself: 'Yes.' Then he clapped his hands and called for food.

# Twelve

THE BOY Saad saw the canoe first, but only by a fraction of a second. Plandok knew at once that it was important to her as it lay, half covered with seaweed and palm wrack, on the flotsam line of the spring tide. It was a small canoe of the type used by boys in Java to learn the lore of the sea and the techniques of fishing. It was sea-battered, the float of the outrigger was gone, and one of the struts as well. The other still cocked up from the canoe as it lay over on one side, with ends of sennit drooping disconsolately from it. They pulled it over until it was upright, and with quick hands cleared it of flotsam and leaves.

The boy said: 'It is broken.'

With a discerning eye Plandok answered: 'There is nothing broken that cannot be mended. This is mine.'

'I saw it first,' protested Saad. She did not even answer him; she merely turned her head and looked at him for a moment, and he said hastily: 'It is as you wish.'

'It is mine,' she repeated, 'and it is my secret. We will hide it now in the bushes. Afterwards I will see what can be done with it.'

Between them they carried it away from the beach. There was an iron-wood tree just inside the line of the shore palms and a flurry of young trees and scrub and nipa palm beyond. In the middle of this they placed it and covered it with fronds.

'Now,' said Plandok, 'you can go where you choose, but see that you say nothing of this now or hereafter—nothing.'

'I will say nothing.' The boy went down the beach reluctantly.

Plandok swung off the opposite way, her head down, thinking. She was light-hearted, elated even—not that she could see any immediate need for the canoe, but it was still a symbol of independence, a symbol of freedom.

They had been on the island three months now. Hare had organized a method of life that suited him absolutely. The women looked after him with an enhanced devotion; they intrigued for a place in his bed; they quarrelled amongst themselves; they were indolent and inefficient, but they were also languorous. He was the master—more now than ever. He moved from the big hut late in the mornings to bathe and the women followed him, adoring, to bathe with him. They hung flowers round his head and he looked like an incongruous bearded Pan with a powerful admixture of Silenus. Food was ready for him if he clapped his hands, drink was always there.

The halcyon days went by in timeless succession, each day precisely like the last except that the shower of cooling rain changed its hour at times. It was neither too hot nor too cold at the Cocos. It neither blew too hard nor grew too stiflingly still. The water was always warm, but not too hot to be refreshing in the midday, and all through the hot afternoons the cool trade winds blew.

Hare did no work now. He had expended all his inclination for work in the building of the kampong. Now it was no longer necessary for him to work: he had the women.

Downie worked. He drove the eight Malay men whom Hare had established ashore with an endless nagging energy. They fished, they sent down coconuts, they cleared scrub; and the women whom Hare was not using at the time worked with them, under the lash of his tongue. The oil presses were set up. Hare had told him that they must have a cargo of palm oil for the ship when she next passed through, and in the pressing of the oil he could work out his obscure revenges. He drove his own two wives more harshly than any of the others. Oddly enough, they loved him. Even the children worked, carrying in the coconuts to the husking, carrying the white meat to the presses, gathering shell-fish. The older boys went in the boats with the men. The whole village turned out at times to use the seine net. Everyone worked on the island, Downie hardest of all, a slave to his need to establish his own superiority.

Only Hare did not work at all—Hare and Plandok. The girl had the quality of invisibility; she was never there when work was necessary. Sometimes to please herself she would go out with the boys in the boats. She gathered shell-fish when she wished to wander in the shallows. She would go up the leaning palms that hung out over the water to get young nuts if she was thirsty. But she did these things when she chose and in her own time, and she ignored Downie. Short of beating her, there was nothing that he could do.

The wives had tried to starve her—that was the first of the Kling woman's plans. But when she was hungry she sat herself down at Hare's table, and he laughed, guessing the probabilities, and let her eat. They had tried not talking to her and she had appeared unaware of it. They had made the children keep away from her for three whole days once, but the children themselves had brought that to an end.

Hare used to send for her in the afternoons. He had developed an inquisitive passion for her stories, always sensing the personal emphasis that she put on the legends that her Dyak nurse had woven into her being. He knew that she thought of herself as the mouse-deer—weak, small, cunning, and infinitely resourceful. He knew that she had a profound conviction of triumph.

Occasionally he fondled her a little and she would allow it with a humorous gleam in her eye, as if she knew perfectly well what his thought was and was prepared to allow him so much indulgence and no more. Improbably a real friendship grew up between them, but when he tried to evaluate it, he knew that it was perilously poised.

Each morning as a ritual she went, he knew, to the north-east to look into the sunrise.

No ships came.

On the evening of the second day after the finding of the canoe she went back from the nightly sport of the frigate birds. The boats were not in yet and, with the children, she went down to the landing place to watch them approaching. They were working towards the south end of the lagoon now, and they came drifting in with the light evening air in their sails, silhouetted and very beautiful against the sunset. Looking beyond them, she knew suddenly what she would do with the canoe. Underscoring the boats, very dark against the last glow of the light, the line of the palms of the west island became a promised land and the promise became accessible. The canoe made it accessible.

The next morning, after the ritual search of the horizon to the east, she went to the hiding place. The canoe was safe.

It had dried out now. One triangular piece was smashed out of the side almost amidships: there would be no difficulty in putting a patch on that. An ironwood branch would serve for the broken strut. She could steal enough cord from the stores to make the lashings. There remained the float. She considered the boy for a while and decided at last that it was beyond him. It would have to be shaped out of a solid block, streamlined, and balanced so that it would not make the canoe too heavy or unmanageable. The whole thing had to be light enough for her to handle and she knew the limits of her strength. She would appeal to Pa Abas. Pa Abas was the shipwright, the skilled carpenter, the man on whom Hare relied for all the woodwork of the colony. The wife of Pa Abas would object, of course, but that was unimportant; the wives always objected when she asked their men for anything. Pa Abas would do it, but how could she stop him talking?

She thought for a little and then said to the boy: 'Saad, you would like a small boat to sail in the shallows.'

'I have a small boat.'

'None the less, you would like another—a bigger one.' She bent over the sound strut and stretched her arms to indicate the length. 'A boat as large as this.' He grinned at her suddenly, grasping her meaning. 'Pa Abas would like to shape you such a boat.'

'He would not!'

'But if I asked him he would.'

Saad laughed outright. 'What devilment do you do now?'

'No devilment. I need a canoe so that I may be by myself when I wish to be.'

'You will not take me with you, then?'

'Sometimes,' she replied graciously. 'There will be occasions when I need company.'

'Who is to ask Pa Abas?'

'You,' said the girl firmly, 'but I will help you when he says no.'

It took two weeks for the float to be made. In the end it was a thought too fine in the bows, being shaped like a prau, but it would serve well enough. She and the boy bored holes through it to take the lashings of the struts. They had to make a fire to heat an iron and it took eight days for them to get through the hard wood, but there was no hurry.

She had not yet learnt that the Kling woman was advocating the use of white arsenic, of which there was a canister in the store. The Kling woman was especially angry with her now, for Plandok had prejudiced Hare against her with an amusing mixture of derision—the Kling woman's breasts drooped shamefully and the skin of her neck was scrawny and dry-looking—and parodies of her inexhaustible supply of stories. How much Hare understood she did not know, but there had been three separate bursts of trouble between him and the Kling woman, and that was sufficient.

The lashing was easy enough; she had done much of it on her father's prau. She took pride in it, working out the traditional patterns with care and memory.

When it was all finished the canoe was too heavy for the two of them to carry.

The boy said: 'I will fetch Neh Basir and Batin Alam.'

'You will not! This is our secret only. We do not share it.' And she began to undo the lashings so that they could carry the heavy wooden float separately.

A month after they had first seen the canoe they carried it in moonlight to the lagoon beach and hid it, the canoe and the float together, in a safe patch of scrub. It required much effort.

Two nights later, with the lashings renewed, they launched it and in the still brilliance of the night they paddled over the lagoon shallows with their mysterious luminescences until they were sure that it was sound and that she could handle it alone. Then, grunting and gasping in the darkness, they dragged it back to the security of the scrub.

The Kling woman used the white arsenic two days later. It was a remarkable coincidence. She had been awaiting an opportunity for a full month. Plandok ate one mouthful of the curry that hid it, but one only. She recognized at once that there was something evil in it.

The Kling woman had a daughter Halijah. Watching her mother, Plandok pushed the plate across to her and said: 'I am not hungry. Eat!' Then, as the Kling woman snatched the plate away, she said: 'I am Plandok. Next time she will eat it or she will feel my kris.'

Nothing more was said. None of the other women, not even the three who knew about the plan, offered comment or even talked. They sat quietly eating, and the girl sat placid with her beautiful hands in her lap and gave no sign either of anxiety or of anger.

At nightfall, with the boy Saad to help her, she dragged the canoe down to the water again. She had brought things with her: rice, dried fish, a line and hooks, a parang, a small mat, a length of cloth, tea and a cooking-pot, flint and tinder.

As they dragged the canoe, the boy kept whispering: 'Where are you going? To where are you going?'

At last, when they had dragged the canoe into the water and it floated, she answered: 'To be by myself. This time you do not come. But brush out the marks of the keel before you go home, and if the Sush'nong'— this was the derisive diminutive she used for the honorific Susuhunan— 'grows too angry tell him that the Kling woman tried to poison me.'

'Then she will poison *me*,' said Saad reasonably.

Plandok shook her head in the moonlight. 'No, she will not try to poison anyone for a time now.'

'None the less, I am afraid of her.'

'But you are afraid also of the Sush'nong. You must choose.'

One gleam of light showed through the palm trees, but only for a little, then it disappeared and the palms themselves diminished. From a dark cliff they sank slowly to the dimensions of a wall. The water became very lonely. It was not still this night. The wind blew softly and easily across it, making ripples that beat against the bow of the canoe with gentle liquid noises. She was not afraid. Often enough in the past she had moved at night in the dark refuges where the Pangaran's prau had anchored. She was aware of the special qualities of darkness and of water.

The canoe was not easy to manage. It took time to acquire its rhythm and its character. At the beginning she discovered, looking back over her shoulder at the light, that she was being set to the southward. And then one time, looking back over her shoulder, there was no longer a light, and she chose a bright star in the arc of the horizon where she knew the west island lay and steered by that.

The star paths were broken on the water but, as she looked down through the parallelogram of the outrigger struts, she could see other lights: the pulsing glow of the jelly-fish, the vague, creeping green of unidentifiable creatures in the coral, the darting flash of a startled fish. She came to a stretch of water that was milk-white in the moonlight, the white sand bottom of the anchorage. Fish paths crossed it at intervals, but for the most part it was as if the sea bed itself shone up at her and the canoe floated on a pool of milky light, the float and the outrigger very dark against its brilliance.

She was aware of the west island first as a strengthening of the horizon. Then it was like a low edging, a fringe, a palisade, and at last a cliff stretching out wide on either hand, losing itself in ultimate darkness. She came to dark water and broken coral, and finally to the insubstantial crystal of the shallows, and the canoe's bow struck softly on sand.

The tide was falling but she knew that it would rise again with the sun. She dragged the canoe far enough on to the beach to grip firmly, and went ashore with the line of the painter in her hand. It was long enough to reach to the stem of a bush, and she fastened it there.

She was very tired. Her arms were aching, there was a burning pain in the joints, her back was stiff and sore. She took the cloth and the tinder and the flint and a little bundle of coconut husk, and in the warm darkness of the beach palms she lay down to sleep.

Here in the lee of the palms the wind was still. There was a rustle only in the uppermost leaves and over it occasionally the night squeak of an uneasy bird. In the leaf trash below the palms she could hear rustling and over the sand the soft, all but inaudible whisper of the land crabs moving down to the water to moisten their branchiae. She lay quite still.

She was almost afraid.

The light woke her, for she lay with her face towards the east. She had planned exactly what she meant to do, and she woke clear-eyed and ready. It took her no more than a moment to gather the cloth and the unused tinder, then she tore off a branch and wiped out the foot-marks on the beach.

The canoe was broadside on in the shallows, already afloat. She went down to it backwards, brushing out the footsteps of the night and of the morning and, as soon as she was afloat, moved down the coast towards the south. The men who had gone over to loose the pigs on the west island had told her of a deep bay, a small interior lagoon, halfway down the length of the island. As she paddled, she looked out over her shoulder but there was no sign of searching boats.

The sun was well up when she came to the recurved point of the inner lagoon and she slipped round it at the top of the tide. They had told her that most of it was covered with soft mud but that there were deep pools in it. She headed north again and found what she was searching for, a creek that led in through the arching palms, a place secret and inviolable, and, moving her gear from the canoe, she tipped it until it filled with water and added lumps of coral to it till it sank. Then she covered it with weeds and wrack until it no longer had the shape of anything that floated.

While she worked at it she became aware of the terns. As on the first day on Direction Island, they floated silently like moths, watching her with their black, bright eyes. The terns on Direction Island had de-serted her after the first few days, frightened by the clumsy insistence of the children, scared by the older women, intimidated by the axe noises and the tearing at the palms and the building of the kampong, and, above all, afraid of Hare's enormous, noise-filled progress. It could be that these were the same terns, but it did not matter. The birds had come back to her; it was auspicious.

She made a bundle of the things in the cloth and moved back towards the lagoon beach, seeking for a mark by which she could identify the place. The jungle growth was denser here than on Direction Island. There was more ironwood, more dadass, kamiri, more small palms, but close to the lagoon beach it was clearer and she found almost at once a configuration of rocks that was enough for guidance.

She moved lightly now. A gaiety overtook her and occasionally on the open ground beneath the trees she skipped. Sometimes she sang in little snatches. An immense and indefinable happiness encompassed her. She was alone. She possessed herself.

After a long while, up to the north at the edge of a pool that struck suddenly blinding blue through the pillars of the palms, she made herself a camp of sorts. She was utterly confident. They would not search for her this morning. They would not discover that she was gone until the day was almost done. After she had eaten she would look out to identify the sails of the fishing boats but they would have put out long before her absence was discovered. Not until tomorrow would they search for her. When she had eaten she slipped out of her sarong, unwound the silken bandage of the kris and stood, grave and wholly relaxed, as if freed of a burden. Yet when she went towards the water she took the weapon with her and laid it on a log by the water-side. The pool was cool, the water only faintly brackish. The bottom was brilliant white sand but the blueness persisted. She swam in it naked and free, her skin outlined in tiny silver bubbles. Now and then she laughed. And the terns wheeled and floated over the water.

The search did not reach the west island until the third day. A furious Hare had harried the men down the islands of the eastern side, certain that she had waded or swum across the shallow channels. They had found nothing. He had sent the boats to Horsburgh, the northernmost island, and there too they had found nothing—only their own footprints on the wind-smoothed sand and the marks of their own boats when they had gone there to release the first of the pigs.

The boats reached Panjang, the west island, late in the afternoon when they did come, and the girl watched them, lying on her stomach in the fringing scrub, her eyes brilliant with mischief and her whole small body like a leaf on the wind with the intoxication of freedom.

They searched perfunctorily. Twice men passed within touching distance of her. She watched them with stifled laughter, and when they were out of earshot she laughed aloud. Once, as Downie came plodding along the beach, the terns swooped down low and flashed through the bush which hid her, and she whispered: 'Do not betray me. Go!' Downie plodded on, unseeing. The men went away in the end, Downie calling them back to the boats. His voice was rasping.

She had an impulse to go out on the beach as their sails filled for the homeward run, but the remembered caution of her father held her safe. She lay still, laughing, and the terns came down again and perched on a bough above her shoulder.

In the days that followed she explored all the island. Three times she saw the pigs that had been loosed. There was a boar and four young sows. They were rooting amongst the fallen coconuts, but already they had acquired the instinct of wildness: they fled when they heard her. For the rest she had the company of the indignant gannets, the frigate birds that eyed her from the palms and the ironwood trees, the stupidity of the noddies, and always and incessantly the silent friendship of the terns.

On the outer beach there was wreckage: a mast, a cabin door, carvings, and a broken spar. There were tree trunks, one of them with a bright lizard basking in the sun upon it, and sprouting coconuts, and crabs' backs and shells, and the fragile puff-balls of the Portuguese men-of-war. The island was a treasure chest of sea wrack.

She carried her bundle with her where she went and she slept where the sunset found her. She made her fires deep in among the palms where no light could betray her to the outside and even the smoke was attenuated by the branches and the wind. She sang and she laughed and she was utterly free.

But on the tenth day—she had not counted but it was the tenth day—she took the cooking-pot and the cloth and the few things that were left to her, and she went back round the head of the inner lagoon and searched for the creek where she had left the canoe. That night she slept close to it, and in the morning, after she had gone to the eastern beach for her bright ritual of the sunrise, she began to free the boat of the coral lumps and the rubbish and the weeds.

At sunset she headed back for Direction Island, the wind behind her, helping her this time. The sense of freedom persisted in her. It had been vital for her to get away from the intrigues of the women and the importunity of the children and the acrid bitterness of the man Downie, but that necessity was now past. She could go back with a sense of victory.

She landed in the night close to the southern tip of Direction Island. She could make it out clearly by the darkness of the palms against the low stars. It took an hour to get Saad silently out of the family hut, an hour of cautious manœuvre, through all of which she bubbled with silent laughter as if her whole entity were iridescent and lighter than air. When he came whispering with inquisitiveness she drew him down to the canoe.

Only when they had pulled it into the depths of the beach scrub and brushed over the sand to the water's edge would she answer his questions, and then she said: 'I went where I wished to go. I wished to be by myself. There is nothing to tell.' As they went back towards the kampong she asked: 'Was the Sush'nong angry?' Her voice was light and indifferent.

The boy replied wonderingly: 'He was more angered than I have seen him. The Kling woman was beaten, but she has not done anything to me. My mother says that she will be quiet now.'

'Ha!' said Plandok, skipping a little.

Her mind darted from the Kling woman to the community as a whole. She asked: 'Has the child of Mai Munah come yet?'

'A girl,' said Saad affirmatively. 'It cries much. I think it will not live.' Then, as Plandok made no comment: 'It is the Sush'nong's child. Pa

Kadok thinks it is his, but its hair is the colour of the Sush'nong's and the women say that they know.'

'This they know,' agreed Plandok equably, 'the matters of the bed and the cooking place. They have no other knowledge. Their minds are like the minds of sheep.'

# *Thirteen*

THE BOY flung the jala, the small cast net, in a wide, beautiful curve and stood for a moment in the frozen mobility of a Greek bronze. The net sank and he drew it in to him and the fish leapt, furiously enmeshed in it, in a splendour of colour.

Plandok said: 'Put it with the others.'

As he waded into the shallow keep pool, she stood meditative. When he came out again she murmured, hardly bothering whether he caught the words or not: 'I have said all the prayers of the Illanun women for the safe return of the praus. I have made the sacrifices.'

Saad, gathering the net to make another cast, caught the word 'sacrifice' and cocked his head up. 'It was you, then, who stole Ma Ngah's chicken.'

'It was I,' agreed the girl, as if the matter were of no importance at all. 'Also I took rice and turmeric and sugar from Hang Tuah's hut.'

'The sugar also!' The boy nodded, as if things were adding up. 'And the sweetmeats . . .'

'From the Sush'nong.' The girl smiled at him delicately. 'But those were for myself.'

'For that I was beaten!'

'I know. It is the hikayat of Plandok in the pit.'

'Wah! You are a devil, as the black girl says.'

'What is she to you?'

'Nothing,' replied the boy. 'Only she is angry because after you talked to her at the full of the moon she did not go to the Sush'nong, and he was angry with her and *she* was beaten.'

'With unmerited beatings the soul acquires merit.' The girl misquoted from the Chinese.

'Wah!' said the boy again and made a fresh cast with the net. 'I missed. *Insh, Allah!*'

'*Pulak!*' said the girl with an unusual outgoing of sympathy. Saad looked at her suspiciously. 'I made the proper sacrifices but nothing has come, therefore I must try other things.'

'What?' His voice was uneasy.

'All that my Sea Dyak nurse taught me I remember,' Plandok answered obliquely, and waited while her memory ranged back.

'What did she tell you?'

'That a woman can become a manang. This she told me, but it requires ceremonies.'

'What is a manang?'

'A priest, a worker of miracles, a healer.' She poured out the words as if they interfered with her thought processes. 'I do not know the ceremonies. Moreover, it requires the help of other manangs. But if I had a head . . .'

'God alone is real!' Saad dropped the net, his eyes bulging. He made the familiar exclamation into an oath.

The Kling woman crouched on the matting, her shoulders down-bent and disconsolate. Occasionally she picked at a ragged thread of palm frond. She looked old and weary.

Hare said: 'This is your own doing. These things you bring upon yourself. Leave her alone!'

'She says that she will kill me.'

'You have tried to kill her.' Hare's voice was brutally realistic. 'It would be no more than just.'

'I do not wish to die!'

'Nor did she,' Hare's voice rasped. 'But you tried to kill her with arsenic—*my* arsenic!'

'She will make trouble—always she will make trouble!'

Downie, standing against the other chair, said: 'She's right there! That girl will make trouble always. Give her her papers and send her on when the *Borneo* comes back.'

'We would have been contented without her,' said the Kling woman morosely. 'Now we are against her, all of us, but we do not trust each other. The young girls scorn us and talk against us, and . . . and . . .' She halted and looked up pleadingly to Hare. 'And they do not always come to your bed when they are called. It is her doing, all of it!'

Hare grunted. 'That is because you are fools, and the young girls are fools also. In the end'—he shrugged his shoulders—'they come. It is no matter here on the island. We have time; other things we may lack, but we have all the time that there is under God.'

The woman muttered something piously, and in almost the same tone went on: 'But what of this word that she will kill me?'

'Who told you?'

'The boy Saad.'

'Ah!' exclaimed Hare quickly. 'If he told you, she told him to tell you.

And if you were told, she will not do it. She does not give warnings, that one.'

Downie, anxious not to be left out of the discussion, said: 'That is true, Mr. Hare, sir. That is true.'

'Why has she said this? Why do you think she has said this?'

'Because,' answered the Kling woman naively, 'I told the black girl to put the gall bladder of the poison-fish in her rice.'

'That's why she's bolted again,' said Hare ruminatively. He scratched his chin. 'I thought we would get to it sooner or later. Did you know this?' He glared at Downie.

'The Zulu girl told me.'

'Did she do it?'

'She said: "Why should I do her harm for her?" ' He nodded down at the Kling woman on the mat. 'She told Plandok.'

'And Plandok took the canoe and went. Where is she this time? Horsburgh? Panjang? Pulau Atas?'

'God knows!' replied Downie, intimating his opinion that God also did not care.

Hare shrugged his shoulders. 'It may be'—he stood directly over the Kling woman, his face bent over her head—'that she will kill you. That is in her mind and it is in her hands also. If she does I will not punish her, for you have brought this thing upon yourself. It is no more than justice. I will not this time have you beaten, for it may be that you are about to die.'

On her hands and knees the Kling woman went out of the great hut and, as she went, he heard, floating back over her shoulder, the words: 'I am forsaken.'

Downie said: 'I don't understand you.'

Hare glowered at him. 'I do not require your understanding. I should have sent *that* one on to Malacca.'

'I don't understand,' Downie repeated defiantly. 'The Kling woman is right: the girl has destroyed the peace of this island.'

Hare roared at him: 'What do you know of peace? What do you know of her? She is worth all these women. She has spirit, she has fire, she has life. These . . . !' He dismissed them with a gesture of contempt. 'You could not understand her. You are from the gutter of a Liverpool slum. She is the daughter of a leader of men. You could never understand the mind of an aristocrat.'

Four days later, when the boys came running up the path to shout that the canoe was coming—Plandok no longer crept back in the darkness—Hare himself went down to the beach. She handled the canoe beautifully now, her shoulders moving with the paddle in an exquisite economy of effort. The upper half of her body was bare, her sarong adjusted below her breasts. Hare felt a rich, impotent fury of desire sweep through him.

As she came up the beach she lifted the paddle in salute. 'The turtle are laying on the northern beaches. It would be well to collect the eggs. I have a score myself.' She offered no apology, no explanation of her absence.

He laughed at her. He was always surprised and impressed by her candour and her contempt for custom.

The children rushed in and hauled the canoe up, taking the turtle eggs from her.

She said, still sitting in her place: 'If you want them you had better send the boats before nightfall. There is a big wind coming.'

He nodded to her on adult terms. He no longer attempted to treat her as a child or even as a young girl. 'I have seen the cloud.'

He looked over the line of the western breakers. They were high and very brilliant in the sun, angrier than ordinary, a continuous line of white from which leapt brighter summits. Beyond them on the horizon there was a small flower of cloud. It was hardly bigger than the sails of a ship. It was very distant, so far that he could not even judge the distance, but it had an evil light, a mingling of purple and silver wholly different from the cumulus that built up day after day in the hot, upward currents of the air. Hare watched it carefully, according it a wide measure of respect.

The children lifted the canoe from the water and began to carry it up the beach to its usual place.

Plandok stopped them in mid-stride. 'No, take it there!' She pointed to the place where a clump of ironwood came close to the sand edge. 'Push it in as far as—wait! I will show you.'

She walked down the beach with it and Hare watched her curiously. He sat on a boulder of coral, and on the horizon the cloud grew, spreading on either hand so that the central flower of it rested now on a podium of livid greys.

Before the children returned Downie came down to the beach. 'Have you see the glass?' he asked.

Hare nodded curtly.

'Bottom's falling out of it,' Downie went on with a morose relish. 'It's going to blow.'

Hare grunted again.

Downie picked up the direction of his eyes. 'Ha! That's it.' Sobered by Hare's look, he sat down on a lesser boulder.

Plandok came back. Almost indifferently she said over her shoulder as she passed them: 'It is a Tai Fung.' She sat down behind them in the shade, her eyes also fixed on the rising cloud.

The children played noisily for a while in the shallows and then appeared to catch the contagion of apprehension. The air was lifeless, no leaf moved in the palm trees. Even the birds were still. The water was glass smooth. Only the roar of the surf was unnaturally loud and distinct about them. They came up from the shallows and sat with Plandok, demanding a story.

The girl silenced them and sat on, silent herself, except that once she said: 'I was with my father in a Tai Fung north of Tambelan.'

And when a child asked, naturally: 'What happened?' she replied:

'Be still! It took our masts and our sails, and three men drowned.'

Oppressed by the silence, the children left them at last, drifting quietly in through the palms.

A full hour later Hare said: 'It will miss us. It is moving across the north. We will get the edge of it, though.' By a physical effort he broke himself out of his lethargy. 'Get everything lashed up! Get the boats in! There's no telling what it will do. We have not got more than six feet above the water at the highest point of the island.' After a pause he added: 'We could be swept.'

Downie said: 'Never been swept before with all these palms.'

'Palms grow,' said Hare, more to himself than to the other man. 'The ironwood and the dadass are a better guide. I'd say the island has not been swept for a century, but that's not to say that it could not happen now. Get the men to work!'

Behind in the shadows the girl said: 'It is wise. This will be a very great wind.'

The tornado hit them at the edge of darkness. All through the afternoon the wind had risen; beginning with cat's-paws from every point of the compass; settling to a steady blast from the west that bent the trees over and held them there almost without relenting, the fronds streaming downwind like the hair on a woman's head as she swims through breakers. There was nothing to fear in such a wind. Here and there the crown of a palm snapped off with a sharp pistol shot and went whistling, but these things had no importance. It was an honest, steady gale of wind, and under it there were even sudden brilliances of gold and scarlet and purple from the sunset.

Then, with the sunset, the foul wind hit them. It came almost from the north across the island from the outer sea. It came so suddenly that it was impossible to note the lull that there must have been between the steady wind from the west and this new brutality.

They were not prepared for a wind from the north; they had no expectation of it. They had come to believe in the western gale. In its relentless procession through the palm trunks it had possessed them, so that the new direction affected them with a sense of shock.

At its first onslaught it cut a wide swathe through the trees as a sickle cuts through standing corn. The swathe was clear of the kampong, beyond the last of the Malay huts. They could just see in the final silver of the twilight the approach of the spume that came with it, blotting everything out. Then they were enveloped themselves and could hear only the crash of the crowns, the snap of the boles, and the shriek of twisted wood. Water came with the spume. The hut roofs went with the very first onrush.

In the half-dark Plandok and the children could hear Hare roaring, and to his voice they crawled, unable to breathe against the wind, their eyes full of sand and spume and tears.

It was not possible to remember afterwards in detail what happened. Plandok could recall only the shriek of the birds as the foul wind hit them. They had been insanely restless all through the early evening; had cowered, bemused and unseeing, in the steady rush of the western wind. Now it seemed that they exploded in an instant despairing fury and disappeared with the brutal rush.

Hare was in a corner where three trees close together made some sort of wind-break. He had four of the smallest children with him already. As the others reached him, he grabbed at them, packing them into a tight, compact bundle in the exiguous shelter. All the while he kept up a tremendous shouting, unintelligible most of it, some of it ribald, using his voice as a guide. The women began to come in towards it. Plandok felt the Chinese girl next to her and one of the Cape girls. There were others beyond. Once, when the fury of the noise for a moment relented, she heard Downie's voice shouting beyond them. After a while no more women came, and even as she was certain that no more would come, the wind dropped.

It was possible to hear Hare's words now. He bawled: 'We must get to the ironwood trees. We will have the sea over us if there is another gust like that.'

It was hardly possible to believe that the sea was not over them already. Wind-driven water under the spume had flooded the belt between them and the reef beach. They crouched in a streaming flood that even in the hot tropic air chilled them as they waited.

Hare moved when he thought that they understood his intention, and they crawled with him and behind him, touching one another in the darkness, a bruised, rippling line of children and women. None of the men had reached them.

The lull held, a lull in relative terms only. It was stronger than the wind from the west had been in the earlier evening. It was punctuated by the snapping of trunks. Twice, as they crawled, crowns crashed down to the ground close to them. The thud of nuts torn away from their stems was incessant.

The lightning blazed for the first time as they reached the edge of the clump of ironwoods. It produced a high, simultaneous shriek from the children. In its blue glare Plandok saw 'Timah, looking old and terrified, and the boy Saad, and Hare, moving crouched with three small children in his enormous arms.

Suddenly everything was easier. Even the wind seemed lighter. The flashes were continuous. They moved on their feet now, hurrying towards the protection of whatever plan Hare had in mind. Their trust in him was absolute, his stature among them gigantic. He went ahead of them in the intermittent light and when they came up with him he was lashing the small children in the forks of the gnarled and arched branches of the ironwoods.

He gave the boy Saad a length of cord and another to Plandok. 'Get up! Make yourselves fast!'

'*Ya Allah!*' said the boy in a high exclamation of relief.

Hare was helping the old women. One by one he got them into place. he began to shout again, bellowing for Downie and the others. There was no answer. They could hear nothing above the wind and the deep, shuddering bourdon of the surf against the reef. While they still stood with their feet on the ground they could feel it trembling underneath them. The whole island had acquired an impermanence, as if it might at any moment disappear from beneath them.

The second blast hit them, still from the north, an hour after they had fastened themselves into the ironwood, an hour of cold and exhaustion. Its roar was more terrible even than that of the first because perhaps their ears had permitted themselves to hope. Spume came with it again, blotting out even the nearer trees. They could hear the crash and hurtle of the broken palms, the terrible wood noises again and then, behind them, another and an altogether different noise—a noise that had the deep thunder of the reef itself in it and that came roaring up in a slow, intolerable crescendo. Then they were aware of deep water sweeping under the foam, broken and split by the tree trunks, ghostly white and racing. It passed beneath them, lapping some of the lower places where they clung.

Quite suddenly, it was gone and the roar of the wind with it, and the foam was gone too, and they could see the nearest trees straightening themselves. Through the ruin of their crowns Hare saw a ragged patch of sky and three pale stars in it. They were left with only the immeasurable crash and thunder of the surf.

A long while after they heard voices shouting. Hare, already down from his own refuge in the ironwood, bellowed back, and the voices came towards him—Malay voices, men's. They came slowly, picking their way across broken tree trunks and frond wrack and the wreckage of the kampong. They were very close before their words came clear above the reef thunder: they were shouting that the Kling woman was gone. When they came up finally to the grotesque, Gothic safety of the ironwoods they seemed to transfer their terrors and their reponsibilities to Hare. The fear went out of their voices.

To his questions they said, shouting still, for they had to shout to be heard: 'The Kling woman is gone. She was with us when the water swept us and after—she was gone!'

Hare's voice, portentously angry, roared: 'And the Tuan Downie?'

'He is in the shelter of the stores hut with the rest of the women.'

'Has he sent to search for her?'

'He has done nothing,' said one of the men simply. 'Therefore we came to seek for you.'

'Stay with these!' ordered Hare abruptly to the leader of the three men. 'If the wind comes again tie them in the branches as they were before. Pa Abas, Kassim, you come with me.'

He began to fight his way through to the lagoon beach. Flashes of the now distant lightning gave enough brilliance still for the women to see him. He appeared heroic among the shadows, sure and powerful in his movement in the splintered world. They took hope from him.

He crashed his way through to the beach, the two Malays following him. At the edge of the water he stood shouting. Plandok could not make out what he was shouting: it was the Kling woman's name that she had never heard. After a little he worked his way down the beach to where the pathway had led to the kampong. Everywhere was cluttered with wreckage. He moved in a crashing of broken fronds. The path itself was choked with timbers from the houses, rafters, broken furniture even. He thought that he saw the ruins of his great chair but the lightning flash was not long enough for him to be certain. He moved up the path, shouting all the time. There was no answer except that when he came close to the kampong he could hear an unintelligible babble of hysteria, women's voices and children's; they seemed to be berating the man Downie.

In the twisted cage of their refuge the others heard his voice again, mastering the thunder of the surf. He was calling to them to make their way to the kampong. The women stirred uneasily, their movements slow and indecisive, as if they no longer had power over their own wills.

Plandok climbed down first. She loosened the end of the rope that Hare had given her and that had held her to the branch through the worst of the wind. Stiffly, she felt down with one foot, found the shoulder of the boy Saad, used it as a foothold, and dropped to the ground. Her movements had no spring. The boy watched her, silent, and fumbled at the knot of his own lashing. After a moment he felt for the knife that he carried and cut it. They moved off together towards the kampong.

The girl's body was slack, her shoulders drooped, her head bent forward. She was still frightened. For the first time in her life she had recognized real fear, the fear of something that man had not made and that man could not control.

She had little memory of the night except the explosion of the birds, the first roar of the foul wind, and the heart-shattering thunder of the sea that swept the island. Superimposed on these was the image of Hare. It seemed twice life size: Hare, with his enormous shoulders, carrying a fountain of children, Hare standing against the lightning like a latter-day Ajax, securing their fastenings and bawling coarse, obscure comfort, Hare managing the hysterical women, slapping them into sober caution, helping them into security, Hare plunging through the dawn light and the wreckage, searching for the Kling woman on the wrack-strewn beach. He had acquired new stature in her mind, an heroic dimension, though she could not put it into words even to herself.

When she saw him again in what had been the kampong, with the morning sun flooding down through the ravished palm crowns, it frightened her once more to see that he was only his own size, that he was stooped with weariness, that his face was grey and haggard. For the first time and with a sense of having come into collision with a fundamental truth she realized that Hare was a man no longer young, in no way immune from the limitations of mortality. She was aware of a sympathy with him, though she could not have given it shape—something that transcended the friendliness that had grown irregularly since they had come to the islands. Only the hoarse, bull-throated voice remained of the night's proportions.

He was savaging the man Downie, who still lay in the lee of the boulders that they had used as a foundation for the vanished stores hut. He lay there, wet, bedraggled, and almost invisible under a tangled heap of women: his own two wives, Mei Ying, the Portuguese-Malay Meriam, and the Zulu girl. The children who had been with his group sat apart, watching them. The man was paralysed with fear. Gradually, under the lash of Hare's tongue, he lifted himself from the ruck. There was something inherently comic about him, but Plandok could not laugh; she was still too shattered in herself. Eventually he sat up.

The other Malay men had come up from the beach. Hare made a swift count: they were all there except the Kling woman.

He bellowed at Downie: 'You white-spleened scoundrel! Sit up straight and look at me and tell me what happened!'

Under the lash Downie answered: 'She was with us and the wave came. We had a rope and we hung on to it. And then she screamed, and after that we saw nothing more of her.'

The woman Meriam said: 'It was the girl who did it.'

Hare took three quick strides forward and stood over them as they lay on the ground. The water had washed all resistance out of them. 'The girl? What girl?'

'The girl Plandok.'

'Fools! Imbeciles! The girl Plandok was not here. She was with me over at the ironwoods.'

'She hated the Kling woman.' Mei Ying hardly breathed the words. And the Zulu girl said: 'She wished her dead and now she *is* dead.'

'Be silent! Get up from there—stand up! The girl had nothing to do with this. She was with me. I will not have this talk. She could have done nothing.'

Mei Ying rose to her knees and held her hands forward in a gesture of supplication. 'She called up the wind.'

And the other women came in in chorus: 'She is a witch.'

Even Hare hesitated for an instant, as if appalled by their unanimity. Then he said: 'You are half-wits, cowards, all of you. You have not all of you together the strength of this one child. This is not to be said again or I will myself beat the woman who says it.' He turned and looked at the girl.

She stood there as she had stood from the very beginning, her shoulders stooped so that she looked, in the pulsing flicker of the lightning, even more childish, more fragile than she was.

She was still frightened.

# Fourteen

SHE FOUND the body on the second day after the storm. It was caught between two coral boulders in the shallows just below the south point of Pulau Gangsa. For a long time she stood quite still, the water halfway up her calves, staring at it. The sarong, secured round the waist with a length of rope that Downie had given the woman, had reversed itself like an umbrella blown inside out. It covered the upper half of the body. One leg had been torn off halfway up the thigh, either by sharks or on the sharp spikes of the coral, half the other foot was gone. Fish had nibbled at the flesh elsewhere. It had a macabre cleanliness, tide-washed.

Plandok asked it, her voice expressionless: 'Is it true, then, that I am a witch?' And when she got no answer she bent down at last and pulled the sarong back.

The fish and the crabs had been kept away from the head. The face was almost undamaged except that one ear had been torn—again perhaps by the coral.

She looked into the dulled eyes of the Kling woman. 'You hated me because I was young and you were old,' she said in judgement. 'You made the women believe that I was a witch. Now I will be a witch—and for that I require a head—your head!' Again she paused as if waiting for a reply, her head a little to one side. 'Wait while I fetch the parang.'

She stalked back gravely through the shallows, the limpid water splashing in little bright gem sprays from her shins.

The canoe was at the north point of Pulau Selma across the shallows. It had survived the tornado. At some time in the early gale of the evening it had been flung into the ironwoods to which she had secured it and it had jammed there, with one outrigger strut broken, and escaped the grasp of the great wave. One of the three boats that Hare had brought from the ship had disappeared altogether, the other two were badly damaged. The canoe, when the outrigger strut had been spliced, was the only thing that still floated in the lagoon.

For two days now she had worked, searching for stuff that had been washed down the lagoon to the other islands. Mostly the boy Saad had come with her, hanging on to the canoe and swimming. They had found a net and three paddles, one of the boat sails, badly torn, and one mast un-scratched. There was a trunk that had belonged to Hare, washed clean of its contents. They found clothing and bales of cloth. These things she had ferried back to the landing beach or had stacked in safety on the islands.

This afternoon Saad had not come with her: he was wanted to help with the roofs of the new huts. The kampong was coming to life again. But she would not work there herself with the eyes of the women follow-ing her about as they made atap or cooked or tended the children or husked coconuts from the unlimited store in the wreckage. She seemed to hear always the whisper: 'She is a witch!'

Striding through the shallows now, she said aloud: 'Therefore I will be a witch.'

The parang they had found with the heavy tools half-buried in the sand two-thirds of the way towards the beach where the wave had washed them. Only this morning she had made Pa Abas sharpen it.

When she returned to the body she stood silent as she had stood before, staring down at it. The crabs had come up while she was away and were exploring tentatively at the neck and shoulders. She said: 'Go away! This is mine. After I have done you may take what you wish.' And suddenly, with no more premeditation, she slashed down at the neck.

Instantly the water became tinged with red. She had not expected this. It seemed inconceivable that the body could still hold blood despite the gaping ruin of the thigh. There was blood congealed in the great arteries of the neck. The scarlet spread through the waters, and small fish came up and explored the body and its colour and swam away again.

She hacked at the neck with unhurried, accurate strokes. Despite the sharpness of the parang, it had an unexpected resistance. The flesh seemed to have acquired a solidity in the water. The larynx opened and emitted a ghostly, bubbling sigh. In a moment it washed clean and ex-hibited a yellow cartilaginous ugliness against the pinks of the flesh.

She hacked on. Each time she slashed, the water spurted up, thinly red. It was difficult to get at the vertebral column because the flesh flowed back after each cut. In the end she was forced to lift the shoulders and prop them with a lump of coral. The head fell back then, opening the whole of the neck, oozing blood that washed away with each ripple of the water. Two strokes sufficed now, and the head rolled clear, the long hair streaming through the red water.

She stood staring at the stump of the neck, sorting things out in her mind. Then she put the parang down and withdrew the kris from its hid-ing place. Deliberately she began to cut round the stump of the neck in little stabs. Aloud she said to herself: 'This will look as if a shark had taken her head as she floated in the lagoon. The leg beyond doubt was taken by a shark.' She studied the nature of the wound on the thigh and made one or two tentative cuts to match it. 'This, and that which the crabs will do to it after I go.' The water gurgled obscenely in the open windpipe as if the corpse were answering her at last, and she said: 'Be still! I am all but done.'

She made three more cuts, obscuring the transverse hacking of the parang, and then, removing the coral lump, let the headless shoulders sink back below the surface.

The blood had almost ceased to dissolve now in the sea water. The streaming current of the tide took the red patch to the south. She could see it growing always more faint. In a little the water at her feet was clear and the head lay, grotesque in profile, the long black hair streaming and alive beyond it in the movement of the water.

From her memory came, abruptly and without warning, sentences of the invocation that men used when they took the head of an enemy. She knew that it did not matter what head was taken; this her Sea Dyak nurse had told her over and over again. It did not have to be a man's head—a woman's, a child's, would do. It could be taken by simple murder, a knife thrust in the back—anything. The head was the one thing that was important, not how it was obtained. The stories of the courage, the single-ness of purpose of the head-hunter were stories for the white men.

The crabs came back slowly. Three of them, bolder than the rest, attached themselves to the stump of the neck. A fourth went towards the head.

'Do here as you wish, but that is mine!' she said, and, taking two strides forward, she bent down, grabbed the head and lifted it.

It was astonishingly heavy, but she walked through the shallows with it towards the damaged palm groves of Pulau Selma.

It was the middle of the afternoon now. She rested in a patch of shade, sitting cross-legged with her delicate hands in her lap, and remembered the Sea Dyak women. There were certain things to be said and certain things to be done in the preparation of the head. The brains would have to be drawn. To draw them through the nostrils was the way an artist would do it. The easier way was to draw them through the base of the skull. After that, it would have to be smoked. Certain woods were better than others, but she could remember only that hard woods were neces-sary; it would not perhaps matter. Some of the rituals she would have to do without. The main thing was the head.

When she was rested she began the grisly task of cutting through the thick muscles at the base of the skull. The kris was not a good cutting weapon, the parang was too clumsy. After a long while she separated the first of the vertebrae, and then, cutting more freely, slashed the remainder of the neck clear of the skull itself. Walking deep into the battered palm grove, she flung the gobbet of flesh containing the bones away. The rats and the land crabs between them would deal with it.

Her hands were bloodied with the work. She looked down at them distastefully and decided to go back to the lagoon. Again the water performed its miracle, transforming the flesh from a red anger to a pallid acquiescence. The kris seemed to work better in the water. Exploring with its needle-sharp point, she worked through the hole into the white pulp of the brain.

After a while it was obvious that she needed a more spatulate tool and she went back to the high-water-mark to search for a section of bamboo. As she stalked back through the shallows to the head, she saw that a cloud had come up. Now, as she crouched down over the head again, the cloud hesitated on the edge of the sun, edged itself with unbearable brightness for a moment, and then overran it. The green light of the lagoon went out as if snuffed. The water surface became leaden, and she heard behind her the onrush of rain, great drops stabbing at the water and raising return dropules greater than themselves.

She did not even bother to look round, but to the head she said: 'It is well that the rain has come. Now there will be water for all.'

The wave that had overrun the island had turned the wells brackish. The new wells that Hare ordered dug on the morning after the disaster had been only a little less brackish. The whole water table of the island was contaminated. It was Downie who had remembered the South Sea Island trick of tying a bunch of leaves round the bole of a palm so suspended as to direct rain water from a heavy shower into a jar or a basin. There were few jars left on the island. For the most part they had had to be content with gourds or giant clam shells, but even so she knew that this shower would give them drinking water until the wells cleared again.

She felt the sting of the rain on her bare shoulders and against her head. Her hair became limp and bedraggled, but she worked on, digging the bamboo sliver deep into the hollow of the cranium. All through the rain she talked to the head, and sometimes, as her hands moved or the water caught at it, the mouth seemed to open in a terrible parody of answer.

The crabs collected in rings round her, stepping with little sideways movements, holding up their claws in idiot supplication. Occasionally she talked to them too, telling them of the power that the head would bring her.

All the while the sun sank in the western sky. It was late in the afternoon before she prepared, deep in the tangled scrub of the big island, a
tripod and built a fire below it. She hung the head from the apex of the
tripod, calmly and without a tremor, on a knot of its own hair. She had the
flint and tinder that she had always carried in the canoe. With its paddles and her fishing lines and the small hand net, it had remained safe in
its lashings through the tornado. Now she lit a fire, using dry palm wrack
that had been sheltered from the rain by fallen fronds, and coconut
husks. She piled chips of ironwood to make the smoke.

For a long time she sat silent, watching it. A tiny handful of birds had
survived the storm. They circled her, inquisitive, but at last they settled,
and she knew that it was almost evening. The fire was low enough to leave
now. She built up a screen of branches and leaves that would hide the
tripod from an accidental eye and at the same time keep the smoke in as
long as the fire smouldered. Then she went back to the canoe and tipped
the rain water out.

The sun set when she was midway between the high sand island and
the kampong. The tide was full now. An unaccustomed loneliness as-
sailed her. Some of her self-sufficiency seemed to have drained itself in the
bloody work of the afternoon. Once, in the red of the last of the sunset,
she had looked herself over with immense care to see if blood, in fact, was
left anywhere on her body or her garments, but she had bathed before
she started for home and everything, even her sarong, was clean.

The canoe was heavy to handle and she moved very slowly, for behind
her she towed a barrel, another oar that she had found, and a little raft of
odds and ends of shaped timber. In the canoe itself she had another bale
of cloth, and three gourd dippers with handles that she had found, oddly
enough, within five yards of one another.

The soft and exquisite lights of the afterglow faded and lost themselves.
The deep blue velvet of the night covered the lagoon. The stars blazed in
it. In a windless silence, broken only by the dip and splash of the paddle
and the occasional rap as it knocked against the side of the boat, she came
at last to the beach.

Hare himself was waiting for her. 'You are late!' His voice was rum-
bling and almost kind.

'I had much to do,' she answered. 'I have a barrel and another oar.
Also there is yet another roll of cloth and a part, I think, of your great
chair.'

The canoe grated on the sand, and the boy Saad and two of the other
youngsters rushed forward and dragged it firmly in.

Hare stared at her in the starlight. 'What else?'

'Three dippers. They floated together and I found them together.' And then, as she turned to go up the newly cleared path to the kampong, she added casually: 'And the body of the Kling woman.'

'My God!' exclaimed Hare, startled, 'You found her body?'

'It is her,' replied the girl with her voice still unconcerned, as if she were discussing only another piece of wreckage. 'It lacks one leg and the other is torn, nor is there a head to it, but it is the Kling woman. I knew it by the kain sarong.' She felt Hare staring at her, but she continued to drift slowly up towards the kampong.

Behind her he said: 'How has this happened?'

'The coral,' she answered indifferently, and then a long while after, 'or it might be that it was a shark.' Deliberately she had chosen the less dramatic possibility first.

Hare seized on the alternative. 'Yes, it would be a shark.'

'Or it might be the coral.' The girl repeated herself with calculation. 'It is not possible to tell, for the fish have taken what they would and the crabs also.'

'Wait! What did you do with it?'

'I did nothing. It was too heavy for me to lift. Moreover, it is stuck between the boulders of the coral. There was nothing that I could do.'

He relaxed, suddenly satisfied. 'You will take us to it tomorrow.'

'I will take you, but what will you go in?'

'The boat will be ready by noon—not finished, but patched enough for that.'

'I will take you. Now I am hungry.'

The women were making atap in a furious, quarrelling energy. Plandok sat with her back against a broken log, soaking in the sunlight and wriggling her toes. Mei Ying regarded her balefully. On her seemed to have settled the responsibility for trying to discipline Plandok, the responsibility that had been the Kling woman's.

'It is not in my disposition to make atap,' Plandok explained lightly. 'That is women's work. It is required of me that I go out with the men.'

Mei Ying said: 'It would be better if you went to a beating.'

'Slaves are beaten,' observed the girl cheerfully.

The Zulu girl demanded: 'Where do the men go?'

'*Nonya*'—Plandok addressed herself directly to the Chinese woman, using the prefix of respect—'we go to bury the Kling woman.'

'Timah, working five yards away from the Chinese woman, let fall the two segments of a frond that she was beginning to plait for a screen. Her hands went up to her face. Mei Ying herself stood frozen, with one arm ludicrously misplaced behind her. Hare had said nothing of the discovery.

Plandok herself had kept silence. The shock spread through the whole party, even those too far away to hear the words. The babble of talk and argument that had filled the clearing was abruptly silenced.

It was 'Timah who said first: 'She is found, then?'

'She is found,' agreed Plandok indifferently.

The Zulu girl said: 'It was *you* who found her.' The note of accusation was almost palpable.

'I found her.'

'How?' 'Timah's voice was deeply shocked.

Plandok turned to her. 'Walking on the beach I saw her kain sarong. It showed above the water. The pattern I knew.'

The Zulu girl in her dreadful, twisted Malay asked: 'Why was it that it should be you? What art did you use?'

Plandok rubbed her back delicately against the palm bole. The scratching effect was delicious. At last with a lazy insolence she rose to go and turned to the Zulu girl. 'I am a witch. You have said it.'

The women gathered self-protectively a little closer.

'*La ilaha ila Allah,*' said Munah, Downie's head wife. 'There is no God but God. It is true that she is a witch.'

She led the boat, ten yards or so ahead of its clumsy progress. There was not enough water inshore on the western side of Pulau Gangsa for it to make the beach at this state of the tide and she took the canoe down well below the northern point of Selma before she turned north for the is-let. The boat grounded before she reached the rocks that held the body.

The sarong still floated, patterned, on the surface.

Hare strode up through the shallows, making a tremendous noise in the afternoon hush. Downie had not come. Hare had three men with him. One of them stayed with the boat, the other two followed him. He stood looking down at the battered body. It had swollen evilly since the previous day. The abdomen was distended and ugly, and the stump of the thigh was opened back so that the broken bone jutted whitely through it.

His voice shook as he said: 'My God!' The tone had nothing in it of his customary complacency. Without turning his head, he called: 'Pull the boat up! Bring a blanket!'

He disregarded Plandok absolutely and stood quite still as the men rolled one of the rocks back, lifted the ruined body enough to work the blanket beneath it and folded it over the top. Then he said: 'Take her to the beach!'

'Do you bury her there?' Plandok asked.

'Not bury.' Hare's voice was slow and ruminative. 'I will burn her upon a pyre. She was a Chuliah, a Hindu. I know nothing of their rites, but I know that their dead are burned, and she deserves at least that of me.'

Plandok considered the words carefully. She could not understand the meaning behind them. She whispered tentatively: 'Deserves?'

Whether Hare heard her or not she could not tell, but he went on, his voice still low, so low that she could hardly hear it above the booming of the reef: 'She was from Malacca. She came to me before Banjermasin, before the others except 'Timah herself. She was young then—not as young as you, but as graceful. She had the beauty of a reed in the wind.' There was an immense sorrow in his voice. 'She had soft eyes, like a young deer's—like your eyes—and her voice was soft as the night rustle in a tree.'

He was quiet for a long time, watching the men. They had dropped the body on the sand, and were walking along the tide line, picking at driftwood.

At length Hare said gently: 'Afterwards she grew shapeless and her voice was hard, but I remember her as she came to me a long time ago.' He began to walk heavily in towards the body.

Plandok stayed where she was, holding the canoe steady.

They made a bed of palm wrack and on it they put dry sticks from above the high-water-mark, and then logs—dried driftwood logs—and branches and broken wood. On top of it they put the body, and when Pa Abas made to take the blanket out from under it, she heard Hare's voice angrily: 'Leave it! Leave it!'

He lit the pyre himself, blowing the tinder into a small bright flame with fragments of dry leaves. There was something ritualistic in the way he lit each of the four corners of the fire, passing ceremoniously round it to do so. When it was ablaze he stood away from it at what would have been the head end if there had been a head, his hat in his hand. There was no wind. The smoke rose with a greedy uprush into the still air, elongated itself with its own interior heat, and stretched up and up and up.

The girl, sitting low in the canoe, saw these things happening as a frieze. On the small elevation of the beach the men were silhouetted against the empty sky. The palms began twenty yards back from them, leaning over in sorrowful curves. Splintered boles reached high above the beachward crests. The three Malays stood in a group, self-supporting; Hare stood alone, and in front of him the fire blazed, red under the grey and blue of the smoke.

She could not tell how long she waited. Time stood still: there was nothing by which to mark it. Only the creeping tide took cognizance of the passing of the hours. It moved in towards the pyre as if it conspired to put out the flames, but before it reached them the thing was done. The

Kling woman was gone, dismissed into the still and uncomprehending air.

When only the ashes glowed and smouldered Hare came back to the boat, leading the three men in silence. A little shiver of apprehension went through the girl. This was the moment of challenge, this was the time when, if he had noticed the difference between the wound of the leg and the wound of the neck, Hare would deal with her. She waited with her stoical courage, her hands tense on the handle of the paddle, but Hare had not even looked at the neck. He walked past her blindly, but even as she thought he was past, he said: 'We will go back now to the kampong.'

She shook her head, though he was past her and could not see the gesture. 'I do not go back now. Your women believe that I did it. They have called me a witch again. I will be by myself until their minds are at rest.'

'Little fool!' said Hare brusquely. 'I will talk to them.'

'Speak to them with a rattan,' suggested Plandok impishly. 'I go now, but I will come back.' This was the first time she had ever committed herself.

She swung the canoe. The men should have stopped her, but they made no movement. Hare knew that it was impossible to pursue her either in the boat or by wading through the shallows.

Only when she was round the farther point of Pulau Selma did she shake off the faint, unidentifiable depression that had settled over her. The smoke of the cremation still hung in the sky, very thin and almost incandescent in the glare of the late afternoon. She grounded the canoe and went up on to the beach. The boat was still in sight, but only as a minute speck already crossing the anchorage off the kampong.

She lay in a patch of shade, giving it time to get clear out of sight. Once again, as in the aftermath of the storm, she saw Hare as a man, subject also to sorrows. It was the timbre of his voice that stayed with her. It had an elegiac quality, a lament for the evanescence of youth and beauty. She did not recognize that it was for his own youth that he despaired—she was not old enough.

When she was sure that the boat was out of sight, she paddled lazily north again.

The head was safe in the tripod. Neither crabs nor rats had got at it in the night. A rank smell hung about it. She wrapped it in leaves, making a large, untidy bundle, and placed it in the stern of the canoe. Then she set off on the long passage across the lagoon, paddling fast and strongly. The sun was low now and it was urgent that she should get there before it set.

The west island had also suffered the blast of the tornado. She could see, as she approached it, that the northern mile of it was a wilderness of splintered boles. No green thing lived there. South of it the damage grew slightly less. She could not tell yet if it had been swept by the wave, but the wave had come from the north-east.

Already it was too late to use the inner lagoon; the tide was too low. She made for a point on the beach level with the blue pool, steering by the rocks that lay off it. As she made the canoe fast she could see that the wave had hit. By the driftwood and the rubbish caught in the beachward bushes it had not been as high as on Direction, but it had been high enough. There was no sign of her hiding place, no sign of the pots that she had so carefully stolen, no sign of the bed place that she had made.

With the red sun breaking in splendour through the palm stems, she set to work with the parang to make another tripod. It was deep enough in the unruined trees here for the light of a fire to be hidden. Now she worked with a steely desperation. She cut ironwood saplings for the tripod. She gathered the chips of the cutting for fuel. The head she tied up by the hair again. This time she contrived a basket of ironwood creeper around it. And at sunset it was ready for the fire. She lit it with the experience of the previous day, fed it with driftwood until it burned clear, and stoked it with green chips. Finally, she damped it down and covered the outside with greenery. Only after that did she make a rough bed.

That night the land crabs bothered her and she slept lightly, changing her resting place from time to time, waking herself up to stoke the fire with fresh chips. Once the light night wind changed and the smoke of the burning and the stench of the scorching flesh overpowered her, and she woke crying.

At dawn, hollow-eyed and desperately tired, she woke again and fed the fire afresh, and lay down in the clean unfrightening light to sleep once more.

The fire was insatiable. All through the day she fed it, while, without interest, without enthusiasm, she made a sleeping place where the land crabs could not reach her, and roofed it roughly with atap against the rain. She had a great confidence in building, born out of her shipboard knowledge of lashings and spars and the sharpness of the parang that she had stolen. With the disappearance of the pots she had no cooking utensils, but there were giant clam shells and the fish that she caught could be broiled over the ashes. There were fresh coconuts and even birds' eggs from the handful of loobies and gannets that remained.

Except for food and the canoe, the fire absorbed her energies. With the servitude to the fire, she had acquired a fear of the head. Even when she had to replace the green palm fronds at the apex of the tripod she did it with her eyes averted. The very hair knotted above the timbers offended her.

She became a slave to the fire, wholly absorbed in it. She did not attempt to explore the ruined north of the island. She did not bother to keep watch out over the lagoon, though she guessed that the second boat must be all but repaired by now. But she bathed herself scrupulously —it was difficult to keep clean with the work of the fire—and she slept exhausted, interrupted by an inner compulsion that woke her to go back every few hours to the smouldering heap.

On the evening of the fourth day she opened the protecting screen. There was still enough light from the low sun to see. The face had shrunk. The cheeks were drawn in in a mockery of the soft hollows of the Kling woman's face. The eye sockets were wide, but one of the lids drooped in a murderous wink. The lips were thin and tight and drawn back from the protruding teeth. The nose had receded, shrinking back, elongating the nostrils upward. It was terrible and inhuman—but it was, beyond all doubt, the Kling woman. It expressed all the evil of which she had been capable, the jealousies and the vindictiveness, the cunning and the cruelty and the bitterness.

All through this day in a frenetic energy she had worked at its permanent resting place. The head should, she knew, hang above the fire in a long-house—a baang; but she had no baang. It should be the centre-piece of a community; but there was no community. She made a small, strong shelter, shaping it according to her memory of what the woman had told her of the little hut used in the mong-hosan, the ceremony of welcoming the head, anchoring it against the boles of two broken palm trees. It had a pitched roof, the gables sealed with strands of frond, the roof itself heavy with atap strongly tied down. The floor was made of flat slabs of coral dragged painfully from the beach.

Now she took the head and, repeating the runes that the Sea Dyak girl had taught her and that came of themselves out of memory, carried it to the shelter. She knotted the long black hair to a peg in a cross-pole of the roof. The eyes seemed to follow the movements of her hands even above the head, though there were, in fact, no eyes now. She replenished the cage of creeper and lashed that to the cross-pole. She passed a fresh lashing of ill-spared cord from the canoe round it all.

Then she brought leaves to it.

To the head she said: 'They should, I know, be isang leaves but in this island there are no isang leaves. It is enough, I think, that I do you such honour as I can. Also there is the matter of the tree. This is a small island, very far in the sea. There is here no mahang tree. The tree that I will bring you is a good tree and should house a good spirit. It is a rare tree also: it is the only tree of its kind that I have seen in the island. You will accept its spirit?'

She shaped the words like a question, but the question had an admonitory air. The mahang tree, she knew, was necessary—perhaps even essential. It was a part of the origins of the cult of the heads, the tree in which lived the spirit of Oton Tawim, the woman from whose misfortunes the head cult sprang.

Last of all, as the brief twilight swept past the island, she lit a fire on the flat coral slabs. Hanging over the hearth in a long-house, a head would expect smoke. The fire gave enough light to illuminate the underside of the fresh atap, the clean green-gold of the palm leaves, the fresh surface of the wood. Gradually the smoke thickened. In the utterly still night air it collected under the canopy of the leaves until the surface of them became misted and insubstantial and the rafters themselves were swallowed. Last of all, it swallowed the head. She could see it only when the swirls of the hot air made clear patches about it and it seemed to peer down out of the mystery of the smoke.

She sat in her customary position, her back against an upright, her hands motionless on her lap, contemplating it as it danced in and out. She remembered Hare's words: 'Not as young as you, but as graceful.' She repeated them softly and, as the clean air swept up for a moment, she said: 'I do not care. You were old when I knew you, and ugly.' She waited while the smoke swallowed the head again and remembered Hare's next words: 'She had the beauty of a reed in the wind.' Again she waited until the clean air revealed the head to the flickering light of the flames. 'What is it to me how graceful you were? You are now dead, and you are mine!' Again she thought back to Hare, remembering and rejecting the sorrow in his voice. 'Your eyes are not like a young deer's now.'

The clean air went up, and in the play of the fire the eye sockets seemed to come alive and move.

'You cannot frighten me!' The girl was startled into a sudden anger. 'I have said the right words and I have prepared the right place for you so far as I am able, and there is nothing that you can do to me whatever you were when you were young.'

The fire grew brighter as the hardwood chips dried and became combustible. The hut had an impermanent ceiling of smoke. All round the eaves it escaped like the veil of an inverted waterfall. Inside it breathed up and down and the head appeared and disappeared with an hypnotic, malevolent effect.

She moved away from the upright, crouching closer to the fire, her head upstretched, staring to detect it at the precise moment when the smoke freed it. It seemed to change expression. She said over and over again: 'It is nothing to me what you once were. You are what you are now, and I need certain things of you. Be still while I ask you!'

There was no moment of stillness. The smoke still billowed up and down. The head seemed to move down and up through its inverted surface.

Finally the fire grew too hot, and she moved away uneasily. The hut was full of small noises: fire noises and noises where the atap was drying and where the creeper was tightening and where the rafters were stiffening in the heat—little whispering sounds. They flowed into the baleful hypnotism of the head, the commanding power of the eyeless sockets.

She grew more and more uneasy, moving farther and farther away till she came to the edge of the hut. Then, as if to re-establish her own powers, she said: 'I will light another fire outside.'

The flames of the new fire leapt up and lit the underside of the palms. She had made the shelter at the edge of a patch of destruction. The palms had fallen here to make a natural clearing, and the night sky was open to the north, its velvet encrusted with stars. The fire lit the little cove in the trees brilliantly, and she stood by it, staring at the hut through the soft corruscations of sparks.

'You are fast in there,' she said softly, 'and I have no fear of you. When the smoke has cleared I will ask what I have to ask of you.'

Then, quite still, she waited.

The wing hit her with the instant shock of a lightning flash. She had heard nothing coming. Only after the thing hit her and swept up did she hear the whistle of the wind through feathers, and almost instantly another wing brushed past, not hitting her but so close that the wind of its passing fanned against her. This time she saw the flash of it in the firelight, a sudden whiteness that was instantly lost in the darkness. Another bird came from a different direction, and another and another and another. As she looked upwards she could see wings flashing as they caught the firelight, diving towards her, sweeping upward in a rustle and sometimes a snap of hard-braking feathers.

She was not sure that they were birds. In the development of the hypnosis of the head she had lost her sense of ordinary things. These were like emanations of the head, like ghosts called up by it from the spirit world, legions of allies for its eyeless intelligence.

She could not know that the great flock of the gannets, blown far out over the open sea by the hurricane, had come back at last to the island. She could not know that, attracted by the fire, blinded by its improbability, they were diving on it, not on her.

The rate of the diving increased. More and more birds seemed to be pouring down in a constant succession of attack. The fire itself was leaping under the beat of the wings. She was brushed again and again. A bird began to scream and other birds took up the crying. The air was raucous and angular and terrible with its dissonance. Still they came, more and more birds, dodging one another at the bottom of their dives, brushing against each other, colliding, quarrelling, screaming, ghost-riding and ghost-ridden.

She put her arms around her head to shelter herself, still standing there, and when they hit her arms she crouched down to the fire. She became terrified, hysterical, but she did not scream; her voice would not have been heard above the clamour of the birds. She gathered herself at last on her knees, her body arched over, her head against the ground, her hands over the back of her neck—sobbing, incoherent, utterly in despair.

She could not measure afterwards how long she endured there. She only remembered that abruptly she told herself that the Kling woman's head was hers and that the ghosts of the head, therefore, were hers also. Rising to her feet, she stretched out her hand, found the stems of a couple of dried palm fronds, thrust them on to the fire, waited till they caught and then swirled them above her head. The brilliant flame of the new blaze lifted high into the night. Looking up it, she could see a vortex of bird wings, wings that went up in an endless perspective to the night sky, that moved in incredibly beautiful arabesques against the stars, and discovered that they were the wings of birds, the wings of birds, the wings of birds.

She waited while the dry stuff blazed to its end. Then she stalked through the still-diving gannets to the shelter of the hut. She sat down again with her back against the upright, laid her hands on her lap, and looked up. The inner fire had diminished but there was still light enough to see. The smoke had risen so that the head hung clear of it. There was almost no flicker from the glowing charcoal. The head appeared to be subdued and waiting.

Plandok said to it after a long pause: 'They were no more than birds. It was a trick only. I am not afraid. You will do now what I ask of you. You will bring my father's prau to this island.' She watched the head earnestly. It made no sign either of acceptance or of rejection. 'It is a new prau. I cannot tell you how it will look or what its name will be. I can tell you only that it will be the fastest prau on the coast. If, because of this and because of the fact that you are a woman and know nothing of ships, you cannot find my father's prau, you will bring another ship to the island so that I may go away and find my father by myself. Hear this!'

She stretched out her hand and flung a chip or two on the fire. As they caught, the shadows seemed to give motion to the lips and to the eyes in a monstrous, macabre imitation of life. Outside the whistle of the still-diving birds had something of the character of whispering.

'My father's prau,' she said again, 'or at least another ship.'

BOOK THREE

# THE LAGOON

# *Fifteen*

THE BOY'S voice was at the topmost level of the register of excitement. He was shouting over and over again: *'Kapal! Kapal! Kapal!'* A ship; not a boat, not a canoe, but a decked ship. The voice was coming up the track now from the landing place, growing in shrillness and volume with every moment.

Plandok, sitting in the shadow of the big hut, said with the utmost complacency: 'Now indeed it is true that I am a witch.'

Her instinctive knowledge of sea matters told her before the boy reached the kampong that it was the second part of her request that had been fulfilled. This ship was not from the east. Mat—she recognized the voice—must have seen it from the lagoon beach. With the wind that was blowing it must be beating up towards the entrance. Therefore it was not her father, but it *was* a ship.

To make quite certain she asked, as the boy reached them sobbing for breath: 'Is it from the east?'

'No, from the west.'

Hare was up at the oil-pressing shed where they were trying to rebuild the presses. He came down now. Excitement enveloped the place. The children came running from the vegetable patches, the women from the wells and from the coconut gathering, the men from the endless, intolerable work of clearance. They surged down the path towards the beach, Hare moving in the middle of them like a flock master enveloped in his sheep.

Plandok waited till they were all on the path before she walked, skipping a little, at the tail of the procession, hugging to herself the knowledge that she had done this thing. For five days she had waited, five days since she had come back from the west island—thin, worn, spiritually exhausted by her experience.

Hare, meeting her on the path as she returned from the west island, had said: 'God! What have you been doing to yourself, child? Go and get food.' And, as an afterthought: 'The women will not trouble you—now.'

She did not bother then or after to ask what Hare had done to ensure her security. It was not important. She might, of course, have asked the head to look after it, but she was wholly certain that this was within her own power.

The ship was there all right, but, despite the shrieking of the children and the buzzing chatter of the women, there was almost a sense of anti-climax about it. It was no more than a minute pyramid of white sail on the horizon just clear of Tanjong Ujong, the northernmost point of the west island. It hung there while Hare adjusted the long glass that they had recovered, half buried in sand, halfway to the sea after the wind. Water had got into it and a small area of a lens was clouded. He fiddled with it, growling angrily. Downie came up the beach, hearing the tumult.

After a long while Hare got the glass adjusted. 'It's a brig. It could be the *Borneo*.'

Downie said: 'There's plenty of brigs.'

Hare disregarded him. 'Seems as if she's heading up for us, but there's no telling. I want a big fire built up at the end of the island. We'll light it when she gets close in.'

The children raced up the beach, shouting, laughing, electric. The men began to drift up, the women followed them. It had become suddenly a holiday. All thought of work was abandoned. Downie went up behind them to direct the placing of the fire. Hare stood watching through the long glass.

When he lowered it again, Plandok said casually: 'I told you a ship would come.'

He put his head on one side and looked at her. 'You did. And how the devil *did* you know?'

'I knew,' she answered distantly, 'and now it has come. There is no need for a fire. It will enter the lagoon.'

'If it is the *Borneo* it will be John Ross come to see his seeds.'

'Whoever it is,' said the girl calmly and with absolute certitude, 'it will come.'

She began to stroll leisurely up the path to join the others. She moved, holding back the flame of a secret victory. The head had worked for her. A new world was opened.

The boat was close alongside the brig. There was much shouting back and forth. People lined her rail from bow to stern. There were women on the quarter-deck. The brig had a festive and holiday air to match the wild excitement along the beach.

Plandok lay farther away in the canoe, her paddle poised and glisten-ing in the sun, her eyes taking in every movement, every sound, every new shape, as the *Borneo* glided through the calm water and the men on her fo'c'sle stood ready to drop the anchor.

She heard Hare's bellow: 'You're about right now. I'd let go.' And watched the brig's head swing right into the eye of the wind with the last drifting movement that was left to her. Then she saw the splash grow under the forefoot as the anchor dropped.

Hare was aboard before the splash had died down, Downie with him.

Plandok dipped the paddle and moved slowly in. She had from the deck something of the appearance of a water insect, tentative, nervous, exhilarated.

In the waist there was a line of young men's heads and shoulders leaning over the bulwarks. A deep voice from among them shouted: 'Ma God, it's a wee girrl!'

She sensed rather than understood that the words were meant for her and she looked up and smiled, and there was a wide outbreak of smiles along the rail and a craning of necks and a chorus of calls. She put her head back and laughed delightedly.

One of the young men threw her a line, and she made it fast and allowed the canoe to be hauled alongside. She went up the ladder and hesitated at the top of it: she did not want Hare to see her for the time being. The young men crowded about her, but she stepped on to the deck with dignity and downcast eyes, and she found at once a corner where she could settle down with her back against a timber.

She was less than three yards from Hare. It was apparent from his stance that something had gone wrong. He faced a tall man, taller than himself, broader, even more powerful. This, she knew must be John Clunies-Ross, brother of the captain of the *Hippomenes*—that much she had gathered from Hare's talk with Downie during the hours of waiting —and it was clear that John Ross was angry. The first words that she heard as she settled herself on the deck were his.

'I established rights to the island. I planted it.'

Hare's shoulders were squared and already angry. 'Rights be damned! Uninhabited islands. Did you expect me to up anchor and sail a thousand miles because of a few withered seedlings?'

John Ross said stubbornly: 'They are *my* islands!'

'Nobody's islands! Anyway, there is room enough for both of us— room enough for five of us with a big island apiece, if it comes to that.'

'It is not the room. It's the principle.'

'Principles be damned!' retorted Hare.

The young men had fallen back a little. They stood in a small compact group, watching. Plandok allowed her eye to consider them once, but the fascination of the meeting of the two men held her.

Ross said: 'You were determined to take them from me.'

'God damn it!' roared Hare. 'I didn't know that you'd been to the islands. If you had kept to the time you promised——'

'I promised no time,' Ross broke in angrily. 'My orders were to pick up a load of pepper and call at the Cape on my way to London.'

'And you spent a week piddling round this atoll on your private ploys. If you had come when I expected you I'd have known you had plans for these islands.'

'You knew.' Ross's voice rose indignantly. 'It was on my list.'

'Lists! Lists! You made lists of every damned island group in the Indian Ocean, and the Atlantic. St. Paul, the Falklands, Christmas Island, Chagos, the Andamans—there was no end to your lists. How was I to know which one you had chosen?'

'Why did you set out for the Cocos?'

'Damn your obstinate hide, John Ross! I never set out for the Cocos! I set out for Christmas Island. Ask your brother when you see him! Ask him to show you the log: "Cape Town towards Christmas Island." We stood off that damned island for days before we gave it up. I near lost a boat's crew in the landing place.'

There was a brief silence as Ross considered this. The ship's company, the young men, stood gaping.

And then from above them on the poop a voice came down, acidulous and rebuking: 'Mr. Ross, is it not your intention to introduce your wife and myself to Mr. Hare, if this indeed is Mr. Hare?'

Hare looked up as if he had been utterly unaware of the presence of women. He lifted his hat in one of his splendid gestures. 'Your servant, ma'am. I am Alexander Hare of whom no doubt you have heard.'

'I have heard,' replied the woman, thin-lipped.

Ross said hastily: 'Mrs. Dymoke, may I present Mr. Hare?' The second woman came forward. 'My wife—Mr. Hare.' His tone seemed to have not merely a reproof but a warning.

Hare turned away from him and went up the ladder. Plandok watched him from her position on the deck, craning her head upwards. He moved quickly and easily with the lithe young man's grace that he always assumed when there were strange women present.

On the poop deck he doffed his hat again, almost sweeping the ground with it. 'It is a pleasure to be able to offer to you the slender resources of Direction Island, ma'am.' He addressed himself particularly to Ross's mother-in-law. 'After the months of shipboard you must be anxious to rest yourselves ashore.'

Over his back he heard Ross's voice belligerently: 'I will make my own arrangements for my own people.'

Hare disregarded the interruption. 'Such as we have, it is yours, ma'am, but we have, as you must have seen, been swept by a hurricane.' He turned to Ross lightly, all trace of anger gone even from his eyes. 'When we saw your sails we were deeply thankful, for Direction was swept by the sea.' He turned to Mrs. Dymoke again. 'One giant wave in the night, ma'am, but it took our stored foods. You would not have rice to spare, I doubt?' The last question was addressed to Ross.

Ross replied shortly: 'We come from the west. We have no rice.'

Hare shrugged his shoulders. 'No matter. My people will survive until the *Hippomenes* returns. We expect her daily almost.'

Grudgingly Ross said: 'I can let you have flour. Something in the way of dry stores perhaps. The meat has gone.'

'We have no need of meat,' Hare answered grandly. 'The ocean and the sea-birds give us a livelihood. They have come back to us, the birds. They returned five nights ago.'

Down below on the deck Plandok shivered. Presently she turned away from the tableau on the poop where Hare still exerted his charm on the two hostile women, and considered the young men. There were ten of them. They formed a group quite separate from the crew of the ship, which was partly native and partly international. They were young, all of them; the eldest not more than twenty-two, she judged. Most of them were fair-haired, sun-blistered, red, but they had an air of energy and purposefulness that was non-existent in the scheme of island things.

She heard Ross's voice again. 'I shall settle on Selma or on the south island, as I judge to be most suitable.'

Hare, flooding his immense animal magnetism on Mrs. Dymoke, answered: 'As I have said, there is ample room for all. The islands look small in this waste of waters but they have a richness of their own. We will help you with our boats and our people.'

'I require no help,' said Ross furiously, his anger stirred up again by the older man's attitude. 'I have ten young men who settle with me and I have my own boats.'

'There is water in plenty on Selma,' said Hare equably, 'but it may yet be brackish. Ours is still affected by the wave. There is little damage on Selma—a few palms, hardly more than that. The west island suffered worst of all. It was a tornado that wreaked the damage, something that swirled off the main hurricane, circling back to strike us.'

Mrs. Dymoke asked: 'Do they visit the islands often?'

'No, ma'am.' Hare bowed slightly. 'There cannot have been one like this for a score—for fifty years perhaps.'

'Ah!' Mrs. Dymoke's voice was relieved.

Ross coughed angrily.

Mrs. Ross spoke for the first time. 'That child?' she asked, looking over the rail to where Plandok sat, quietly gentle, a small brown image of total innocence.

Hare looked down after her, though he had no need to do so. 'She is the daughter of a noted pirate. She was rescued by an Indiaman after a battle. I brought her with us to return her to her people.' There was an unctuous smoothness in his tone.

'Poor thing!' Mrs. Ross hesitated for a second and then called down to the deck: 'Davie, bring the child up to us!'

A boy detached himself from the group. He looked younger than the others, no more perhaps than sixteen. He was fair, but his skin, unlike the others, took the sun. Against the brownness of it his hair shone like burnished gold. He held out his hand to Plandok. 'The mistress wishes tae speak wi' ye.'

She took his hand with the trustfulness of a little girl. From the first she had singled him out in the group as being nearest to her age. Even in her quick side glances she had assessed the moulding of his head and the strength of his young body. She allowed herself to be helped to the poop ladder and she went up it childishly, giving the impression that she needed support.

Downie, waiting below on the main deck, watched her open-mouthed.

She moved very delicately across to the women, her head down, her eyes hooded, her hands lax. Opposite Mrs. Ross she stood, vernal and artless.

Even Hare was shocked.

Elizabeth Ross said in her deep, maternal voice: 'You poor child!'

And inside Plandok bubbled with a sheer and beautiful wickedness.

# Sixteen

THE BOY Saad was busy paring down a new strut for the outrigger. The hasty repair after the big wind had served its turn, and Plandok needed a permanent fixture. Moreover, she had used a length of the line that had bound it for the last support of the head. She herself was working, repairing a hole in the jala. The hand nets were her own special province, and she would allow no one else to touch them except Saad and herself.

While they worked they watched the boats plying backwards and forwards from the brig to Pulau Selma. It was a long haul up to the big island.

The brig herself lay head to wind in the ruffled anchorage. She looked graceful from where they watched her. John Ross had built her himself in the wild days on the Karroo river from timber that he had selected and in part seasoned, with workmen that he had trained, to his own design. And when at last he had sailed her to Java, where Hare had removed with his harem, she was a thing of beauty. Ross had had few prouder moments in his life than when, at the end of her first passage to England, she had been surveyed by Lloyds and classified A1. By some financial chicanery that he did not understand John Hare, Alexander's brother, owned most of the vessel; Ross himself owned eight sixty-fourths; Alexander Hare one sixty-fourth only, and yet he was still the dominant partner—the aegis of the Borneo appointment still hung over him like a patent of nobility.

Plandok said: 'She is deep in the water.'

'I heard Tuan Downie talking,' Saad answered. 'She has cargo for Singapura and for Pinang. Afterwards she collects spices and pepper and some tin from the Bugis.'

'She will take me to Singapura,' said the girl confidently. 'In a little the women of Selma will send for me—you shall see. Meanwhile . . .' she dropped the net across her lap and stretched back against the palm root, looking up into its fronded heart to see if the fairy terns that had come back after the wind were still sitting companionably there, '. . . meanwhile there are ten young men who will stay in the islands, all of them devils.'

'Ha!' muttered Saad noncommittally.

'The oldest of them has hair upon his belly and upon his chest—black hair, much of it. We shall call him Tun Mai.'

Saad giggled, remembering the hairy caterpillar so called.

Plandok murmured dreamily, still watching the beady eyes of the terns: 'He has been at sea for a long time without any women except the foolish one with the deep voice'—she meant Elizabeth Ross—'and the old one with the voice like the juice of a lime.' She puckered her lips meditatively. 'Therefore,' she said positively, after a little pause, 'he would be suited to the Zulu girl, being, as it were, half black himself—at least as to the hair.'

Saad looked at her in alarm. 'What devilry is this?'

'It is not proper that young men should endure too long without women,' replied Plandok demurely, avoiding all words which might have a sexual implication. 'Also the Zulu girl has herself had no satisfaction since the wind. The Sush'nong has not sent for her. It might be that they would find favour in each other's sight.'

'Beyond all doubt,' said Saad, as he had said it so often, 'you are a devil!'

'But you are not afraid of me.' She lowered her eyes from the birds and stared fixedly at him.

'I am nothing in your eyes. You will not take the labour to destroy me.'

For the first time in a long while her smile was complete and natural. 'You are my friend, Saad.'

The boy rested the strut on the ground and looked at her gratefully.

On the morning of the third day Elizabeth Ross sent for her. In the intervening period Plandok had kept close to the landing place. Saad, wanting to go fishing on the reef, had had to go by himself. Plandok had found something to keep her busy always within sight of the *Borneo* and the boats that worked from her. Early on this morning the boat headed in towards the kampong. Hare had broken down Ross's first antagonisms. His boats were helping to put the gear ashore and half the Malay men were down on the big island.

The mate of the *Borneo* was with the boat. He came ashore and strode up the path to find Hare. Plandok drifted up the path behind him. He was a shifty, brutal-looking man, and she kept a wary distance from him. But she was close enough to the big hut to hear his voice as he made the request and to hear Hare's amused answer.

'To look after the children—Plandok! To look after children?'

'Why?' demanded Leisk.

'No, no reason.'

'She said that the child seemed gentle and was kind with the children when she took her below. She wishes it for a matter of days only—until the huts are built.'

Hare snorted. 'She has seen the girl, she knows her. It is her own choice. I will send for her.' He called over his shoulder to the Chinese woman. 'Mei Ying!' In Malay he said: 'Tell Plandok she goes to the big island to be of help to the white women.' Even the impassive face of Mei Ying creased into a look of surprise. 'Fetch her! Fetch her!' ordered Hare testily, and began to pour a drink for Leisk.

'Early in the morning,' said the mate, and tossed it down.

Hare asked: 'When do you sail?'

'Ship sails as soon as the huts are finished,' replied Leisk shortly.

'I want the girl back before she sails.'

'I'll tell Mrs. Ross.'

The Chinese woman had found Plandok. They came into the hut together. The girl walked soberly, her eyes downcast.

Hare said: 'You will go to the big island to help the white ladies. There will be no devilry.'

She bowed submissively, putting her hands together in a gesture of absolute obedience.

Leisk looked puzzled for an instant before he said: 'All right, we'll go, then. Does she need anything?'

Plandok said: 'I will go in my own canoe. I will not go with him.'

Without bothering to translate, Hare said: 'She will go down with the canoe. She can fish as well then.' Privately he chuckled at the thought of the possible situation that could develop. Aloud he observed: 'A masterful woman, Mrs. Dymoke.'

They were enchanted with her. In a single morning she accomplished the conquest of the six children. To the women she was gentle, submissive, and entirely willing. To Ross she was respectful. To the young men she was laughter. An unquenchable gaiety seemed to emanate from her. The children—it was their first full day ashore—she instructed in the ways of fairy terns or showed them the shore crabs and the little rockfish. She found turtles' eggs for Mrs. Ross and shell-fish for Mrs. Dymoke. She instructed the young men in the art of climbing the easier palms to the accompaniment of gales of laughter and lost time. She helped with the proper placing of the atap, and the Malay men watched her with awe and suspicion.

The young men gravitated towards her in the rest periods, but she was immensely careful. Always she had a protective screen of children around her or moved towards Mrs. Dymoke as if to seek the shelter of her robe. She made an exception only of the youngest of the young men, the fair-haired boy Davie. Occasionally she gave him a shy smile for his own that was quite different from her laughter. Once or twice she spoke to him. She could understand his English when he spoke carefully.

Mrs. Ross said: 'She is a friendly little soul, gentle and kind.' And Plandok, understanding less than half of what she said, none the less laughed inwardly.

The day passed with an almost inconceivable swiftness.

At sunset they made a fire large enough to illuminate the new clearing of the Ross kampong. Mrs. Dymoke sat on a chair that had been brought ashore. Mrs. Ross sat close to her with the baby and two of the youngest children beside her. The other three children sat with Plandok a yard or two away. The men sat all together in a little group while Mrs. Dymoke read an evening prayer. Ross watched her uneasily out of the corner of his eye, holding a lantern to reinforce the flickering light of the fire.

Plandok, with her instant imitativeness, followed the movements of the others, clasping her hands when they clasped their hands, bowing her head when they bowed theirs. She even managed an unidentifiable but acceptable sound at the deep 'amens'. Mrs. Dymoke held on too long with an extemporized prayer for the benefits of heaven on the new settlement. The lantern in Ross's hand wavered. It was altogether different, Plandok decided, from the first day on Direction Island, the day on which she had mocked Hare with the imperial titles of the Susuhunan. None the less, she preferred that day.

Mrs. Ross, not reading her thoughts, regarded her benevolently.

When it was over, Ross told the young men to sit. He made a short speech—a rehearsed speech, clearly. Plandok understood almost nothing of it, for he spoke fast and his accent differed altogether from that of Hare; but she caught Hare's name from time to time and saw his hand point up to the northern island, and read enough into the anger of his voice to know that he was talking of the other kampong.

He had, in fact, evolved a series of rules for the control of the new situation. None of the young men was to go to the northern island on any pretext whatever except with himself or with Leisk. None of them was to have contact with anybody from the northern island—particularly the women. None of them was to take instructions from Hare if Hare should come to Selma. They were not to interfere with boats from Direction or allow boats from Direction to interfere with them. They were not to fish close into Direction or chase turtle into the bight of the crescent island. They were to keep clear of all trouble at all times. They were to come to him—or to Leisk when he had left—with any news, however slight, that concerned the people of Selma, and they were to watch Hare whenever he came abroad. Above all they were to keep away from the women. Above *all* they were to keep away from the women.

Plandok was aware of eyes looking at her.

When he had finished he stood by the fire, waiting for questions. A voice from the group asked: 'Dae we hae a celebration tomorrer?'

'Why?' demanded Ross abruptly, jerked out of his contemplation of the wrong that Hare had done to him.

Two voices answered: 'St. Andra's Day!'

Ross said, at a loss: 'Are you sure?'

'We're guid Scots,' replied the first voice.

Plandok, watching the group in the glitter of the fire, identified the tall man whom she had christened Tun Mai.

Ross replied: 'I'm a good Scot too, Dougal' Shepherd. But this is no time for celebrations.'

Mrs. Dymoke said: 'There will be no drinking.'

'Hech!' exclaimed an unidentifiable voice in the deep dusk.

Ross looked at her hesitantly, uncertain as to whether to assert his authority.

One of the four sailors who had come ashore protested: 'God, Mr. Ross, it's aye been the custom!'

'There will be no celebration,' announced Ross firmly.

Three voices like a chorus said: 'St. Andra's Nicht an' a'!'

Plandok could not understand it, but her eyes darted from voice to voice identifying the speakers, storing their identity in her mind. It was obvious that there was disagreement here, a crack in the solidarity of this other kampong. The boy Davie, she noted, took no part.

For a minute or two the argument went on until Ross ended it with a brusque: 'That's enough! Away to your beds now!' And a sidelong glance at Mrs. Dymoke for approval.

Plandok stored up the fact that he was afraid of Mrs. Dymoke. She stored up the fact that the obedience of the young men, at least in this matter, was reluctant. She went to bed with the children, snuggled into the first shelter that had been put up on the island. The big huts were nearly completed now but they were not yet ready for occupation.

Mrs. Ross was almost as gentle with her as she was with her own children.

In the exquisite perfection of the morning Plandok took the children down to bathe. They splashed, happily naked, in the shallows. The boy Davie passed them, going down the beach to fetch a load from a pile of gear. He laughed gently at her as she drew her wet sarong with a modest urgency about her body.

Ross himself came down the path and stood watching and laughing too. But when his laughter was ended he said to the eldest of the three girls: 'You had better put your clothes on before your grandmother sees.' And they sobered and came out of the water.

At the first work break of the morning she manœuvred the children close to the resting place. Davie Knight sat at the edge of it, nearest to her. She heard almost at once again the phrase that she had heard the night before: 'Sinandrasnicht.'

She whispered to him: 'What is this thing?'

'St. Andra,' he answered softly, 'is the patron saint o' Scotland.' And then, with a simple understanding, recognized that she could not possibly grasp the meaning of his words and added: 'He was a saint. D'ye ken what a saint is? Na, ye wadna. He was a great man.'

That at least she understood.

'On his day we drink tae him.' He raised his hand in the gesture of holding a glass and tipped his head back and gurgled in his throat, and she laughed delightedly.

This too she understood. Her quick intelligence linked up the hints that she could gather. There was a great man and it was customary to drink to him, and from what had happened last night and from the tone of the voices now there would be no drink. She arrived at this in a miracle of perceptiveness, basing it all on the boy's single unmistakable gesture, and her mind raced ahead towards the glimmerings of a plan. She said no more, but sat there with the children twining around her, listening.

She heard Dougal' Shepherd saying: 'It's the auld bitch. She doesna ken the needs o' a Scot—or a mon, come tae that. Heigh, but I've a got a dryness in ma throat!'

Leisk came down on them. 'Stop belly-aching! Get on with it! You've got the stores to bring up and get stacked.'

A voice said: 'He's no' your saint.'

And another, an English voice, added softly: 'Supposin' you ever had a saint.'

Plandok gathered the children, grinned companionably at Davie Knight, and went away. At least she was certain that they were thirsty men.

In the middle of the afternoon someone sighted a boat coming down from Direction Island. Plandok, making a pool in the falling tide to hold starfish and hermit crabs, and a baby turtle that she had triumphantly captured in the morning, heard shouts and stood up. It was the best of Hare's two remaining boats and it crawled, deep-laden, in the water. Downie was in the stern-sheets. Two of the Malay men paddled; it had not been possible to make a new set of oars yet. The middle section of the boat was piled high with something that was covered with palm fronds and leaves.

Ross himself, warned of its coming, came down to the beach. He stood waiting.

Downie climbed out of the boat uninvited and came up the beach to him. 'Mr. Hare, remembering that it is St. Andrew's Day, has sent an offering.'

Shepherd fished down into the boat and pulled up the leaves. 'Roast pig!' he cried before Ross himself had chance to refuse. 'St. Andra himsel' would ha' appreciated it.'

Downie said: 'They are three parts cooked. An hour over a slow fire will have them ready, and there's a keg of rum.'

'Rum did you say, b'God?' One of the English sailors strode towards the boat.

'Leave it!' Ross ordered.

Shepherd, already alongside, snatched at the leaves and a small keg stood exposed. 'A wee bar'l!' His eyes were wide.

Ross surrendered. The mischief was done.

Downie, facing him, said smoothly: 'It is all that we can spare. We lost the great part of our store when the sea swept us. Mr. Hare regrets its inadequacy.'

'It will be adequate, I have nae doubt,' answered Ross gratingly, his anger overcoming his accent.

Plandok judged her moment with a fiendish precision. Shepherd up-ended the empty keg and squinted into the hole with an air of comic despair. Even watered, the rum had barely lasted three full rounds. Shepherd had gathered to himself the rounds of two of the non-drinkers, but he was not drunk—no more than stimulated.

'No' a drap an' the nex' St. Andra's Nicht's a fu' year awa'! It's a dry worrld.' Shepherd saw her laughing at him. 'Lassie, it's no' a matter for frevolity,' he admonished her.

Her eyes held his, and he frowned for a moment, puzzled. Then he saw an almost imperceptible gesture of her hand towards the north and his wit, thirst sharpened, leapt at a possibility. Very softly he asked: 'Is there mair where this came fra?'

She answered his eagerness rather than the actual words with a nod.

'Heugh! Sandy lad, we'll tak' her awa' up the beach an' pit her tae the question.'

She grinned at him in a companionship of utter mischief and shook her head. 'Davee,' she said. She could understand him: he could understand her alone of them all.

It took time for her to make Shepherd understand. She sat serenely quiet until he did. Then he said drolly: 'She's no fer us, Sandy. That wee deil Davie's oot ahead o' us. Davie, ye bluidy young ram, tak' her awa' an' sift the matter oot o' her!' She rose as the boy rose, and Shepherd slapped lightly at her bottom. 'Heugh! She's got a neat wee hurdie.' His enormous hand gathered in the small bottom and squeezed.

Plandok's hand brushed lightly over the resting place of the kris, but it was not a threat, for the young men knew nothing of the knife. It was a personal gesture of reassurance. She shook herself, remembering, and went out into the fresh darkness.

The boy followed after.

# Seventeen

THE WARMTH of the night wind streamed over them. Davie, lying in the bows of the boat with his head clear of the stem-piece, felt it ruffle through his hair like a teasing hand. He watched the diaphanous wake of the canoe ahead of them, the phosphorescence swirling in light, delicate whorls. In the moonlight he could see the girl, her body silvered on the eastern side. She leaned forward, paddling with a strong, easy stroke.

Behind him Shepherd said: 'Pull, ye thrawn buggers! Pull! She's fetchin' awa' from us agen.'

'Quiet! The sound carries ower the wa'er. I can see th' island.' Davie could see it as a dark bank against the moon haze over the reef. It lay in a nimbus of soft light.

The canoe altered course, and he passed the information back in a low voice. Plandok was heading apparently for the open sea. He judged that she was keeping to deep water as long as possible before turning in for the southern horn of Direction Island. The current caught them a little here and the pulling was heavy. The light canoe skimmed ahead with the assurance of a night bird. Then, quite suddenly, they were grounded at the very edge of the beach. The distance in the moonlight had been deceptive. Plandok was already standing motionless in the shadows, waiting. They pulled the canoe and the boat up on the sand, clear of the rising tide.

She said: 'Three come,' holding up three fingers. 'You'—she indicated Shepherd—'you'—her finger picked out Hugh Johnson, the Englishman—'an' Davee.'

One of the others asked: 'Whit aboot us, then?' his voice instantly aggrieved.

She patted the ground in a gesture of sitting down.

'We'll bring the stuff here,' said Shepherd. 'It's no' a howff we're gaein' to, mon!'

'An' the girrls? I dinna trust ye the length o' a cud, Dougal'!'

'Efter three months at sea I dinna trust mysel'.' The big man began to laugh internally, stifling the mirth.

'Come!' said Plandok.

She led the three up the horn of the crescent and along the seaward beach. They walked in silence, the girl picking the way through the piled wreckage, the logs and the broken timbers that had been left by the last of the hurricane. There were new boulders piled up, broken from the edge of the reef and rolled in by the force of the seas and the wind. But she picked her way unerringly through it all, the light of the moon ample for her purpose. At the end of eight minutes or so she found what she was seeking: three big boulders in a conspicuous group at the edge of the seaward palms. She had half feared that they might be missing, but she knew that they marked the end of the short path that led to the site of the hut of Pa Abas. Now she would level with Pa Abas.

Four full months back three jars had disappeared—big, capacious jars. Inevitably she had been accused; every disappearance was put down to her. One of the jars she had seen already on an early morning at the back of the hut of Pa Abas insufficiently covered with palm fronds. Three times since she had seen Pa Abas drunk, not obstreperously drunk but gently, happily drunk. She had stored up then the useful knowledge that Pa Abas was making palm toddy. He had, of course, denied all knowledge of the jars, had made no attempt to shield her from the wrath of Downie—not that she cared for Downie.

The hut itself, like the others, had gone in the hurricane. Pa Abas, she judged, had been too busy since to investigate his cellar. Now he was safely on Selma with the other men whom Hare had lent to Ross.

She led them up to the rocks, turned in along the path that was partly obstructed by fallen palm boles, and found the clearing. Two of the uprights of the hut were still there to fix the position. She stooped and began to pull fronds and palm trash away to get at the sand. They found the first jar in five minutes. She cleared the sand from the stopper, opened it, and put her nose to it. It was beyond question full of matured palm toddy. She laughed and beckoned Shepherd to put his head down.

He drew in a long, deep breath. 'For Godsake!' A grin of enormous admiration split his face. 'Ye're a cunnin' wee de'il!'

She pointed her finger at Johnson and made a motion of digging, throwing sand away from the side of the jar. Then she said: 'Come!'

Shepherd took her meaning instantly. 'Ye stay behind an' dig oot the jar, Hugh Johnson, an' if a drap is spilt I'll hae yer tripes!'

Since the hurricane the women had slept in three small shelters: the children and the young girls in one, the younger women in the second, the older women in the third. Plandok, on her stomach on the ground, worked her fingers through the thin and temporary screen. The black girl had pre-empted this corner. Plandok was resting her luck heavily on the black girl's innate and inordinate curiosity. Presently she had a hole big enough to put her hand through. She groped delicately in the darkness until she found the warm, polished ebony skin. She found it with no more than her finger-tips but at once the girl stirred. She stroked delicately, trying to give to her finger-tips a touch of reassurance. After a moment the girl stirred again, more positively. Plandok gave to her fingers a feeling of urgency, almost of imperiousness.

Then, sure that the Zulu girl was awake enough, she whispered: 'It is I, Plandok. Come outside!'

The girl stirred once more and murmured foolishly: 'Who?'

'I, Plandok.'

'What . . . ?'

Plandok ssh'd her into silence, withdrawing her hand. She knew that curiosity and perhaps a degree of fear would bring the Zulu girl out now. In a moment she saw a darker shape than the darkness under the eaves. She stretched out a hand, caught the Zulu girl's, and pulled her over beyond the edge of the clearing.

'The Sush'nong has not sent for you, I have a man for you.'

The black girl backed away. 'Beyond doubt you are a witch!'

'The man I bring,' said Plandok smoothly, 'is, none the less, a man. Come!' Again she took the black girl's hand.

She led her down the path a few yards. In an open clearing Shepherd stood in the moonlight. He looked enormous, intensely virile. The black girl walked towards him, wholly fascinated. Her movement had the attributes of somnambulism. As Shepherd opened his arms to her, she almost flung herself into them.

'Heugh,' he muttered, 'there's an armfu' here!'

Plandok gave them only a minute to establish contact. Then she separated them—small, imperious, and eager. 'Go back now to the hut and waken Anita—and softly! If you rouse the others I will indeed use my witchcraft. Go now and quickly, for there are more men at the horn of the island and they have been at sea too long.'

This at least the Zulu girl could understand, though she understood little of the rest of what was happening. She gave a deep gurgle, itself an expression of her sexual hunger, and hurried up the path.

Plandok said: 'Davee!'

'I am here,' he answered out of the shadows.

'You want girl?'

She saw him shake his head in the dim light. 'No,' he said, 'I have no need for one.'

They arrived back at the horn of the island in an hour. Shepherd and Johnson carried the great jar between them, slung on a pole over their shoulders. Three women walked with them: the Zulu girl, Anita, and the half-Portuguese girl, Meriam, who had wakened and perforce been brought with them.

They were greeted with querulous whisperings. The four men who had been left behind had acquired anxieties.

'Like a lot o' bluidy auld wives!' exclaimed Shepherd witheringly. 'Ye should hae trusted the wee wonder here.' He put his arm across Plandok's shoulders. This time she slipped from under it with an abruptness that contained a warning.

They unslung the jar and collected half-coconut shells from the boat.

Shepherd poured, holding the whole weight in his strong arms. 'It's no whusky, but in a bit island like this in the middle o' yon vast, unthinkin' ocean it's in the nature o' the manna that the good Lord brought to the Hebrews i' the wilderness. Drink, ye humpty-backit, ghost-glowerin' buggers!'

The taste was wholly foreign to them; it was deceptively mild. It required all the assurance of Shepherd, the knowledgeable one in the field of alcohol, to make them drink enough of it; but in a short while it established its own authority.

The women drank hardly at all, so that the whole thing started slowly. They were shy. Even Shepherd was shy, standing with his arm about the Zulu girl's shoulders and unwilling to acknowledge that he was shocked by the appearance of her bare and splendid breasts in the moonlight.

Plandok withdrew herself, first within the confines of the group and then physically away from it, and Davie followed her. He had drunk only a little.

The lighting of the fire sparked it all. It was the Englishman's suggestion. They built it rapidly and efficiently out of driftwood and dry rubbish, and it lit in a single, up-leaping blaze.

Davie protested anxiously, remembering Hare: 'It will bring him down on us!'

But Plandok, considering the position carefully before she spoke, said: 'It is no matter now.' With her inevitable, unchildlike judgement, she had arrived at the conclusion that these young men, introduced once to the possibilities of drink and the willingness of women on Direction, would thereafter harass Hare in their own ways. Her part was accomplished. Hare was paid for the beating.

She sat on, watching the simple drinking develop into a saturnalia.

The men became lightly drunk, excited, emulative. As if the light of the flames had fired them, the women became part of the pattern. They moved about the fire first. Anita slipped away from a passionate embrace and was chased and brought back screaming with laughter. The Zulu girl began to dance in a slow, unmistakable rhythm. They all laughed. They rushed backwards and forwards. The women's voices were shrill. They drank more and more. They piled the fire higher. The tempo of passion leapt upward with the flames.

There were six men and three girls. Early there was a fight. It failed of drunkenness, but they pulled the women between them and the women screamed with laughter. And then, with almost no precedent fondling, Shepherd fell on the Zulu girl, and Plandok, sitting quietly with her hands, as always, still on her lap, watched the primitive, urgent copulation while the rest of the men and the two girls stood around and cheered and shouted.

Johnson, the Englishman, pulled Meriam's legs from beneath her and they wrestled on the ground. The watching group split and coalesced again. Somebody began to sing. Davie, watching intent, the furrowing of his forehead accentuated by the firelight, recognized the words.

> '. . . an' I were ne'er sae weary;
> I'll lay thee ower the lea-rig
> Bonnie Anne, my dearie . . .'

The other voices caught up the thin, lilting melody. The laughter punctuated it.

Shepherd rolled away at last and lay gasping and crowing with laughter. Somebody carried him a drink, and he propped himself on one elbow and lay back again, shouting unintelligible bawdinesses between the gusts. The Cape girl, Anita, dropped on him where he lay and his arms folded round her. The standing men cheered and a voice said: 'The randy stot'll tak' them a'!' Two of them fell on their knees beside her and tried to claw her away. Shepherd struck out, still laughing, and the girl laughed with him, and they clung together.

The men began to sing again, a song that this time Davie could not recognize. The two who had been kneeling next to the Cape girl moved to the black wench, who lay outstretched and still inviting, and she chose one of them with a single clutch of her arm.

Plandok watched entranced, her eyes dancing with malice. From time to time she stole a side glance at Davie, who sat, his face puckered with ununderstanding.

After a little Shepherd was quiet again and, as he lay there, he said softly in the ear of the Cape girl: 'Whaur wad the young lass be?' And then, when he got no understanding from her: 'Whaur's Plandok?'

The girl answered him in clear English: 'With the boy.'

'God's teeth, and ye speak English as weel! Whaur's the boy?'

'Leave her 'lone! She carries a kris.'

'A kris?'

'A knife,' the girl explained savagely. 'Between her legs she carries it.'

'Heugh! That's no a place for a knife.'

Somebody poured more drink. They sat up. The singing went on through the drinking. Somebody else threw more dry wood on the fire. The night was full of the sound of flames and laughter and wildness.

Hare came out of it with a spectral suddenness. One moment there was only the light of the fire against the tarnished silver of the palm stems and the white of the beach and the nothingness of the inshore water; and then there was Hare with a gun in his hands, and Downie a safe ten yards behind him, and one of the Malay men behind him again.

It was the Cape girl who saw him first. Her shriek was wholly different this time. The reality of her fear was instant and communicable. The other women scrambled to their feet and ran blindly.

Hare's voice began, as always, to bellow.

Shepherd rose. He was not so drunk but that he could see the gun and assess its danger. He shouted: 'The boat! Push out the boat!' And the men ran in one confused pattern of arms and bodies lit red by the flames against the darkness of the lagoon.

Hare was bellowing: 'Stop or I'll shoot!'

They saw him raise the gun, and Davie rose on one knee, staring with an almost painful intensity. As he rose, he felt Plandok's hand on his arm. He heard her voice in a long sibilant warning 'Ssh!'

The boat was half afloat already. The men pushed her into the water in a flurry of firelit spray. Their own legs flung up more spray. They were tumbling aboard her. Under the palms Plandok could hear the thuds as men scrambled inboard, as the oars were struck and struck in their turn against the thwarts. The last man, Dougal' Shepherd himself, pushed ferociously and, as the water reached his waist, flung himself upwards over the bows and lay with his legs kicking.

She could hear a roar of laughter, and again above it Hare's thunderous voice: 'Stop or I'll shoot!'

The boy said: 'He must no' shoot.'

Plandok whispered softly: 'He has no powder. Now we will go to the canoe.'

She had beached it farther down, almost at the exact point of the southern horn of the crescent of the island. She slipped through the beach palms like a small ghost, and Davie, still shocked, still half hypnotized by the riotousness of the night, followed obediently behind her. Over the water, as they went, they heard the thud of the oars between the thole pins and the splash as the men began to row. The boat drew out of the firelight, out of distance, out of range. The men began to sing again:

> 'The cats like kitchen;
> The dogs like broo;
> The lasses like the lads weel,
> And th' auld wives too.'

And then came the ribald chorus:

> 'An' we're a' noddin',
> Nid, nid, noddin',
> We're a' noddin' fou at e'en . . .'

The girl stopped level with the canoe and surveyed it cautiously. Less than half of it was in the water. She turned back and watched Hare. He was raging at the water-side, Downie behind him, and the other man with them. Their heads were drawn to the singing. She judged that it was wholly safe, and walked quietly down to the water's edge.

She said: 'Lift!'

The boy grasped her meaning at once, and between them they walked the canoe out until it floated. She sat herself in it and then motioned him to go into the space between the outrigger struts, and herself placed his hands at the point where the struts grew out from the hull.

'Swim!' she said, and he laughed softly, achieving an instant understanding.

He walked the boat out until he too floated and then began to kick as he felt the paddle drive in. They slipped swiftly out of the ring of the firelight. At any moment Hare could have seen them, but he was still facing outward to the deep water, shaking his fist after the retreating song. The ballad had changed now to a coarse bawdiness.

# Eighteen

Ross WALKED down the line with his head low, thrust forward with something of the appearance of an expectant vulture. 'You—you—and you!' One by one he picked out the six who had been around the fire.

There was small problem in this. They were bloodshot, bleary-eyed, tousled. It had taken them three hours of blind rowing to find their way back to Selma without the canoe. Plandok, already snuggled down between the children, had listened to their whispering, stumbling, still half-drunken return. Davie was already in his sleeping place.

She had landed him at the north point of Selma to run down the beach and warm himself, but he had waited to drag in the canoe with her and in the darkness going softly up the path to the huts he had put his hand lightly on her shoulder.

Ross separated the six from the others. He passed Davie by without a glance. 'I warned you yesterday morning. By God, I'll not warn you again! I'll set up a triangle and I'll flog the next man who goes to Direction. I'll flog the next man who gets drunk. Damn, I'll flog the lot o' ye! How did ye find the drink? Come on, how did ye find it?'

They stood silent, not answering. Shepherd at least was sure that the rage was assumed. He watched intently for an opening. Before it came Ross was aware of a figure on the lagoon beach. The boat from Direction had come down unsighted. The whole settlement was concentrated in this scene of accusation.

Downie came up to him without greeting and held out a note.

Shepherd relaxed slightly.

For a moment Ross read in silence, then suddenly he spluttered and read aloud: ' "I thought when I sent rum and roast pig to your sailors that they would stay away from my flower-garden . . ." Flower-garden —flower-garden, by God! He calls it a flower-garden. The island's a brothel, no less, and he calls it a flower-garden!'

Shepherd relaxed completely. He was sure that he knew enough of Ross to know that the crisis so far as it concerned them was over. He watched the captain towering over the wretched Downie.

'Who is he to send me letters like this? Who does he think he is? Damned, man, these are *my* islands! My men will go where they will. If he wants to keep his women let him keep them. I'll no' help him.'

Plandok, with the children gathered round her half fascinated, half terrified by the excitement, watched with her eyes glistening. Her absolute and complete wickedness was like a particular joy.

Ross went on and on, and Downie cringed and made no attempt to answer him. When he was almost exhausted Ross said: 'Get back and tell him that. No, by God! I'll away up and tell him mysel'. You'—he turned to the group—'get the boat in the water, damn your hides!'

Downie found his voice again. 'Mr. Hare requests that you shall send back his men with my boat. He no longer wishes them to be of assistance to you.'

'Tak' them and be damned to them, the pack o' lazy, skulkin' bastards!'

'And the girl,' said Downie with surprising firmness, 'the girl Plandok.'

Somewhere behind him Ross heard his mother-in-law clear her throat. He said: 'Tak' her and be damned to you!'

Again Mrs. Dymoke cleared her throat. This time it had an implication of warning, but it was Mrs. Ross who came forward. 'Don't send her back!' she begged. 'She is so young, so gentle.'

Downie, in his most irritating manner, said: 'Mr. Hare insists!'

Mrs. Ross asked: 'Can she not stay, John? She has been good with the children; I think they love her already. She is a little thing. She does not need to go back there.' Ross turned and faced her. She stood with her hands clasped, her face anxious and pleading. 'I do not like to think of a child with a man like that.'

'Child be damned!' returned Ross abruptly. 'She has been in his harem for the best of a year. Do you think she is still a child?'

Mrs. Ross put her hands to her mouth. 'No, no! You cannot mean . . . ?'

'What do you think Hare bought her for? I have told you enough of him.'

'So young,' murmured Mrs. Ross.

'He's had 'em younger,' he said indifferently, and suddenly, wheeling on Plandok, he demanded: 'Where were you last night?'

She looked at him with her enormous fawnlike eyes. 'With these, Tuan,' she answered softly, immensely enjoying the situation. It was even, in a sense, true—or in part true. She had been with them for the last of the night.

Mrs. Dymoke, from behind, said: 'Send her back if it is as you say it is. You cannot keep her here. You should not have allowed her to come here. It was monstrous, Mr. Ross!'

He muttered abstractedly: 'Ma'am,' staring all the while at the child. At last he said: 'I believe you are a finished little devil.'

Sorrowfully Mrs. Ross said: 'At least put her in safety on the *Borneo* and take her east with you so that she may find her father.'

Downie had somehow reacquired his customary self-assurance. 'You are right, Mr. Ross! She is a finished devil. I would myself gladly see her go. She is at the root of all the troubles of the household. Ask your children where she was last night!' And then, as if he had gone too far, he added: 'But Mr. Hare would not permit it, sir; in no way would he permit it. He is in a sense besotted, sir—'

'Damn Alexander Hare and damn you! Get your men and get the hell from off my island!'

Plandok lolled back in the canoe, ridiculously idle. She could see no reason why she should paddle when she was tied to the stern of the boat. Downie had taken his orders literally. 'Keep a tight hold on her till you get her back here!' The boat was sluggish, well astern of Ross's cutter. She could, of course, escape: it required only a slash of a knife at the line and a few strokes of the paddle. The overloaded boat would never catch up with her. The knowledge was itself a strength, but her curiosity as to the outcome of this affair was enough to overcome the idea of it. She lay lazily, occasionally putting a foot over the side and trailing her toes in the water. The glittering spray ran up under her knee and trickled down her thigh. Once or twice she dipped a hand into the water and patted her forehead with its coolness.

The young men in Ross's cutter were sweating. He drove them remorselessly. They worked out their hangovers in a fierce, pounding rhythm, hammered out by him on the gunwale with a fish cudgel. At times he swore at them but there was no malice in his swearing. He was driving them only so that he could get to grips with Hare.

The girl heard his voice long before she had thought it necessary to raise herself enough to sight the island. There was no one on the beach, but Ross was bawling in the thunderous voice that he had used in the old days of the whaling ships, the voice of the harpooner.

'Ahoy, there! You, Hare—don't you know that rum and roast pig are not a sailor's heaven?'

Shepherd laughed and, when Ross glowered at him, he laughed again. The sweat was racing down his face and over his chest but that was little enough to pay for a riot that would have not disgraced a howff in Glasgow on The Night.

They lay on their oars, waiting, and presently, as Downie's boat went past them, the girl, looking beyond it, saw Hare come out of the path from the kampong, his gun cradled in his arms, and stalk, furious, to the water's edge.

'Keep away,' he shouted out. 'I'll shoot the next one that tries to land!'

'Shoot and I'll burn your kampong over your head!'

She listened, convulsed with inner laughter as Hare's voice grew stronger and Ross's voice diminished with the progress of the boat. The bawling went on: old accusations, recriminations, new insults, sheer fury. It was not worth while attempting to dissever the meaning out of the thunder of the words. She was content with the knowledge that she had stirred this up.

She steered the canoe to one side as the heavy boat grounded and, clambering out, pulled it up on the sand. Then she walked demurely, wholly submissive, to the thin shadows of the path.

Hare watched her with suspicion out of the corner of his eye. He had recognized the marks where the canoe had been dragged up when they searched the scene of the orgy at sunrise. He became distracted in his vituperation. Over the water Ross redoubled his efforts.

Plandok went on towards the kampong and the battered palm trees swallowed her.

The hut into which Hare thrust her had been reinforced. New uprights had been driven in all round it, filling in the spaces between the original posts. To her eye it had at once the appearance of a prison. It was, in fact, a prison: they had salved the padlock, and she was locked in— and she knew at once that escape would be difficult.

She lay there, alone. At noon Kam Ho brought her food.

The Chinese girl whispered: 'Never has he been so angry—but never, never!' And stole out again.

An hour after the meal she heard Saad's voice, low and apprehensive. He was lying on his belly on the far side of the hut from the path. 'He is more angry than he has ever been. The hut is watched. I will bring what I can, but there is no escape from here. 'Timah watches now and the men will watch at night: it is his order, and they are afraid of him.'

She giggled and she saw that the boy's eyes looked scandalized. 'I have been working. Now I will take a rest. He will not beat me again.'

She settled herself comfortably, and one by one the older children came up on the path side and talked to her through the bars of the cage.

She slept well that night. In the early morning the birds woke her. She was acutely sensitive to the birds now and when the gannets had gone, their cries diminishing in the distance, she thought back over the riot of the night and the splendour of the morning quarrels. From time to time little gusts of laughter took her. She was completely happy.

It was not until the evening of the second day that she began to have doubts. Hare had made no move. Since he had thrust her into the prison hut he had not come near. She had heard him from time to time giving orders, berating the women, crashing once through the undergrowth, but she had not seen him.

Her food came when the others had their meals. The children drifted up and were chased away and drifted back again. There was always someone to talk to if she chose, but the watch was constant and effective. It was clear that the people were terrified of Hare in his present mood. Once or twice Downie came and looked in through the bars, smugly satisfied.

It was Downie perhaps who aroused her doubts. She began to wonder if she could not have stayed on the other island. Mrs. Ross—she thought of Mrs. Ross as kind but foolish—had said something about the *Borneo,* about the ship, but she had not gathered it completely in the quick-fire of the exchange. Perhaps if she had chosen she could have stayed with Mrs. Ross. Perhaps if she had stayed Mrs. Ross could have helped her to sail with the *Borneo.* It took a long time before she formulated this idea but when she had accepted it the depression was instant and absolute. She knew now that she had made a mistake. To get aboard the *Borneo* by herself would require immense cunning, and she was locked in this stupid prison. For the first time she began to consider escape.

In the early evening when Shuk Yi, Mei Ying's child, drifted up to the cage to talk, she sent her for Saad. The boy came a long while after in the darkness. She heard his whispered greeting close to her head as she lay, her mind pounding over the possibilities of her mistake.

'I must get to the *Borneo!*' she said.

'You cannot,' he answered softly. 'He will not let you go. Tonight the men watch, and you cannot break out of this place without noise. They will not dare to sleep. He has told them that he will lash them against a tree if you so much as break one pole of the hut.'

'And you?'

'What can I do? I am a child. I could bring you a knife but you have a knife already. If you need a parang I will bring it, but it will not help you because of the noise; I have heard the men say this.'

'I could dig my way under the posts.'

'You could not. They go too deep. He made it that way, thinking of this.'

'What am I to do, then?' She began to feel a stirring of panic.

'It is not for me to say,' replied Saad softly.

All through the night she lay restless and afraid. She knew now that she had mishandled the affair. It was humiliating to admit even to herself that she was wrong; it was destructive of confidence. If she had used Mrs. Ross she could have stayed; she was sure now of that. Ross himself would have given in in the end. And now she was in this accursed cage, and the men were terrified—and there was no chance of escape.

Unless—unless perhaps she could do something with the men themselves.

She spoke to Kassim when he came to the hut to make certain that she was still secure. 'I must get to the ship. If you aid me there will be great reward.'

'There will be unmeasured beating,' said Kassim soberly. 'For myself, I would let you go, for I believe that there is an endless succession of mischief in you, but he has beaten the Zulu girl and she still lies sick in the women's hut, and he has beaten the Cape girl, and I will not make a third in the beatings.'

'You will not be to blame——' she began, the wheedling note coming into her voice.

'It is not a matter of blame,' Kassim broke in with finality. 'If you escape I will be beaten. Even if a djinn came down from the sky and lifted you out through the roof I would still be beaten. Therefore I will not help you.'

She spat the single word 'Coward!' after him, but it did not seem to weigh particularly heavily.

When the watch was relieved a little before dawn she tried again with Pa Abas.

He asked: 'Who revealed to them the hiding place of my jars?'

'I did, but a jar of palm toddy is a small thing against the reward that you will get from my father.'

'We have been here the most of a year and your father has not come,' Pa Abas pointed out firmly. 'I do not any longer believe in this reward.'

'Then, because I am a witch, I will bring a curse upon you.'

'I fulfil his orders,' said Pa Abas uneasily, but still determined. 'I know how he will punish me. I do not know about your curses.' And he walked away.

On the morning of the fourth day she heard the singing. She heard shouts, and the creaking of the blocks, and the rhythmic, repetitive clacking of the pawls.

As the *Borneo* went out to sea, she put her head on a pile of leaves and wept with deep, shattering sobs. It was not simply that the *Borneo* was gone. It was not alone that her chance of escape had vanished. It was that her faith in herself was damaged.

# Nineteen

SAAD FLUNG the jala. It hung for a moment lambent in the evening light, acquired its full and perfect circle, and dropped. Plandok remembered the morning when she had stood with him fishing in the lagoon—months ago now—in the almost forgotten period before the wind. He had been more amenable then; it was time to make him amenable again.

She waited until he had gathered in the net and was ready to make another cast before she said: 'It was my error. I did not ask my head for aid.'

He took her meaning in a flash of time. Precisely as he had done on that other day, he dropped the net and jerked out: *'Insh' Allah!'* And then, gasping, as he crouched down to recover it: 'What head, in the name of God?'

She answered loftily: *'You* surely should know. It was the head that brought the ship, but I did not ask it to permit the ship to take me away. This was my error.'

'And now?'

'Now I must go to it and make the prayers and the spells.'

'Why do you tell me this?'

'Because I do not wish to go alone.'

'I do not go!' The boy gathered up the net and clasped it to his chest. 'I do not wish to hear of this.'

'You have heard,' she said smoothly. 'Last time she called the birds down on me, and I wish to have someone to stand at my back as it were.'

*'I* will not come!' Saad was frankly terrified now.

She shrugged her shoulders. 'Then I must go alone. At least the canoe will float now.'

Hare had put a hole through its bottom as a secondary guarantee against escape. It was not a very big hole and, with the help of Pa Abas and the boy, she had repaired it, Hare raising no objections now that the ship was safely gone. She had been let out early in the morning of the departure. No one had said anything, not even Downie. All the kampong had heard her sobbing. The women at least were afraid of what would happen next.

It had taken her a full seven days to re-establish her confidence in herself. For the first of them she had crept round the kampong like a wounded bird, and Hare, his own anger appeased now, had watched her compassionately. As much as anything it had been the complacency among the women that had restored her faith in herself. It had become necessary to deal with them.

She cast her mind back over these things for a minute, then she said to Saad: 'I will go tonight. There is no moon but it does not matter, there are at least the stars. And I am not afraid.'

She did not add 'like you', but Saad accepted the reproach. After he had meditated over it for a little he said: 'It is true—I am afraid. I was afraid of her in her life but in her death I am many times afraid. I thought when they said that a shark had taken it . . . but I put the thought away.'

'That was wise. It will be wise if you put the thought of talking about this away also.'

Hare was coming down the path as she went back towards the kampong. He grunted at her, and she could not tell from his bearing whether he were angry with her or pleased. 'You are coming back to life again?'

She decided to say nothing.

'Saad passed me like a frightened rabbit.'

'Rabbit?' she asked, putting her head on one side.

He bent down to look into her face and actually laughed; her innocence was so exquisitely fabricated. 'You don't know about rabbits. Any of the small animals in your stories, then, when Plandok has frightened them. What are you planning?'

'I plan nothing,' she replied airily. 'It is that things happen.'

'You had better get it into your small head that you can't escape me,' he said, half menacing, half humorous. 'It is time that we were friends.'

She opened both hands in a gesture of appeasement. 'It is my wish to be friends with all.'

'It was in friendship, then,' he said as if trying to follow her line of reasoning, 'that you brought the young men from Selma to the beach, that you uncovered the palm toddy of Pa Abas, and that you persuaded the girls from the hut?'

She looked at him full in the face, her voice disarming. 'The young men had been many months without women and for what I know without drink also.'

Hare exploded with laughter. 'Beyond doubt you were born in the pit itself!' He went on down the path, still laughing. Over his shoulder he tossed back: 'Sleep well!'

'I will sleep well,' she called back musically, and added softly so that he could not hear: 'When the time comes for me to sleep.' And went on her way to the kampong.

The birds grumbled and were querulous in the darkness as she crept beneath them. They could hear her passing though she moved as softly as was possible. They could see the spark of the coconut fibre torch that she carried in her hand—more for comfort than for its minuscule light.

She found the shed lonely at the end of its storm clearing, untouched, silent, and waiting. It took no more than five minutes to gather fuel for the fire beneath the head—this night there was no question of a fire outside. As she blew up the spark of the fibre torch to light the fire she saw the head for the first time—vague, undiminished, and baleful. Then the fire caught and the eyes began to move with its flickering and the mouth to change its shape as if in speech. When the fire had taken, Plandok moved back to her place against the upright, settled herself and contemplated it.

The head had suffered a little since she left it: the skin had cracked in places and the corners had lifted up in a mockery of wounds, the eye-sockets were deeper and dustier, and some small bird had perched on it and there were droppings. Strangely, the cracking at the corners of the mouth had altered its expression. It had seemed baleful in the first red glow of the fibre but now in the full light of the fire it took on a macabre cheerfulness. The mouth had almost the appearance of laughter.

She said: 'You may laugh at me. This is your right, for it was my error. I should have come to you.' She thought of adding in explanation: 'But I am young,' and rejected it.

The lips appeared to move in sound formation with the play of the light but no sound came.

She said: 'Laugh, then! Laugh! But now I shall say the words that the Sea Dyak woman taught me and then you will again do my bidding. Laugh while you may.'

She leaned her head back against the post and closed her eyes, digging deeply into her memories. The words came to her of their own volition. She found herself pronouncing them without conscious formation of the sounds. About her she could hear the squeak and protest of the birds but there was no whistle of diving, and this she could disregard. For a long time she sat quite still, allowing the little rivulets of words to coalesce and stream from her mouth. Half of them she had never understood, of half of the rest of them the meaning was forgotten, but the words were the thing that was important. When at last her mind became utterly empty with effort, she sat in silence. Far away the surf boomed; the bird sounds and the rustle of wings, and the occasional clap of feathers in clumsy take-off came under the eaves to her.

The smoke had filled the inverted bowl of the roof. The head once more was swooping in and out of it, most of the time invisible or at best half-seen, and once again she waited for the fire to die and the level to rise.

When at last it did so, she said: 'I need another ship to come. See to it!' And almost as if she were not saying it herself, but that the phrases were formed independently of her as some of the spells had been, she went on: 'Also I have been afraid and am sad, and I need happiness.' And a long while afterwards, drowsily and about to sleep: 'See to it!'

Davie came down the narrow stretch of the high-tide beach disconsolate. Once he kicked at a shell, shaped to kick at it a second time, boy fashion, and then abandoned the intention. More than anything else the failure betrayed both his indeterminate position between boyhood and manhood and his unhappiness. Shepherd had been at him again.

Shepherd was not cruel. It was only that he lacked perception of other people's feelings. Since the night of the saturnalia he had maintained a constant harassing of the boy.

'Ah! But where were ye, ye wee bugger, when we were in trouble? Awa' in the bushes wi' the lassie—and you the youngest o' us a', ye randy wee stot!'

He meant it in laughter. Another man might have held a grievance against Davie for escaping from the wrath of Ross, for not admitting that he too had been of the adventure. He, however, bore no malice; and, anyway, Leisk, the mate of the *Borneo,* who had been left in charge on Ross's island when the *Borneo* sailed, had long since discovered his share in the affair and Leisk had a sour and a brutal temperament.

Davie walked on, not even bothering to kick a shell that lay directly in the path of his feet.

The girl watched him from her place in the shade of the shoreward palms. She sat, as always, utterly still, completely absorbed in his approach. She was not sure that she had asked the head to bring Davie to her. In the moment between waking and sleeping she might have asked anything of it: memory stopped at the sad appeal for happiness. Had the head brought Davie to her or had she come to him of her own volition? Did she want him or had the head ensured that she should have him? She was wholly unsure of her own feelings and of the reasons that had brought her here.

She knew only that she had woken early, long before the first light, that the tide had served, and that she had come straight across the lagoon to Pulau Ampong and hidden the canoe in the bight of the island. It was as if she had moved like a puppet of the shadow plays, given life by invisible hands. She had left the canoe at Ampong and had waded up through the shallows. And all through the day she had sat here, waiting—and now he had come.

He walked framed under the arch of the outward-leaning shore palms. The blinding glare of the afternoon made an halation about him. The thin green of the shallows relieved it hardly at all, and he walked in a glory and in the centre of the glory he looked like a lost child, sad and lonely. She was aware of compassion; it was an emotion she did not know how to deal with. She had once felt compassion for Hare; but she had never before had the urge to show it. He came under the last half-arch of the palms and walked straight past her, unseeing and self-absorbed.

She said softly: 'Davee!'

He stopped instantly as a man would stop at a gunshot, turned and then ran, half stumbling, towards her. With a wholly unadult impulse he dropped to his knees in front of her and held out his hands, groping for her hands.

His eyes on her eyes, he said: 'What are ye daein' here? Oh, Plandok, but that man Leisk will be angry if he finds ye! What made ye come?'

For the first time in her life she was at a loss for a positive answer. Instead she murmured: 'I wished to see . . .'

'Och,' he cried, bubbling over, 'but I am happy to see *you!*'

There was something important in the touch of his hands on hers, some communicable companionship that was new to her, different from anything that she had ever known with Saad, a new and perhaps irrational feeling. 'Davee, I have gone . . .' She loosed one hand and swept it up to indicate Direction Island. 'I live—there.' She pointed towards the thin line of the palm tops of the west island. 'You come!'

'Tae the west island?' The words themselves were not important, the incredulousness of them was. He sat back on his heels and studied her face. After a long pause he asked: 'Ye mean gang to the west island wi' ye tae live?' And when she still made no reply but kept her eyes steadily on his, he said: 'Lassie, ye dinna think what ye are saying.' And then, after a still longer pause: 'Aye, but b'God ye do!'

He realized that he was still holding her hands, though in the act of sitting back on his heels his arms had had to stretch out ludicrously. He

released them, and then, as she put them back into her lap, he stretched
forward again and groped for them—and in that moment she knew that
she had won.

For a long time, none the less, he argued against it: Mrs. Ross, the
children, his duty to John Ross; and then, balanced against these things,
Leisk and his coarseness and brutality, and Mrs. Dymoke and her thin-
lipped disapprovals, and Shepherd and his endless uncouth jocosity. Once
he got up and walked to the water's edge and picked up a flat piece of
shell and skimmed it over the shallows, all boy again. She waited plac-
idly, quite certain that he would come.

The journey across the lagoon was desperately long, seven miles the
way she took: waiting for the tide to flood the shallows, wading with
the canoe till they found water deep enough for him to swim, going
south back into the shallow water to give him rest times, standing in
the enchanted combination of new moon and starlight. He swam well
with the canoe now, hanging on to the forward outrigger at the point
where it sprang from the hull, kicking in the rhythm that he had acquired on the night of the escape from Direction. She made the rest
periods long as they moved across. He grew cold, though the water
was warm and the night air soft. He looked very young in the delicate
light, and when he stood in the shallows he faced away from her always.
It had taken the best part of six minutes to persuade him to put his
trousers in the canoe at the start.

It was past three in the morning before the bow of the canoe grated
on the lagoon beach of the west island. The tide was too low to take her
round to the inner lagoon, they themselves were too exhausted. They
dragged it with a slow weariness on to the dry sand, and she took the
line in and made it fast.

When she came back, he was struggling into his trousers, wet with
the bottom water of the canoe. She said: 'Tid'apa,' and took them from
him.

He was too tired to argue and too cold, and yet he was aware that
he was blushing uselessly in the darkness.

She led him by the hand in through the palms, sure even in the night
of her direction. Inside their shelter she struck flint and lit a section of
coconut husk and, swirling it to make it glow, went forward again, and in
time they came to the bed place that she had made at the head of the
blue pool.

Davie walked like a man in sleep, his personality completely surrendered, utterly exhausted with the swim and the necessity to avoid the

sharp spikes of coral and the difficulty of walking in the uncertain shallows. He took in the bed place when she whirled the husk into a brief brilliance and accepted it as a place on which to lie down. He accepted the cloth that she spread for him and he accepted, perhaps because he did not even comprehend it, the cover of her sarong when she spread it over him and lay down beside him and pressed herself with an utterly sexless companionship against him.

The boy woke first. He was conscious that he lay in a green pool the sides of which were made of the silver of the palm stems. The surface of the pool was the bright blue of the morning sky, and from time to time the white of the wing of a drifting sea-bird skimmed across it. There were the four colours only: the white, the blue, the green, and the silver—four colours, except where the girl lay, still asleep, the honey-brown of her skin glowing.

He stared at her for a long time before he was fully conscious of the implications of her existence. She was still totally asleep, her eyelids closed and pale, her mouth relaxed and pitiful. He could see a pulse beating in her throat, slow and regular, and the beat of it reminded him of breathing and the thought of breathing drew his eyes to her chest against his embarrassed will, and at once he saw not the slow rise and fall of her breathing but the disturbing swellings of her breasts. They had grown since she had first been brought to the *Hippomenes*. They were no longer the beginning buds of that time but were developed and rounded and firm. Beneath them the skin was lighter in colour, so that at this angle and in this light they looked more mature than in fact they were.

He felt himself blushing hotly and, as it were against his will, he put out a hand to touch her. His finger-tips achieved a sense of shock. He had touched nothing before that was like this swelling softness; it had a quality of unreality. It was difficult for him to adjust it to his own responses. He stroked her timidly, apprehensively, ashamed of what was happening to himself and yet proud of it. And presently and very slowly she woke, and a slow, lazy arm curled round his shoulders, and pulled him down against her.

She was full of knowledge, remembered knowledge of the rapes of captured women on the deck of her father's prau, remembrance of the necessarily public couplings in the crowded boat. She had no inhibitions of convention, no personal reticences. For almost a year now she had had no controls except her own.

She took him joyously, teaching him the knowledge that she lacked, guiding him in the necessities, for he was almost harshly ignorant. With-

out her he would have been awkward and shame-faced and conscience-
ridden, but she brought laughter to it.

Idiotically, under the reassertion of his Scots upbringing, he insisted
on putting on his trousers when they went down to take the canoe round
into the inner lagoon to sink her out of sight in the blue pool. He took on
a consciousness of guilt with them. Plandok left her sarong in the bed
place, splendidly indifferent, and as she walked ahead of him, her small
bottom taut and humorously beautiful, he remembered something that
had fretted vaguely throughout their love-making—there was no knife between her legs. Remembering Downie's warning and the ribaldry of
Shepherd, he could see, or he thought he could see, on her left thigh the
marks of the silken bandage in which it was habitually carried. But there
was no kris now and there had been no kris in the early light when he
had first overcome his moralities enough to look on her young body.

She walked with a jaunty gaiety, quite unconcerned with what had
passed. When she allowed herself to think coherently she thought only
that she had won a victory against Hare. Nothing that he could do could
touch her now. She had escaped him. For a moment she wondered
vaguely if that were why she had conceived the idea of bringing Davie to
the island, but the thought appeared to be unimportant and she abandoned it. It did not matter why she had brought him, whether it was
herself or her necessity for revenge against Hare or the head's inter-
pretation of her need for happiness. The one thing that was important
was that he had come, and that, having seduced him, she was happy.

The boy walked in an increasing oppression of the spirit. It was dark
out of the clearing of the sleeping place. It was sombre in the deep thickness of the palms. He was conscious that he had broken all the moralities of his upbringing.

Occasionally she skipped a little as she walked and allowed herself a
snatch of song. He moved gloomily behind her. When she called back
some nonsense that he could not understand over her shoulder he answered with a grunt, and she turned and laughed at him and held out
her hands, and suddenly the depression lifted. The spaces between the
palms were wider now and they could walk hand in hand, and hand
in hand they came to the edge of the screen and could see the colour of
the lagoon water, the high lozenges of white and green and vari-coloured
blues that she had discovered the first time that she walked across Direction Island.

At the edge of the palms she halted cautiously. From inside the shoreward fringe of them she scanned the surface of the lagoon. There were
no sails on it. She had no fear of Hare's boats but she thought that it

was possible that Leisk might send in search of Davie. Nothing moved on the water. It was too early yet for his absence to be acknowledged. It was difficult for either of them to grasp this fact, so much had happened since nightfall. It seemed as if they were immeasurably removed in time from the quarrelling and the harshness of Selma.

They took the canoe round into the interior lagoon when the tide served, brought her right up to the blue pool and sank her, covering her outline with palm fronds weighted down. They made a game of the sinking, rocking the canoe until it filled with water, swimming out with the stones to sink it, diving down into the blue luminescence of the pool to fix the palm fronds that would mask its outline from the casual eye. They bumped against each other in the water and laughed, and bubbles exploded in silver to the surface. The water was so warm that they had no sensation from it except that it was another element and that they moved differently in it, gracefully in swirling patterns of naked limbs. When they had weighted down the last of the palm leaves, his eyes met hers, and they clasped together wordlessly and without the necessity for communication and without fear, and rose, clinging, through the blue to the brilliance of the day.

When at last they went ashore to the fringe of sand beneath the palms he picked up his trousers and carried them back to the bed place.

That day they made a roof to the bed place. It took time for Davie to learn the possibilities of the parang, but he was quick with tools and he found its sharp edge suited to the task of preparing the rafters. They searched for uprights on the ocean beach, hard driftwood posts that had come from unguessable continents. Plandok did women's work now without complaint: splitting the fronds with a deft assurance, reversing the angle of the leaves, plaiting them swiftly and skilfully into matting. She made baskets to hold their minute store of possessions. She showed him how to bind the thatching down and helped him, and by the time the sun was low they had completed two-thirds of the shelter.

They laughed then and went out to the lagoon beach to bathe, and afterwards they ate the last of the little store of food that she had brought with her from Direction and supplemented it with young coconut meat and drank the milk. But when the sun set she put the fire out and would not tell him why, and because he needed her he did not press for an answer, and they lay together on the bed of leaves.

She slept afterwards naturally like a kitten that has been at play, but he lay awake in the darkness and in the darkness his upbringing crowded in on him again. He could remember denunciations from the pulpit of the small grey church in which he had sat out the long Sunday mornings: the sins of the flesh, of fornication—for the first time he could visualize the word; it had a faintly ridiculous quality, something that was almost laughter-making, and yet it had overtones of threat and doom. He thought of what the succession of dominies who had clouded his boyhood would have said to even this present innocence, and he put his arm across the sleeping girl, and she stirred and turned towards him.

He whispered: 'Ye're ower young, lassie,' and knew that he had borrowed the very words from one of the preachers; and his mind, running at queer tangents, began to examine whether his feelings of guilt were real or whether he felt only what the dominies would have said that he ought to feel. He achieved a high state of metaphysical confusion. It was wicked and it was also beautiful. It was sin but it was also laughter. It was guilt but it was also innocence.

The girl stirred again and pressed against him, and he held her and felt irrationally valiant and protective. The grey church at the head of the loch was three oceans away and this island was perhaps out of the eye of God. And, as if to punctuate the thought, Plandok in her sleep laughed softly.

They woke into a patternless succession of days. They finished the shelter, and they raised the bed place on a low platform that they floored with bamboos from the high-tidemark—Plandok said that it was to keep them clear of the land crabs. They dug a well and, finding the water faintly brack, searched for the giant chama clam shells and put them at the base of palms and tied bunches of leaves above them as Downie had done on Direction after the gale to collect rain water.

His trousers hung to one of the rafters of the roof like a banner of defiance against Presbyterianism. He discovered that it was a simple matter to slip back into a state of nature, that it required only the kindliness of an island climate. He browned slowly but steadily and his muscles hardened with the work. He learned to use the jala almost at a single lesson, but he could never match her with the fish spear, could never challenge her instant and darting eye or the lightning response of her muscles.

She showed him all the secrets of the reef: the young clams that were good to eat, and the great chama clams that lay with their mantles open, ready to close like a trap on an unwary foot. They lay sometimes teasing one and they teased also the octopus that hid in the darkness of the coral rock and whipped out long encircling arms at the unsuspecting. He learned the possibilities of the birds, and though he would never attempt her passion for eggs boiled with the young inside them after the manner of Mindanao, he developed an immense appetite for the fresh ones.

Between the fishing and the foraging they swam. In the heat of the afternoons they lay in the shelter with the wind blowing through the open walls and made love, discovering and inventing. They were lost in an enchantment.

Only Plandok kept a hold on reality. It was because of this hold that they saw the search party. She would break off the idle fantasies of the ocean beach to cross over to the lagoon shore from time to time to scan the water. Always once at least in the mornings she went down to watch for a little. It was about the tenth day that she saw two of the Selma boats coming across to the island. It was too late to slip out and obliterate footmarks across the beach, but the chance of a strong wind from the north-east during the night had sent little seas up almost to the palms. She measured and judged this and nodded, satisfied, and they lay on their stomachs, buoyed up with mischief and freedom, watching.

The boats ran in steadily on what was left of the north-easter. They were steering for a point close to the bechet, the lakelet that lay inside the beach midway down the northern section of the island, and from their concealment the boy and the girl watched them come in to land.

Davie spoke first. 'It's that black deil Leisk in the first boot an' Dougal' steerin' the second.'

She laughed at his tone of indignation.

A wonderful sense of security enveloped them. They knew that they could escape this search. The island was theirs. It brought a contempt for the plodding ignorance of the searchers. They laughed as they saw them splashing out of the boats to stand uncertain on the white sand. They knew there were no footmarks up there; they had not been to the north of the island since they came.

The men from the boats fanned out irresolutely, moving up first a little to the north, then coming south. Leisk plodded to within a quarter of a mile from where they lay, and Plandok and Davie watched him, laughing. They knew that they could get away, that they could never be caught in the thickets of the palms because of their intricate knowledge of the possibilities of the island. At the worst the enemy—they thought of the Selma men as the enemy now—might find the shelter, but if they had to withdraw they would withdraw by way of the shelter and take the irreplaceable things with them: the parang, the flint and tinder, the kris and the clothes. They could retreat to the southern stretches of the island, they could double back, they could swim the mouth of the interior lagoon. They could get away from anything.

It was all unnecessary. Long before the search became dangerous it was abandoned. The virgin whiteness of the lagoon beach seemed to satisfy Leisk. When three of the men struck in through the palms he called them back. After they had been ashore perhaps an hour they took to the boats again. The wind had fallen to an absolute calm and it was necessary to row back all the seven miles to Selma Island.

As the boats pushed off the girl's arm stole round Davie's neck. In a moment she fired his blood and he lay on her, her legs and her arms twined round him, in what was more a gesture of defiance than of love-making.

When it was over, he said: 'Tha' was immoral, lassie,' and laughed at his own pawkiness. When the girl laughed too, he went on: 'But I doot if you hae any notions of morality in this part o' the worrld.' And having discovered, unaided, the geographical differentiations of sin, he was satisfied.

No search came from Direction Island. Hare had known that Plandok would disappear after the departure of the *Borneo;* her behaviour had developed a pattern. He guessed that she was on the west island and he believed that she would come back as soon as she was tired of her independence. She had come back before.

On the fifth day, however, a boat had gone up from Selma, carrying a glowering Leisk, to ask if they had seen the boy Davie. Hare ordered him off the island and went back to the big hut to think. There were the canoe marks at the southern horn of the crescent of Direction on the night of the riot. There were two pairs of footmarks where the canoe had been pushed back to the water. All day he gloomed in the big hut and snarled at the women. But he sent no boat in search. He knew enough of Plandok now to know that it would serve no purpose. So on the west island the beautiful life went on. Slowly for Davie it sloughed off all its overtones of sin. For Plandok herself the feeling that with every culmination she plunged another knife in Hare diminished until she achieved only an exquisiteness of pleasure. Their whole existence became an innocence.

The days divided themselves into the necessities of the search for food, the brief and simple mechanisms of cooking, the need to cool themselves in the water, and the pleasant hours of love. They made an expedition once to the far south of the island to hunt for pigs, but the pigs were timid and suspicious and they had no luck, and their traps were sprung in vain and their pitfalls filled with water, and they laughed and gave it up. After three days they went back to the old bed place and took up the simple pattern of pleasure. Almost their only link now with the other world was the morning ritual of the scanning of the main lagoon for search parties.

It was on the morning of the twentieth day that they saw the ship. Plandok was a little ahead of the boy. She came to the shore fringe of the trees and stood immobile, her slender naked body conveying at once an impression of fear and a sense of warning.

From deep back in the palms he called, anxious: 'Wha' is it?'

She said directly: 'A ship.' And then, less clearly, more as if she spoke to herself alone: 'She has sent it, then. First she sent happiness and now she has sent a ship—and I do not know that I want a ship.'

Davie asked, coming up to her: 'What were ye sayin'?'

And she answered: *'Tid'apa.* It is nothing.'

None the less, he looked at her with the first stirrings of fear.

# Twenty

THE SHIP looked lonely on the still water. No boats moved between it and the shore. Plandok had rested her plan on this, certain that Hare would be taking his afternoon rest: it had been the custom in the past.

It was beyond question the *Hippomenes*. She had been certain in her heart that it was at the first moment of the sighting, but now she could see the odd angle of the fore-top-gallant mast and the unbeautiful clumsiness of her bow. Plandok had planned to reach her in this hot afternoon hour and now, as she approached the anchorage, she watched the island beach rather than the ship.

Davie she had put ashore at the Selma landing place, itself lifeless and empty in the noon hush. It had taken all the early hours of the morning to raise the canoe from the bottom of the blue pool. They had accomplished it without laughter, and there was no love-making as they waited for the tide to make so that they could take the canoe out through the shallow passage. They had sat silent and oppressed, looking something like children found out. But they had made the run back to Selma more swiftly than their first temerarious crossing. In daylight the passage was easier. Davie was stronger, his muscles more accustomed to the water. She had cut the rest periods down recklessly, driven by an indefinable compulsion.

Now she felt an equally indefinable reluctance to approach the ship. She moved in fear. The masts and the yards grew. Presently they towered above her. The hull stood like a cliff, though the ship was low in the water with a full cargo of spices. No one saw her, no one challenged her. The anchor watch was asleep like the rest of them in the heat. She went aboard by the ladder, streaming the canoe astern at the end of its line, climbed to the poop deck, and sat down in her particular corner by the locker.

She was sitting there when Abbott came on to the deck, yawning and blear-eyed. He did not see her for a full minute and when he saw her he started. 'They told us you were gone! Where have you come from now?'

'The other islands,' she answered, niggardly of the truth as always. She looked at him with a faint unease.

'Hare is angry.'

Indifferently she answered: 'He is always angry.' And then, smiling at him with a conscious effort of charm, she asked: 'Do you go back to Singapura?'

'We have just come from there.'

'But you go *east?*'

He knew enough Malay now to accept the word 'timor'. He replied: 'No, we go west. We go . . .' he paused for the very smallest fraction of a second and her heart leapt in her; then he said the fatal words: '. . . to England.'

She let her hands, which had been raised in something that was almost supplication, fall dead into her lap.

He looked at her grave and uneasy. 'It would be no use, Plandok! He will search every inch of the ship before we sail unless he has you under his eye. He has said so to the captain, to Roach, to me. He means it.'

'This I know,' she agreed. She was afraid to ask the other question that she had come to ask.

He had enough insight, enough knowledge of her, to know that she was afraid. Idiotically he said: 'You have grown since we left here, Plandok. You are taller.' He tried, knowing that it was folly, to essay a compliment. 'You have grown more beautiful.'

She blurted out, disregarding his compliment altogether: 'You have news for me?'

'I have no news—I do not speak Malay—but Roach has.'

He went down the ladder before she could stop him, and she read all that it was necessary for her to read into the manner of his going, but she still sat there, her face expressionless.

Roach came up the ladder swiftly. He strode over to her and dropped on one knee. 'Plandok, your father is dead. They found his body three miles off the shore.' He stared into her enormous eyes.

She asked quietly: 'Who found him?'

'The man you spoke of—Yussef of Brunei.'

'Yussef of Brunei was a coward.' She looked at him fiercely. 'He is a liar also. I do not believe this!'

'None the less,' said Roach very gently, 'it is true. He has not been seen since that day. If he had been alive they would have felt him along that coast.'

For a moment her lips closed, pursing themselves in an effort to repress pain. At last, with a terrible reluctance, she echoed: 'They would have felt him,' and, getting up, brushed past Roach where he still knelt on the deck and went blindly down the ladder.

The canoe came in with an almost live obedience. She climbed into it without volition, found the paddle and headed in towards the anchorage.

The two men on the poop could not see her face. Only in the droop of her shoulders and the angle of her small head could they sense the quality of her grief.

# BOOK FOUR

# THE HORIZON

## Twenty-one

THEY HAD almost completed the digging of the new well at the hour of the noon break. Leisk kept them at it, for, once the water filled, the work became twice as difficult. Only when it was all done and the fresh water was creeping up off the new-dug bottom did he order the break. They went back across the island to the huts, Shepherd, as always, leading.

It was Shepherd, therefore, who first saw the boy. He lay sprawled and naked on someone else's blanket and the brilliance of the early afternoon, coming in at the door of the hut, lit him startlingly. He was bronzed. He looked fit, and the weariness that had been engraved in his face on the long swim across had already disappeared in the brief sleep.

Shepherd said softly and delightedly: 'Davie, ye pauky staig, whaur in God's name hae ye been?' The others crowded in behind him. Shepherd took a step closer, stuck out his foot, and kicked Davie in the ribs. 'Davie,' he said more loudly, 'wauk up!'

The boy rolled over, stretched, and grinned back at him with a confidence that was entirely new.

'Whaur hae ye been an' whaur's the lassie?'

'Travellin',' replied Davie almost insolently, and Shepherd, sensing a new defiance, laughed aloud.

Johnson said: 'Leisk's going to take the hide off you. Where have you been all this time? What did you do for food?'

Shepherd burst out: 'It's no' food he's been fashin' himsel' aboot!' And demanded again: 'Whaur's the lassie?'

'Gone up tae the ship,' Davie answered slowly, suddenly aware that he need not attempt to keep secret the enormous thing that had happened to him, aware equally that he had acquired from it a new stature in their eyes.

Johnson dismissed the possibilities of speculation. 'We'll hear of it when someone comes ashore from the ship. The thing is now'—he nodded at the boy, who was getting up slowly from the blanket—'what will Leisk do with him?'

'I'm getting tired o' Meester Leisk,' said Shepherd ruminatively.

And from the back a voice chimed in: 'We're a' tired o' him!'

Another voice complained: 'He's ower handy wi' a rope's end.'

Shepherd, sensing like a good leader the temper of his audience, went on: 'An' we dinna like bein' beaten, eh?'

'He has not beaten you, Dougal',' said Johnson.

'I'm thinkin' o' the weaker brethren,' Shepherd explained with mock piety.

Johnson said: 'It's all very well for you—you're too big for him. But the rest of us have all been hit one time and another.'

'An' we're no' slaves.' Shepherd raised a hand on high like a follower of Wilberforce. 'Meester Leisk is growin' oot o' a' proportion tae his proper station. Awa' up, Davie, an' pit on yer trousis! Ye wadna hae Meester Leisk see ye like that, sunburnt right doon tae the end o' yer foreskin—and ye awa' on an island wi' a lassie a' by yer lee lane. Ye wadna want tae pit ideas into his head noo, wad ye?'

Davie felt himself blushing hotly, but the laughter that engulfed him was friendly, envious laughter.

When it had died down Shepherd declared: 'There'll be nae beatin', neither Davie here nor ony o' us. It's time for a stan'.'

An English voice from the back of the group said: 'He bolted. He's been clear of the work more than three weeks. Mrs. Dymoke'll say he's done wrong.'

Shepherd smacked his lips. 'I'd gie a year's pay for a half o' the wrang he's done.' His voice was full of gusty innuendo. 'He's done a sicht mair than that.' His humorous eye took in the whole of the group. 'He's shown us a' the way. There's a whean disconsolate females up tae Direction Island. There a' sorts o' possibeelities. Let's gang an' searrch for Meester Leisk an' remind him o' the scripture text that says there's more joy in heaven ower one sinner that repenteth . . .'

The boy put a lashing of rope round his trousers and walked out of the hut and stood ready.

As Shepherd stooped to leave the hut, he asked confidentially but in a whisper that all the hut could hear: 'Is it true that she wears a kris between her laigs?'

'I never saw it,' answered Davie with an absolute naivety, and was amazed at the weight of the roar of laughter that exploded around him.

Four of the women were husking rice. The first boats had brought sacks ashore from the *Hippomenes* with the excitement and the gaiety of a harvest festival. The loss of the rice to most of them had been the direst result of the big wind. The rest of the women stood in a circle about the four at the rice mortars. The conventional, customary act had become a celebration, almost in a sense a sacrament. It signalized the full and final return of normal life.

And into the noise and the gaiety and the bustle of it Sulim's daughter, Aishah, came breathless and running. 'She is coming! She is coming!' And only afterwards did she gasp: 'The canoe!'

Even before they were uttered the other women knew by intuition that the child meant Plandok. The rhythm of the pestles faltered and broke. The noise of the talk ceased, began again and utterly changed its note.

'Timah, sitting a little way away from the rest, asked the crucial question: 'The boy from Selma—is he with her?'

Aishah had recovered her breath a little. 'No, she is alone. She comes from the ship.'

'From the ship?' Mei Ying snapped the words as if they were a rebuke.

Anita exclaimed enviously: 'Already she has been there!'

Somebody said: 'She goes where she wills,' and the envy this time was hopeless.

'Timah considered the whole thing above the babble. When she spoke, they hushed. 'It is that they have refused to shelter her upon the ship. There is nothing left for her to do except to come back here. This time he will assuredly punish her, he has said it.'

'She must be beaten again,' said Sulim's wife virtuously. She was proud that her daughter was the bringer of the news.

Behind her a voice murmured: 'Three weeks.' And then, after a pause and with her expression changing to the note of envy: 'Three!'

'He will beat her this time as he beat you.' Mei Ying looked at the Zulu girl.

A chorus of voices said: 'It is proper that she should be beaten again. It is right. It is no more than justice.'

'Timah pronounced again. 'There is the matter this time of the boy. She will no longer have the favour of the Tuan Běsar.'

For a long while they were silent, trying to estimate what the inner meaning of this was.

At last Anita said thoughtfully: 'Yet she has been three weeks away and with a man whom she chose herself.'

Kam Ho lowered the lids of her beautiful eyes and murmured down into the bowl of the mortar with its variegated pattern of half-husked rice: 'It is something that is denied to us though we *have* the favour of the Tuan Běsar.'

The Zulu girl said defiantly: 'She has shown us the way.' And a faint murmur of agreement rose from the younger women.

'Timah ruminated and gave judgement. 'That way is not for us. We are the wives of the Tuan Běsar.'

'The slaves!' declared Anita, adding her defiance to that of the Zulu girl.

Kam Ho murmured softly: 'There are many of us but there is only one Tuan Běsar. They say that the young men on Selma are strong.' This time she looked directly at Meriam, and the half-Portuguese girl flushed under the brown of her skin.

Anita said again: 'She has shown us the way.'

'And for that,' Mei Ying broke out venomously, 'she must be beaten and will be beaten. This time the Tuan cannot pass the matter over lest' —her eye took in in quick succession the Zulu girl, Anita, Meriam, and Kam Ho—'others be corrupted by her example.'

'We are already corrupted. Three weeks . . .' Kam Ho sighed as softly as a leaf in the wind.

Meriam edged back a little into the crowd, away from 'Timah's eyes. 'We could, any of us, do this thing,' she announced speculatively.

'We do not, any of us, have what she has.' Kam Ho's delicate voice was clear.

Another breathless child came running up the path. 'She is at the landing place!' she called, and all the women turned towards the beach, though they knew that they could not see the landing place from where they stood.

Mrs. Dymoke towered over her daughter like a figure of justice carved with an inadequate chisel. 'He must be lashed,' she announced with the absolute conviction of her authority.

'Not *lashed*.' Mrs. Ross spoke hesitantly. She was at a disadvantage, sitting and feeding her youngest child.

'Lashed,' repeated Mrs. Dymoke firmly, 'or all rule is lost on the island.'

A little less hesitantly Mrs. Ross said: 'He is so young.'

'He is old enough,' answered her mother positively. 'Three weeks alone on an island with the girl! You must give your weight to Mr. Leisk. You must speak for the captain.'

Mrs. Ross shook her head. 'I saw his mother,' she said irrelevantly. 'A very small woman. I remember she had a blue shawl.' Across the content of the child's sucking she saw in the eye of her imagination a long vista of palm trees and in it two figures, golden-brown and naked. She acknowledged that they would be naked, though she would not have admitted it aloud.

Mrs. Dymoke said sharply: 'It is necessary that Mr. Leisk should make an example of him. There are other women . . .' She indicated Direction with the very faintest of movements of her head. 'He has taught them that it is possible. For that alone he must be lashed—and as a warning to them.'

Mrs. Ross had acquired confidence now. 'I will not agree.'

Mrs. Dymoke leant over her. 'You must! The whole discipline of the island is at stake.'

'No,' her daughter answered calmly. 'I will tell them that they must wait until John returns. It is for him to judge. This is beyond Leisk's powers.'

Her mother straightened herself. 'Your husband placed him in charge.'

'He is a brute.'

'His personal qualities have no part in this. They have defied him. His authority is in the balance.'

'It can wait until John returns.'

'It can not! You will have a boat-load away at night-fall. They have rebelled.'

'That is not reason enough to lash the boy.'

'His wickedness is reason enough.'

'Not wickedness,' murmured Mrs. Ross dreamily, her eye deep again in her vision. The two golden figures were diminishing in the perspective of the palms. 'Not wickedness.'

'You heard what that man said.'

'What man?'

'The man Downie from the other island. She carries a knife.'

'Perhaps,' said Mrs. Ross softly in a bright flash of perception, 'she needed it in the past to defend herself.' When her mother looked at her, shocked, she added: 'Davie at least has no wounds.'

'Timah herself took the news to Hare. He lay unbuttoned and dishevelled in the great chair that had been re-created out of the recovered fragments. Robert Ross sat opposite him with an almost empty glass in his hand. Downie squatted on a rough stool.

She said without preamble: 'The girl comes.'

Like the women earlier, Hare had no need of further detail. He said instantly: 'Plandok.'

Downie straightened himself so suddenly that he almost fell.

Hare nodded. 'She's come back. I thought the ship would bring her.'

'Timah whispered insinuatingly from the doorway: 'This time you will beat her properly.'

'Go away!' Hare ordered brusquely.

'If you will not beat her send her away!' Downie almost gabbled out the words. 'We've had three weeks of peace. Now there will be unceasing trouble. Send her away!'

'Arrh!' Hare snarled at him.

The captain looked from one man to the other alternately as they spoke. Now he waited.

After a pause Hare called through the open doorway: 'Send her to me!'

At once Downie plucked at his courage. He muttered: 'This time there was the boy.'

Hare called out again. 'Where does she come from?'

Another voice, not 'Timah's, answered: 'From the ship.'

'By God she does!' exclaimed Ross. The look on Hare's face stilled him.

Hare lifted himself in his chair. 'Someone will have told her.'

Ross grunted in agreement: 'Someone will have told her.'

Downie, unable to understand their meanings, said: 'If you will not send her away with the ship, Mr. Hare, thrash her. Thrash her as a warning for the others.'

Hare turned on him savagely. 'Will you thrash her then!'

'I?' queried Downie, agitated. 'It is not my place, Mr. Hare. It is not my place.'

Hare growled at him: 'Get out! I will speak with her alone.'

The captain climbed to his feet. 'I'll start breaking out the rest o' the stores. Let me know what you need, Mr. Hare.'

Plandok came in through the open door space. She walked slowly, her shoulders stooped forward, her arms hanging limp, as he had seen her once before. Her eyes were stricken. He watched her, sitting upright in his great chair, and when she had reached the centre of the space he said: 'Sit!' and she sat down as if at the end of sleep-walking.

He murmured, his voice very soft and gentle: 'You have heard the word of your father?'

'I have heard,' she agreed sorrowfully, 'but I do not believe.' Her bearing belied the courage of her denial.

Hare lifted his shoulders almost imperceptibly. 'It is a year. If he lived it would be known in the ships. The Bugis would have brought the news long since. If he lived he would have had a prau by now and he must have struck somewhere.'

'Yussef of Brunei'—her voice acquired a doubtful access of defiance— 'is a coward and a liar also. I do not believe his word.'

Hare could see that she was uncertain. It could be that she had admitted the reality to herself but was not yet prepared to acknowledge it to the world outside. He waited while he turned this over in his mind. Then he said only: 'A year is a long time.'

And she sighed so deeply that it was almost like a sob.

He lay back in his chair, still watching her, wondering how he could achieve an understanding with her, wondering how he could penetrate under her scrutable mask. He had the feeling that it was all but tangible, the mask—that, if he discovered the secret, he could lift it, could make contact at last with her interior personality. It was a mask that had a life of its own, that displayed emotions and desires that were other than those of the real Plandok beneath it.

Very softly he whispered: 'There is no longer any purpose in wishing to go east.'

She flinched visibly and as visibly achieved control of herself again. 'I do not know,' she answered him at last. 'I have need to think.'

His eyes were compassionate. What does a compass do when its lode-stone is withdrawn?

Again she sighed in a deep admission of grief.

He allowed her time to think, watching her all the while, closely.

When at last she spoke it was almost to herself, whispering so faint that he could scarcely discern it. 'If it is true what remains to me?'

In two words he put the question that he had all but despaired of asking—whispering it, his tone matching hers: 'The boy?'

She shrugged her delicate, beautiful shoulders in a momentary re-action of indifference and in that movement told him almost all that he needed to know.

He kept silent with a long-acquired wisdom. When he rose at last, he said: 'Sleep there! I will send the women away.' And then humor-ously: 'Tuan Downie wished to beat you.'

Drowsily she said: 'Tell him my kris still remains to me,' and settled herself to sleep.

Hare gazed down on her sorrowfully for a moment; then he stalked out of the long hut and marched into the sunlight, waving his arms. 'Away, away!' he called. 'Crows, vultures—away!'

Downie, from his own hut across the open space of the kampong, regarded him sourly.

'Timah followed him down the path. She moved behind him silently and submissively so that Hare was not fully aware of her until he stopped in the shadow at the edge of the ocean beach.

She waited a long time before she spoke, but at last she said: 'What will you do with her?'

He waited almost as long before he answered: 'Nothing. What is there to do?'

Hesitantly she said: 'And the boy?'

He made a little gesture almost as if he were throwing something away. 'That is over.'

'None the less, it happened.'

He shrugged his shoulders. 'It was necessary for her to prove that she can stand alone.'

'Prove to whom?'

'To herself,' replied Hare with an acute perceptiveness. He was trying, even as he answered the old woman's questions, to analyse his own feelings towards the child. He had an immense, almost an overwhelming, admiration for her defiance, for the strength of her determination to preserve her individuality. He knew that she was not moved by ordinary rebellions or simple indisciplines. He guessed that she had inherited from her father a pride of personality, and under the essential simplicity of his own amorality he could appreciate this quality in her character. His understanding of it was almost feminine in its delicacy.

For a long time they were both silent while he thought and re-thought the problem.

Finally she said with a weary scornfulness: 'You are in love with her. This I had never thought to see.' And, turning, walked slowly back down the path to the kampong.

# Twenty-two

IN A sense Kam Ho, the Chinese girl, fled to Selma as a result of a misdirection of sympathy. In a greater degree she fled for reasons of revenge —Plandok's revenge.

The process began at the moment of Plandok's awakening on the mats in the centre of the great hut. The sympathy of the women was real at first: inevitably it was also temporary. Her loss, when Hare told them of it, had a particular effect on them, for they had no family ties. Not one of them could claim a loss like this. Their parents had disappeared in a process of indifference, of gift, of sale. None of them had anyone direct or immediate to lose, and therefore her loss was the sharper and the more pitiable. They crowded into the great hut and sat around her, waiting for her to wake; and they began, talking softly among themselves, a new approach to her. They were gentle, they wiped the past out of their minds, they ignored the possibilities of the future, they overwhelmed her with kindness.

It was true, of course, that in any group there were always one or two who combined sympathy with satisfaction that punishment had at last fallen disastrously on her, but the general sympathy remained.

For a little, for perhaps a week, she allowed herself to be submerged in it. She had to adjust herself through two reactions: the reaction of the weeks on the west island with Davie Knight, the reaction from the news of her father's death. These reactions interwove themselves so that for the first time in her life she had feelings of guilt and of punishment. Almost, but not quite, she arrived at a conception of sin, but before she fell into that dangerous trap she succeeded in ascribing her punishment to the malice of the head.

Saad, listening to her when at last she achieved energy enough to go out from the women's quarters, heard her say once: 'It was not a mahang tree. An evil spirit must have lived in it—and yet not wholly evil, for at least I had happiness for a little.' It was beyond his comprehension and she did not choose to explain, and he could only be sorrowful for her.

Inescapably, before the end of the first week there was a change in the sympathy. It began with the girls and the younger women. One or two of the more intelligent among them began to wonder why such an outflow was necessary. She had, they recalled, achieved three weeks alone with a man of her choosing on the west island, as Anita had pointed out, and this was something to be set off against the news of the year-old death of a father—however beloved. A tinge of envy began to creep into the condolence. She was no longer given the titbits in the meals. She was no longer accorded precedence.

Anita in the end was wholly frank about it. 'He does not punish you,' she complained. 'If I were to go only to the ocean beach with a man he would beat me until his arm was tired. What is the magic that you have and why should you have such magic?'

Plandok was still too listless to retaliate. She ignored this and the increasing questions and the obscene interest in her relations with Davie. They wanted to know everything: the manner and the method of his accomplishment, his endurance. They asked the questions unblushingly; and still Plandok made no answer.

When she menstruated, the Zulu girl went from woman to woman saying: 'There is no justice! She will not even have a child.'

Through it all Plandok moved like a wraith of herself. She walked without her old arrogance and the strength seemed to have gone out of her spine. She disregarded the rising tide of small pinpricks and spitefulness. She was gentle with the children and kind, but she offered no leadership. She led Saad and the other boys into no mischief. She ignored Downie and made no attempt to head conspiracies against him. She kept out of Hare's way.

By the end of a fortnight the quality of the sympathy had changed again completely—this time among the older women. It was Mei Ying who voiced it. She said in the middle of a flow of aimless, pointless comforting: 'None the less, he is dead. It may be that he drowned or it may be that Yussef of Brunei cut his throat: all death is the same. He will not come here to rescue you, that at least is certain. We . . .' She paused while the girl looked at her with sombre eyes: 'We no longer need to walk in fear.'

It was after this that Plandok began to shake off her lassitude, this and a single remark of Anita's: 'We are many but you are by yourself.' It would be too much to say that she evolved a plan; more reasonable to say that she achieved an intention.

Something of this she put to Saad as she watched him fishing in the shallows one day. 'The Sush'nong will not always protect me. He is a man.' She did not bother to look at the boy to see how he took the insult. 'The Tuan Downie will do me harm always. The other men do not matter, for they cannot help. There are all the women on the one side and myself on the other—for you I cannot trust any more.'

He hauled in the net from the water and inspected a fish. It was true, there seemed no point in denying it: he could not fight with her against all the other women.

She said dreamily: 'There is myself alone and there is the boy on Selma and there is my head. It is time that I went to my head again.'

It was Hare, however, who finally triggered the opening of the war— and that too was due to an excess of sympathy.

Late in the afternoon of her talk with Saad he called her to the big hut. He came to the point more directly than was customary with him. 'Are the women troubling you?'

She shrugged her shoulders. 'They do not like me and they are no longer afraid that my father will come.' The memory of her father brought back, as it always did, the look of pain to her eyes.

Almost unconsciously Hare stretched out and put his arm round her and drew her to him. He meant it as a gesture of tenderness, but, in the very act of making it, desire overcame him.

She felt the change in the pressure of his hand against her back, she felt the physical rise of passion in him; and instantly, with precisely the movement of a mouse-deer frightened, she sprang away from him and stood quivering, close to the door. 'It is enough!' she cried. 'I must go.'

For the first time he yielded to a positive jealousy. He said, the words forced out of him against his will: 'To the boy.'

She stared at him, her eyes wide and still frightened, before she answered: 'No, to my island—to be alone.' Then she turned and went out of the hut and, as she went, moved by some emotion that she could not understand but herself also under compulsion, added: 'I will be back in two days, at the most three.'

Through the passage across the lagoon she thought of this and of other things: of her father's death, for it was necessary now to admit—at any rate to herself—that he was dead; of her defencelessness; of the weight and power of the other women; of the inconsistencies of Hare and of the weaknesses that showed in his blustering and armed façade.

But after the halfway point she thought of the head. What she had said to Saad about the mahang tree was true. She debated the consequences of this. It could be that the spirit that had entered from the tree that she had brought was a mischievous spirit. It could be, on the other hand, that it was a weak spirit and unable, therefore, completely to overcome the spirit of the Kling woman. Or it might be that there was only the spirit of the Kling woman and nothing had come in from the tree at all, but that she had power over the Kling woman's spirit—a potential power at least. And through all this conjecture she wondered dispassionately if she really believed in the head. It had sent ships when she asked it, but might not those ships have come by themselves? Certainly it was obvious that they had set sail long before the head dipped down out of the smoke-filled roof of the hut. It was true that she had found happiness with Davie, but equally it was true that she had marked Davie on the very first day of the arrival of the *Borneo* and she could not be certain whether it was the head or her own heart that had brought them together. It was true that the head had called down the birds on her, but then the birds might have come to any fire in their state of alarm and weariness on their return to the island. At least she had not built another fire in the open.

She landed on the west island half an hour before sunset, and, dragging the canoe up as far as she could, she made it fast and walked in towards the clearing of the hut. She no longer walked arrogantly, her whole carriage was doubtful.

The evening was utterly still. Even the roar of the surf was abated to a whispering. No leaves moved in the palm crests, no air came through between the upright stems. After she had made the necessary noise getting the wood together the silence became profound again. Now and then bird sounds broke out or, rather, splayed themselves across it. She could make out the twittering whistle of the terns and the grunt of a discontented gannet.

The fire under the head began to set up noises of its own, the crackling and the spurt of flame, the out-driven hiss of steam. In its light, and before the smoke swallowed it, the head looked shabbier than ever. The leaves, which should have been isang leaves but were not, were withered. The bird droppings—two fairy terns had flitted through under the roof as she approached—were thicker on it. The skin had dried still further. The grin had changed to a leer. The whole place had a shabby and disconsolate air. Wrack had blown in on to the coral slabs of the floor. The roof itself was damaged, and she made a note to mend it in the morning.

Slowly the smoke crept down. It swallowed the uppermost leaves of the decoration. It billowed down, swallowed the head, released it, and crept down again. In a little while the head was gone.

Plandok sat in her customary place, her back against the upright. She had now to formulate the tasks that she had to ask the head. For almost two hours she sat quite still, trancelike, going over and over her predicament in her mind. She was too young to have the power of true connected thought. She could plan for immediate possibilities, she had an unchildlike power of forethought, but she could not conceive long, complicated designs. All that she could think of now was the need to re-establish her ascendancy over the women, to provide the possibility of an escape from Hare—there was even an element of uncertainty about her need for this—and to ask again for happiness.

When at last the smoke cleared, and the head grew animate and responsive in the fire glow, she had reached no decisions, but, because it was of her character, she began with attack.

'There is an evil in you. How it came there I do not know. Perhaps it was that I brought the wrong tree to you, but there was no other way for me. Upon this small piece of dirt upon the sea there are no mahang trees, nor could I do you the proper honour with the isang leaves because there are no isang leaves. This you must understand. I have done you all honour that is possible for me to do in this place, and no one else would have done this honour. Therefore you are mine and you must do the things that I wish you to do. Do you understand that?'

She stared at the head, and a flame leapt and the mouth seemed to frame a syllable, but she could not tell whether the syllable was yes or no.

'Very well,' she went on, 'if you will not answer me clearly I will tell you what I will do. I will ask certain things of you and if you do them I will continue to honour you and to light fires to you. But if you do not do them, or do again as you have done and put a mischief into them, I will take this fire and put it to the thatch, and you will burn and be destroyed and have no more existence. This is a power that I have in my hands always.'

The fire glow remained steady, but the mask of the face was utterly still. Outside, in the night, bird noises, soft and distant, faltered around her.

After a long silence, and with the fire diminished to a dull rubescence, she spoke again. 'You will return to me my power over the women. You will bring another ship. And you will give me back my happiness.'

At sunset two days later she called to Hugh Johnson from the shelter of a clump of ironwood. She had waited all the afternoon for Davie, but he had not appeared.

The Englishman peered in through the ironwoods. 'Davie's girl, by God! You'd better not let Leisk see you.'

She smiled beguilingly at him. 'You tell Davee I here.'

He came closer into the ironwoods. 'Couldn't you do with an older man? Davie's no more than a boy.' He leaned against a twisted arch of ironwood and grinned down at her.

She knew exactly what was in his mind. She repeated, her voice firm, positive: 'You tell Davee.'

He nodded approvingly. 'I like a girl to have spirit. Davie—he's only beginning like. I've had my pickings o' girls.'

She got up from the ground and turned away from him. When she turned again her right hand was behind her back. 'You tell Davee now,' she said, watching him with enormous care and no vestige of apprehension whatever.

He put out both arms and took the one step forward that was necessary, and instantly the blade of the kris was between them like a silver flame. He said afterwards: 'It was like the tongue of an adder.' He stepped back hurriedly. 'It's true what they say: you are a small devil. I'll send Davie.' He laughed ruefully. He was a kind enough youngster.

It was dark before Davie found her, and he came to her hungry and full of love. As she lay with his arms round her when it was all over, she acknowledged that the head had at least done the last thing that she had asked of it and brought her happiness back to her. She listened to the soft rustle of the land crabs going down past them to the water and wondered if it would fulfil her other askings. She wondered what Hare would say. She had, of course, told him that she was not going to Davie. She had, in fact, gone to the island. Her conscience was totally secure: she had come back to Davie, and the subtlety was quite enough to satisfy her almost indiscernible sense of right and wrong.

At dawn he made love to her again, still hungry, and she watched his face in the growing light. It was more important, she decided at last, to him than it was to her. Even to herself she could not say why, but in Davie's arms she had thought of Hare and, thinking of both Hare and Davie, it still seemed necessary to her to think of controlling the pattern of her life. The three things were in conflict, her mind was in turmoil. When at the end Davie pleaded with her to stay on Selma, she refused, though she knew it might be a solution.

Finally she abandoned the argument and asked about Johnson.

'Why d'ye want to know?' Davie demanded.

She giggled at the transparent jealousy. 'He would have made love to me'—Davie had taught her the words—'if I let.'

'Ye wadna!' he begged. 'Ye wadna!'

She laughed at him and shook her head.

He lay thinking in his turn. At last he said: 'He wants a girl—bad, I think. They've a' been after me since we came back. They're fu' o' envy.'

Again she laughed, this time at the masculine complacence in his voice, but all she said was: 'Does Tun Mai, the black one, like tapai?'

'Wha's tapai?'

Once again she went through her pantomime of drinking, making the faithful gurgles in her throat, and once again he collapsed with laughter. She got to her feet and did her little parody of drunkenness, naked and gay, and full herself of laughter.

When she came back to him, he asked: 'It's no' palm toddy?'

She shook her head. 'Tapai,' she repeated and then, remembering the English word rice, said: 'Rice drink.'

'Rice speerit!' He remembered the name coming up in one of the interminable discussions on drink that were held in the young men's hut in the darkness. 'Dae ye want me tae tell Dougal'?'

'Tun Mai, yes. Tell him. . . .'

It was suddenly necessary to fix a time, a date. There was, of course, no rice spirit. The whole thing had burgeoned suddenly in her head, suggested in a sense by the sex hunger of Johnson, moulded by her memory of Shepherd's drinking. But there *was* rice on the island now. Pa Abas could be induced or, if necessary, bullied into making tapai. There was no plan yet, only a comprehension of possibilities.

At length she said: 'When the moon is thin,' and described in a small, elegant gesture the curve of the sickle moon.

Long since he had achieved complete understanding of her meanings. 'Ye want us tae come at the new moon?' and he copied her gesture.

She held up one hand with the fingers and thumb stretched.

'Five? Right! To the same place?'

She nodded.

'We'll come,' he said positively. His new-found authority had not deserted him.

The stealing of the rice was completely simple. Saad did most of the carrying. It was easy enough to slit a bag and dribble it out through a hole in the outer wall of the storage hut. They did it in the darkness and over three nights moved the rice down to Pa Abas's hut. As she had thought, he was wholly willing. Where he had acquired his skills she did not know, but she knew that he was a drunkard when the parsimonious fates allowed and drunkards were easy enough to handle. They stole a whole bag in the end, and Saad was depressed and sulking for a week after it.

It was at the end of this week that the problem of the women came to a head. Something of it stemmed perhaps from the weather. It was atrociously hot. The trades had failed entirely. On the sand the vertical sun produced a baking heat. From the reef shallows and the lagoon shallows it produced a moist heat, clinging and intolerable. It crept through and under the cool of the palms like sea tides engulfing a sand-spit at the flood.

Plandok sat a little apart from the women. They were washing clothes at the well that was reserved for them. It was full now because the tide was high, but it was not cool as it was ordinarily. The women were ill-tempered and querulous, snarling at one another; and presently, as they always did, they began to talk over Plandok—not at her, over her. In a sense she courted it. She spent more time with them these days: it was necessary that her battle against them should come to a head: but she had made no plans for it, for any plans would have involved alliance and any alliance was predestined to disruption. A harem, she knew from within, was a whole, an entity, but it was an entity composed of disparate bodies. Because it was a community it rested upon its individualisms. Alliance was impossible. She had watched the quick groupings that came together like mercury, and separated as swiftly and as improbably. She sat quietly while they talked.

Out of the ruck of it she heard Mei Ying echo Anita: 'What, then, are we afraid of? There are many of us and she is alone. Her father will not come. For a year we feared him—and all that year he was dead! She is no more than a child.'

Somebody asked: 'And the Tuan Běsar?'

'He will beat us afterwards, but what is a beating? At least we will be free of her.'

Somebody said, as somebody always said: 'There is still the kris.'

'We can take it from her. After that she will have nothing.'

There was a little hush of admiration at the reasoning.

Into the hush Plandok said softly: 'I have still my power as a witch.'

'Do not listen to her!' Mei Ying screamed. 'Do not listen to her!'

'I have my power as a witch,' repeated Plandok more loudly, 'and you are afraid that I will use it. Listen! I brought the first ship to the island— it was my doing. I brought the second ship.'

'Lies! Lies!' Mei Ying burst out.

'Ask Saad. I told him that I would call them up.' Plandok looked directly at Amina. 'Ask Saad—or do you fear to?'

Saad's mother, her voice reluctant, said: 'It is true. The boy told me the story of the ships.'

The Chinese woman glared at her venomously, but the unease was already apparent in the group.

'What I have done, I have done,' Plandok said, deliberately obscure. 'What I will do, I will do. I have the power. Listen!' The inspiration had come to her in the very moment of her declaration. She held both arms out straight before her, the fingers in the imperious convention of command that belonged to the dancing of Malaysia. 'Listen, and in a little it will speak.'

She began to quiver, the movement starting in her hands, spreading up the thin, graceful arms and involving her whole body. Her head moved very slowly backwards, and her eyes rolled until the pupils were altogether lost and they were white and sightless, and her face was set in a mask that was, because of association, uncannily like the dried balefulness of the head.

The women drew closer to her. She kept rigid except for the quivering. The heat seemed to help her, to create an aura of horror about the insistent movement. The softer of the women watched appalled.

The silence grew graver, more portentous. Even the reef was only whispering today. The birds were somnolent and still. Hare's chickens had gone to sleep. The men were away fishing or working quietly on nets, and the oppression of the heat held everything utterly still.

She began to babble formless words, syllables, mute sounds. It was easier than she had thought it would be. Returning for a moment to a pure, childish mischief, she thought: If I had stolen a little of the Sush'-nong's soap, I could have frothed at the mouth. But it was not necessary; she had them hypnotized in horror.

She said suddenly in an intensely strained voice, so like the Kling woman's that 'Timah made the sign to avert the evil eye: 'I will send another ship, Small One. I will send it soon.'

Then in a hard natural voice Plandok demanded: 'What else? What else?'

'One of the women will go,' said the Kling woman's voice.

'Where?'

'To Selma,' answered the voice and relapsed into incomprehensibilities.

For a little the quivering went on, and then Plandok allowed her fingers to droop, her arms slackened, her head came back. But before the pupils came down her eyelids shut, and she slumped, slowly and gracefully, to the ground on one side, her face pillowed on her upper arm. The women stood around whispering. She heard 'Timah's faint acceptance: 'Allah is merciful.' And in a moment, exhausted by the strain of the performance, caught back into childhood and paying tribute to the heat, she slept. The women left her there.

There was no other attempt to challenge her directly.

Inevitably, of course, the young women came to her one by one to ask who would go to Selma—she had been quite certain that they would

do just that. At the third asking she told Kam Ho. She told her of Johnson, describing him to her in terms that had at least an attachment to
the truth. It was easy enough to work on Kam Ho, for it had long been
Kam Ho's own hope that she would go to Selma or, for that matter, to
any island with a man—a young man. The others Plandok cut off with
cryptic sayings and twisted words; that too was easy enough.

Three days before the new moon she went to the hut of Pa Abas in
the evening. The making of the liquor was done. He produced it for her
proudly, already a little drunk himself. It tasted like vitriol. She screwed
her face up on the first impact of it on her taste buds. It was not ordinary
tapai. With a patient ingenuity Pa Abas had built a primitive still on
Pulau Bras, wading to the islet in the darkness. No one had smelt anything. This was a hell brew of rice wine fortified by raw spirit, potent
and inflamable. She went back, content, to see Kam Ho and to wait for
the new moon.

When it rose it shone thinly on a drinking party that was utterly different from the first orgy on the point. Shepherd protested as they landed
that there were no women, but, with Davie to help her, Plandok explained that this was a time for drinking only, that the women were
frightened of Hare's beatings, that there was a watch now at nights in
the kampong. Her earnestness and the first half-shell of tapai were
sufficient. Woman and drink was best of all, but drink alone was better
than nothing. There was no fire this night either: Plandok told them
that the watchmen would spot a fire at once.

When she had settled them to their drinking on the beach she pulled
at Davie's hand, and they moved slowly up the slope.

Shepherd, filling his half-nut, called after them: 'Carefu', ye wee de'il!
Remember th' moraleeties.' And then, to the others: 'He doesna drink
and he doesna gandy wi' th' bawds, but he's twa jumps ahead o' us evra
time!'

Davie went with her, expectant, and found Kam Ho ensconced in the
shadow.

'This,' said Plandok, 'is Kam Ho. It means beautiful peach.' She had
no conception of the fruit but somebody—Hare perhaps—had told her
the translation. 'When Tai Mun begins to be drunk you will go down to
fetch Johnson. She is for him.'

'I dinna rightly ken . . .' he began, puzzled. But he felt her arms on
his shoulders and he forgot what he had meant to say, and Kam Ho
watched them enviously in the darkness.

Presently he fetched Johnson. Shepherd was already too deep in the
brew to care. The moon, the stars, the white sand gave just enough
light for the Englishman to make her out.

They heard him say: 'By God, she's Chinese! And young and beautiful, for all that I can see.'

They sat there, the four of them, deeply involved. They did not know that Saad, posted to keep a watch on the beach two hundred yards up from the boat, had crept down in the darkness to watch the love-making. For that reason the crash of Hare's gun and the flash of the explosion were to them like a catastrophe of nature.

Johnson reacted more swiftly than any of them, even Plandok. He said softly and urgently: 'He will have to reload. We'll have time to get to the boat. Take her arm, Davie!'

Davie turned, clinging to Plandok. 'Come wi' us, Plandok! Come wi' us!'

But she shook herself free. 'I cannot.' She was not sure why she was so positive. 'Go,' she urged, 'go quickly!'

At the drinking place there was a confused babel of cursing, of alarm and of drunken laughter. Already they could hear feet splashing in the water and Shepherd shouting enormous threats into the night.

For a moment longer Davie hesitated. She pushed at his back. 'Go! Go!'

Then the three of them, Johnson, the Chinese girl, and Davie, broke from the fringing palms and moved, silent as night birds, across the narrow sand. They fell into the boat together as it was pushed through the shallows. Nobody seemed very much hurt. The shot had scattered too widely.

Shepherd was roaring joyously: 'Twa in ma hurdies. I'll hae to stan' to row.'

Gavin Wemyss had a slug in his shoulder, Haig had a scratch down his thigh, but these were discovered afterwards. The important thing was to splash the boat through the shallows before Hare, dancing like a wounded bat on the white sand, could charge his gun again.

Plandok stood motionless for a while, watching him, and then turned and walked coolly through the palms. She did not even hurry: he would be there still when she was back at the landing place. She wondered what had warned him. Saad had bolted. After she had gone a short distance she began to skip in her walk—the ranks of her enemies were diminished by one. The second part of her prophecy to the women had been made true. It might even be that it would not be necessary for her to do more. If Kam Ho settled with the Englishman, neither Hare nor Leisk would stop the others. She skipped again a little. She would have sung, but she feared that some of the men, attracted by the shot, might have come down, timorously, to the beach.

## Twenty-three

THE *Borneo* was already in the entrance at the first approach of day-light. John Ross had made out the gap between Horsburgh and Direction Island with the last brilliance of the moon. The noise of her anchoring, the shouts, the squeaking of the blocks came through the palm trees to the still-sleeping ears.

Plandok, in her pre-empted corner of the young girls' hut, stretched herself smugly in the half-light. She could hear the voices twittering about her: 'A ship has come! A ship has come!' She could feel them drawing away a little in fear.

A woman had gone.

A ship had come.

Her ascendancy was secure. She swaggered down to the beach in time to follow Hare's boat out to the *Borneo*. Well down the lagoon she could see a boat coming up from Selma. Somebody must have seen the *Borneo* earlier than the people on Direction Island but Hare would win the race.

He did not go aboard the *Borneo*. The boat lay on her oars just clear of the ladder, and Hare bellowed up: 'John Ross, John Ross! Call your raping blackguards off!' He was beside himself with rage. For days he had been smouldering, now the flame leapt. 'Call them off or I'll shoot them. I'll shoot every damned bastard of them. They're a drunken good-for-nothing pack of scoundrels, and you're no better yourself. Damn your hide, sir, you're not a whit better yourself! Keep them off my island, John Ross; keep them off!'

Ross came to the rail, placed his two hands wide apart, and leaned forward, staring down at the angry man. He shouted: 'What are you talking for, Hare? What are you talking for? I told you before: look after your women! Young blood's young blood—there's no holding it.'

Hare's voice rose almost inarticulately. 'God blast your eyes! Keep your men away. I'll shoot anything that comes from Selma. I'll fire on every boat. I'll fire on every man whose foot touches my beach. I'll give guns to my men. You'll keep them clear, John Ross!'

The Selma boat was almost up to them now, driving furiously, the spray leaping high from the oars.

Leisk rose suddenly in the stern-sheets. He bellowed: 'You murdering sod, you! I'll have the law on you if a Navy ship comes here. By God, I'll have you swung on a yard-arm!' He turned and, cupping his hands, shouted: 'Mr. Ross, Mr. Ross, he's murdering our men, he is! He's murdering our men!'

Plandok lay back restfully in the canoe, wriggling her toes with pleasure. This too was her doing.

Ross shouted, Hare shouted, Leisk shouted, and the triangular brawl went on. The Selma boat swept past, and she could see the half-healed scar on the shoulder of Gavin Wemyss. She saw him now leaning forward like a beggar displaying his sores on the steps of a cathedral, and Leisk bawled:

'Look here, Mr. Ross, look here! A slug in his shoulder, by God!'

The crew of the *Borneo* had come to the side, joyful in their entertainment.

Plandok saw Davie watching her, puzzled and anxious, and she smiled at him so that his heart leapt and the anxiety went from his forehead. She stayed where she was, drifting, utterly content.

Still the brawl went on—Hare at a grievous disadvantage, one bull voice against two, one man against two and a choir of support. Hoarse and suddenly weary, he abandoned the stupidity of it. He spoke to the Malays in the boat and they dipped their oars.

Turning, he shouted his Parthian shot: 'Next time, John Ross, I will load with ball. By God, sir, I will load with ball!'

Five days later the boat from Selma came up again. Hare met it at the landing place with a gun.

John Ross himself was steering. He stood off, backing water, twenty yards from the beach, and said, his voice subdued and formal: 'I wish to talk to you, Mr. Hare. It is best that we should settle this thing.'

Grudgingly Hare allowed him to land, still nursing the gun in the crook of his arm. They went up to the big hut, not speaking.

The women hung back in fear but Plandok went on to the doorway of the hut. There was a panel of well-woven leaves that one could use for eavesdropping.

She heard Hare say belligerently: 'Well?'

Ross answered: 'Aren't you going to give me a drink? It's a thirsty run up.'

There seemed to be a moment's hesitation. Then she heard the clink of the bottle against a glass.

When they had drunk, Ross said: 'We're here, Alexander—there's no controvertin' that. We have got to live together. I'm a peaceful man by nature.' His voice went silent; evidently he was drinking.

Most of his words Plandok could understand. All of Hare's were clear as he thundered: 'You may be a peaceful man, John Ross, though you were not a peaceful man when you had the gun-boats at Banjermasin. I will believe that you have changed, but, by God, you've got some unleashed devils on your island! Leash them!'

'I have talked it over with my women,' said Ross reluctantly. 'We will move down the lagoon.' It was a clear enough admission of guilt.

Hare accepted it as such. 'You would be better off on the south island. It's a long way from the anchorage, but you have got all that you could want there and you will not be swept on the south island—the sand is twenty feet high in places.'

'It's a long way from the anchorage,' agreed Ross, as if underlining the magnitude of his sacrifice.

They drank again. Hare reached for the bottle and refilled the glasses. When he had started on the second he asked suspiciously: 'Why did you make up your mind?'

'The women,' replied Ross morosely. 'My wife most of all. She wants no fighting. We shall be eight miles from you there. I will try to hold the boys in check. By God'—his voice rose suddenly—'I'll sweat it out of them! They'll shift every damned thing from Selma in the boats, every damned thing! I'll take the randyness out of them if it takes me a twelvemonth.'

Hare grunted. His mind cast suspiciously round the thing. He mistrusted Ross, Ross mistrusted him.

'Her mother,' said Ross after a moment or two, 'her mother wants it too. A determined woman, Mrs. Dymoke.'

'You should not have run from that press gang," bellowed Hare, suddenly boisterous. 'There's worse things than serving in the Navy. My wives have no mothers, by God!' He was instantly expansive, bawdy, full of bonhomie.

Ross chose the moment. 'There is one condition—my wife insists upon it.'

At once Hare's suspicions came back. 'Condition?' he demanded.

'That the Chinese girl stays.'

'Ha!' Hare expelled his breath like a pistol-shot. 'You have found her, then?'

'They had hidden her on the north end of the island. Leisk is a bone-idle man.'

'I know that,' growled Hare angrily.

'He did not search the north end. She was there all the time. Johnson went to her at nightfall and sometimes in the day also. He brought her to my wife three days ago. She is quiet and gentle. My wife wishes to keep her.'

'I will send a boat for her this afternoon,' said Hare brusquely, brushing the appeal aside.

Ross shook his head. 'You will have enough if we move to the southward, Alexander Hare. You will not get her back. My wife is a stronger woman than her mother when it comes to fundamentals.' He drained his glass. 'You will not get her back.'

Automatically Hare stretched for the bottle again. When he had filled the glass, he said: 'She must come back.' But his conviction was palpably uncertain.

Ross drank before he spoke again. 'My wife is monstrous fond of her. There is nothing you can do about it'—he leaned forward confidently— 'nor I either, Alexander. We will move to the south island and I will do my best to keep the young men close. Leisk is a fool.'

They drank to that: Leisk was a fool. The brandy was an honest solvent. They sat on late into the afternoon.

The boat's crew, watched over suspiciously by Downie, made much of the young women who strayed down close to the landing place.

# Twenty-four

AT THE end of the third month from the return of the *Borneo* Anita went. This was not Plandok's doing—at least, not wholly. In the hot hours while the boat's crew waited for Ross and Hare to finish their drinking the Cape girl had established a *rapport* with Gavin Wemyss. She had an odd beauty of her own: Hare's taste was rare. Her nose had a fine Arab cut about it; her eyes were Malay eyes, soft and deceptive; her forehead was high and bespoke an intelligence that she did not possess—but it would take Wemyss two years at least to discover that fact. Wemyss made the plan himself. Plandok acted as no more than the go-between. He outlined the plan to her one day when she took the canoe up to one of the New Selma boats, which was fishing against the west island.

After she had agreed to the plan she went ashore for an hour with Davie, but in the hour it was impossible to recapture the delicate memories of the west island. The shadow of Hare was between them.

That day she did not go near the head.

The seeds of jealousy are not often planted in vain. It would be impossible to put a precise moment upon their planting as between the women and Plandok. Perhaps it was the hour when she was brought aboard the *Hippomenes* under the blue shadow of Table Mountain. The hour was not important: what was important was that with everything she did, with every move that she made, the seeds germinated and sprouted and grew.

Jealousy permeated the whole of Hare's establishment now. Kam Ho, the soft, the willowy, the exquisite, was gone, was safe on the south island with her man. Anita, forceful, loud, irritating, and irritable, was gone, safe on the south island with her man. Plandok . . . Plandok ranged as she willed, and the younger women without exception were jealous of the youth of Davie Knight.

The final manner of Anita's going was simplicity. Gavin Wemyss and Davie rowed the lighter of the New Selma boats all the way up by themselves. It had to be accurately timed because of the tides and the endless shallows at the head of the lagoon.

Plandok led her to the meeting place. Her own moments with Davie were hurried and anxious. There was no time for beauty. Again the presence of Hare was almost palpable.

The urgent passion of it was ended by Saad, who had been outposted up the beach and had crept in again, inarticulate.

Saad too had achieved an awareness of jealousy.

Hare was angry, but he was not as angry as Downie had expected him to be, for he was tired of the stridency of the Cape girl. As Downie railed over the drinks, Hare said: 'It does not matter. She would have grown ill-favoured and she has the heart of a shrew.'

'I said that where one went others would follow.' Downie disregarded the evasion. 'You should have sent Plandok with the *Borneo*.'

'You grow monotonous.'

'It is the truth, the exact truth. First Kam Ho went—she would never have been a shrew.' He slipped the retort in obliquely. 'Now Anita! There will be another in a week or two as long as you fail to put a rope on that girl.'

Hare watched him with his head on one side, his eyes squinted as if blurring the morose apparition in front of him. After a long silence he said: 'I have told you before: you are unable to understand her—too stupid. You are a fool, James Downie. She is worth all of them, and in time she will come to me of herself and that will be worth waiting for.'

Downie crouched forward and stared up, trying to see into the eyes between the narrowed lids. 'By the horns of God, I think you're in love with the girl!'

Meriam went almost three months later. It took her most of that time to make up her hesitant mind. Again this was not Plandok's doing. Sandy Haig made the preparations. He came three nights to the landing place before Meriam overcame her scruples, and then, because Ross had chained the boats at night, she went in moonlight by the reef path to the south island.

It was Plandok who had discovered that it was possible to wade across the channels between Direction and the south island provided that due attention was paid to the state of the tide. She made the survey over a period of weeks, nagged at by Downie for the small quantity of fish that she brought back to Direction in that time. Between Direction Island and Pulau Bras there was a long, deep ravine in the coral that ran parallel with the main reef, but inside it there was safe wading. Between Pulau Bras and the reef there was another chasm; that too could be avoided. For the rest there were dangers that took one sometimes wide

over the face of the reef and that was itself peril, but there was nothing
that was impossible to the determined spirit.

Saad took them part of the way. He was still prepared to help if
Davie were not there.

'Timah died four days after the fury and anger at Meriam's flight had
ebbed. This too was not Plandok's doing. She died as an old woman
of some nameless failure, more perhaps of her spirit than of her body.
Plandok grieved for her, for the old woman had been kind to her between the upsurges of the women's anger. And now the anger of the community surged up again, and there was no 'Timah to check it.

Plandok heard them talking in the distance on the morning after
'Timah's death and disregarded it. Her ascendancy over them was complete, more complete now perhaps than ever.

Except that she forgot about the boy Saad.

An hour later she heard the noise of them in the path that led to the
kampong and then she heard shouting at the centre of the kampong,
somewhere about the big hut. They had gone in a body to Hare, and
Downie tailed behind them. The boy Saad was held almost as a prisoner
in their centre.

Mei Ying was their leader now, Mei Ying grown harsher, more spiteful, with the passing of time, more angular. She pushed in through the
door with a solid phalanx of the women behind her, crying: 'She is a
witch! She has done this thing!'

Hare barked at her from the depths of his chair. 'Be still! What is
this?'

'The girl is a witch!' Mei Ying flung it back at him. 'The girl Plandok!
She has powers. She has shown them to us. This we have seen with our
own eyes: that she prophesied and that the prophecies came true. Is this
not so?'

The other women shouted behind her in chorus: 'It is true. She proph-
esies. She is a witch. She has power over spirits. We are afraid of her.'

Mei Ying's voice dominated the babble. 'And she must go!'

The rest of the women had crowded now into the big hut. The whole
of the doorway end of it was full of them. They waved their arms; they
moved; they surged; they swayed forward, seeming to have a cohesion,
to be a single entity.

The Chinese woman was the mouthpiece of that entity. She kept on
screaming: 'She is a witch! She is a witch! She is a witch!'

Hare towered over them, bellowing: 'Be still! Damn you for fools,
be still! I do not require to be shouted at. You!' He nodded sharply
at Mei Ying.

'She sat on a hot day at the washing well and when we told her that we no longer feared her because her father was dead she answered that none the less she was still a witch.'

Hare barked: 'Is this true?'

And the women replied in a single voice: 'It is true, Tuan.'

'And she sat there and she put her hands forward'—the Chinese woman imitated the action angularly—'and she quivered, all her body quivered, and she passed from us into the spirit world. And when she spoke'—a deep shudder took Mei Ying and Hare, watching her narrowly, knew that it was real—'when she spoke it was in the voice of the Kling woman.'

Behind her the pack shouted: 'It is true. It was the voice of the Kling woman, Tuan.'

'And what were her prophecies?' Hare's voice was growing harsher.

'She prophesied that one of us would go to Selma.'

'Was that all?'

'She prophesied that a ship would come.'

'And what else?'

'It was enough, Tuan.' Mei Ying relaxed suddenly. 'The ship came and the girl Kam Ho went.'

'Perdurable fools!' Hare relaxed a little in his turn. 'What is there in this but children's talk? She knew that the ship would come, for it had to bring back Tuan Ross—all of you knew that the ship would come.'

A voice said: 'But not when it would come.'

'That is nothing. She did not tell you *when,* only that it would come. As for the girl Kam Ho, she helped her to go to Selma; she knew that she would go. This is less than the talk of children. If this is all, you may go.'

'It is not all,' said the Chinese woman. 'Tuan, it is not all. There is the matter of the head.'

'What head, by God?' Hare took a fierce pace forward and overshadowed her. 'What head, you witless fools?'

Mei Ying seemed to sense in his anger a tension that arose from fear. For the first time she attained control of herself. She watched him, her eyes unblinking for a long moment, before she answered: 'The head of the Kling woman, which she took.'

'By God!' exclaimed Hare uncertainly. 'By Almighty God!' He went back to his chair. 'This is more children's talk,' he shouted, but his tone lacked conviction. 'What proof have you?'

They produced Saad from the centre of the group like a conjuror producing an unimaginable prize.

'She told him! She told him!' All the women were shouting now because all the women were overcome by fear in this final moment of crisis: fear of Hare, fear of Plandok, fear of the head itself and of the incomprehensible spirits behind it. They were shouting at Saad, they were shouting at the Chinese woman, they were shouting at Hare. The place was submerged in a torrent of sound.

Plandok, walking up the path to the kampong, had a faint memory of the taking of a pilgrim ship off Labuan. Then she heard Hare's voice, quelling the riot. He was bellowing curses, almost beside himself with anger.

When at last he controlled them he roared: 'Speak, boy!'

And Saad said, so softly that Plandok, coming up the path, could not hear his words: 'She told me that she had taken the head of the Kling woman and that she had dealt with it according to the ways of the Sea Dyaks.' He hesitated.

Plandok heard Hare's voice roaring: 'Go on, boy! Go on!'

And again she did not hear Saad's answer as he murmured: 'She said that it did her bidding.'

It took Hare and the men two full days to find the baang which sheltered the head. In a sense Saad misled them, for Plandok had told him of the blue pool and the sleeping place, and that information he had also passed to Hare. They found the sleeping place an hour after sunrise on the first morning and, while Hare drove them, they pulled its shelter roof to pieces and stripped the mattress of leaves and tore the screens. They searched the area about it, driven and anxious, afraid of Hare and afraid of the head. All that day they found nothing.

That night as they slept in the wet shelter of the palms—it had rained through the afternoon—Hare said: 'If that boy has lied I will thrash him to the edge of his life!' But he knew that Saad had not lied, for Plandok, charged with the enormity, had denied nothing. Equally she had admitted nothing, but Hare knew that the accusation was true.

They found the baang late in the afternoon of the second day. Hare was close to the man who gave the shout and he went forward alone. The men came hurriedly together, coagulating like raindrops on downward glass, ready to run. The baang was still solid. Plandok had repaired the roof twice, and the extra thickness of the thatch had held. He regarded it sombrely from the outside and at last brought himself to stoop and creep into the shelter.

For a long time his eyes would not accommodate themselves to the gloom but in the end he saw. The head, inadequately smoked, had cracked and stretched still farther. The bone showed through the bound-up lower jaw, and the mouth had split towards the left ear, giving the effect of a shriek of torment. The eyes were terrible, grotesquely over-lined by the droppings of the terns.

None the less, he knew at once that it was the Kling woman.

He sat almost where Plandok ordinarily sat, for a long while, pondering. At last he said: 'I have remembered before that you were beautiful, but I know that you had malice and envy and a spirit of vengeance. It may be that she brought you back to break our quiet.' Once more he fell silent. When he spoke again it was wearily. 'No, I do not believe these things. I do not believe in the power of spirits. All you have given to her was the power to frighten the other women, and it might be that she needed that power. She is still very young against them all.'

When he came out of the hut he was no longer angry, but outside he said, turning and looking back at it: 'The rest of your body I burnt. It is proper that your head too should join that smoke.' And he called for firewood.

The men brought it apprehensively. When there was enough he struck flint on tinder and again, remembering what he had done on the beach at Pulau Gangsa, he lit each of the four corners of the hut.

On the beach at the landing place below the kampong Plandok watched the smoke of that burning. For two days she had sat there. The children had brought food to her. Even the women had come, timorously and uncertain, afraid of the angers that they had awoken. Saad watched her from a point perhaps a hundred yards along the sand, sitting with two or three of the smaller boys who drifted away from time to time. The smoke rose in still evening air as it had risen on Gangsa, a high, thin plume, blue at the base of it, brighter where it snatched the last of the sunlight, bending over at the top where it caught a moving air. She knew, as she saw its first flag above the palm trees, its whole significance.

Early in the darkness Saad went. He took the wading path down to the south island. There was no longer any place for him with Plandok, and though the fear of the head was gone, other fears remained. Plandok did not see him go, nor did the small boys who earlier had sat with him—they had come to her now. This was another happening in which she had no direct part.

She sat on in the darkness, waiting for the return of the boats. One by one the children slipped away till at last she was left alone. There were other women waiting, but they were farther down.

It was difficult to think connectedly. How important was that wisp of smoke? What did this day's work mean? What was the depth of her betrayal? She asked the questions of herself in an extraordinary variety of forms before she realized that there was only one single question: that the one thing that was vital was the reality of the head—not its physical reality, its structure of cracked skin and appearing bone, its empty sockets, and the terrible silent laughter of its mouth, but the reality of its power.

Was it the head that had brought the ships? She knew on the plain level of ordinary life that it was not, that the ships had started, one of them at least, before the Kling woman died, that the others would have come in due season dependent on no more than the decisions of men and the agency of the winds.

Had the head brought her happiness? She was not sure now that she had ever been happy. The bright image of the days on the west island had faded. She was possessed by the need to establish herself against Hare, and because Hare was the dominant point of her possession his shadow was dark between her and the boy's simplicity.

Had the head made it possible to break up the solidarity of the women? It was true that three of the young girls had gone, but they would have gone anyway: she knew enough of the heat of the blood now to be positive of that. They had gone and more would go, and though she had first shown them the way, it had been because of the heat in their own blood and not because of the head.

Should she herself go south with the others? The question seemed to have no relation to the earlier ones that had been so insistent, but she was instinctively aware that it was of the very core of them. The canoe was thirty yards up the beach, the paddle was lashed in it, the net, the flint and tinder, and the fish spear. Between her and escape there was no more than a minute and a half of time. None the less, while she knew that she could not go, she did not know what made her stay.

She sat on with these things moving in her anfractuous mind, illogical and irrelevant. A little before midnight she heard the thud of oars in the thole pins.

Hare came ponderously from the boat, moving through the starlit shallows. His voice, when she heard it, was almost meditative. He asked, of no one: 'Where is the canoe?'

And down the beach a woman, hearing him with an incredible acuity of ear, called: 'It is here, Tuan; it is here!'

He turned towards the voice and walked, still heavily. He was bowed, the steel gone out of that triumphant back. His shoulders sagged. He walked slowly towards it, and some of the men busied themselves with the hauling in of the boat and some followed him. The second boat was coming in now. They could hear the slow thud and return of her oars and the susurrus of the oar splash. When he reached the canoe he stood for a moment or two in thought.

At last, reluctantly, as if the words were drawn out of him, he said: 'Bring wood and palm trash for a fire.'

They drifted into the night. Everyone moved slowly like shadows passing with the drift of small fleece clouds against the moon.

Plandok sat still.

They brought the palm trash and dumped it on the ground. They brought small branches and driftwood and odd rubbish. They piled it together and when the pile was made he said: 'Bring the canoe.'

She could see it all through the starlight, but the tenuity of the light took its realities away from it. It had no meaning for her.

They lifted the canoe and placed it on top of the pile and Hare himself struck flint to the tinder once again. He blew and the small flame mounted, and he put it to the trash and a larger flame upleapt. In a moment it was blazing. The night took on a different quality. The starlight was beaten back. The underneath of the palms became scarlet and imminent, the trees attained form and solidity and stature. And on top of the fire the canoe was black and formal and beautiful, floating, as it were, on a sea of flame.

Hare, standing back, watched it morosely. The men of the second boat, coming in, gathered between Plandok and the fire and stood, acutely silhouetted, against its dancing brilliance.

She sat, quite still, in the place that she had chosen. After a while the canoe caught and began to burn also. It was the end of a chapter of her life, but it was the chapter that was important, not the ending. She had no real need now for a canoe. Before it had been a way of escape; but there was nowhere now to go, she had no destination. The head was burnt and there was no longer any importance in the west island. There was too still a way of escape—the shallows along the reef. She sat quite still, cold in spite of the leaping flames.

A long time afterwards Hare stirred and went up the pathway to the kampong.

They heard Hare quarrelling with Downie over half the island. Plandok heard it also, but she made no attempt to eavesdrop at the door. An awareness of fate had engulfed her. What would happen would happen. If she had believed in Allah it might have been well, but she had no belief in anything—now.

At length the brawl died down, quenched with liquor. The two men sat opposite each other, as they had sat so many times before, faintly drunken.

Hare was reiterating his attitudes. 'I have burnt her head. I have destroyed her canoe. The women know that she is not a witch, and there is no more that she can do. I will not send her away.'

Downie, emboldened with rum, said: 'You are a fool.'

'Damn your hide!' returned Hare, but without belligerence.

'You are a fool because the women still believe that she is a witch.'

Hare demanded brusquely: 'What do you mean?'

'They still believe that she brought the big wind.'

Hare opened his arms in a gesture of hopelessness. 'There is nothing they cannot believe! None the less, the head is burnt and she will change now.' He leant forward confidentially. 'She could have got clear months ago had she chosen. She did not. Now she will come to me of her own will, and it will be worth everything that I have lost. You are not able to understand her. You come from a midden.'

'Before that happens she will have destroyed everything,' retorted Downie sourly. 'Everything! The boy Saad has gone.'

'The boy? The boy! Before it was only women.' Hare sat upright with his glass poised halfway between his knees and his mouth.

He sat silent for so long that Downie framed a question. 'What will you do?'

Hare disregarded him, his mind working. He had thought this over in the boat on the long passage back from the west island. When at last he was ready to speak his voice was soft, slow, and ruminative. 'This island is indefensible. It is too long. A boat can land anywhere along the shore of the lagoon. We cannot watch the whole of it.'

'What do you plan?'

'To keep sentinels posted always would take too much of the life of the men, nor would it serve—they can be bought!' The contempt flooded into Hare's voice.

Downie was possessed with curiosity. 'But what will you do?'

'I could lock them up at night here but it would serve no purpose. Somehow they could get away, somehow she would help them.' Quite suddenly Hare's manner altered again. He drained the glass and put it down with a thud. 'The older women I do not want. I will marry them off. The Zulu girl will go south when she chooses and I shall not stop her. She is like a bird when the migration begins. But I shall build a stockade on Pulau Bras and I shall move the children and Plandok there. If you want one of the other women you may have her. I shall build a stockade at the summit of the rise; it is the highest place in the atoll. A man can watch from there—there is no point of the islet that you cannot see.' There was a hard determination in his voice. 'A stockade, yes! There is the answer, a stockade! They will not get them out of a stockade.'

'And this island?'

'You will manage it,' replied Hare distantly, 'and I will oversee you. I will need more guns when the *Hippomenes* comes again, but meanwhile I will build a castle.'

Downie stared at him doubtfully.

## Twenty-five

PULAU BRAS lay midway between Direction and the eerie, evacuated half-ruin of Selma Island. The scrub there was already pressing back on the clearing that Ross had made. The wells were shallow and silting.

Hare planned the stockade with extraordinary energy and vigour. The man had an incomprehensible resilience. After the finding of the head he had been for a brief time inert and exhausted but now he rampaged round the island searching for sound timbers, driving the men along the high-tide-mark, hunting for stout trees. They rafted timber above the landing place and floated it in to Pulau Bras on the tide. They dug furiously for a well. The whole settlement was driven to the task, Hare's enormous voice booming through them like a slave-master of Egypt.

Plandok watched it all, indolent and catlike. With the burning of the canoe she had ceased to do anything of practical value for the community, and Hare bore with her as if he understood the inner state of her mind.

Pulau Bras was wind-blown sand built up by the succession of the gales to a height of almost twenty feet at the inner edge where it fell steeply like a cliff, veined and bonded with the creeping plants and the thin, coarse grass of the islands, crowned with palms. It looked like the heap of rice that gave it its name.

Hare measured and thought and planned. When he was ready, he lopped the boles of the trees nearest to the edge of the cliff and used them as the anchorage of the high edge of his stockade. He ran it for forty feet along the cliff and brought it down the incline, using a steep declivity to guard one edge. Outside he cleared the nearer palms to give it a field of fire, and used their trunks, deep-buried, to add to the stockade.

The shape of this was determined by the contour of the hill. To the north, towards Direction, it followed an eroded gully that climbed up through the cliff. On the reef face it came across a simple slope. To the south, towards the islet of Pulau Gangsa and Selma, it came close to the natural line, and before they had finished the building of the stockade itself Hare had set men to work to cut back the face of this slope to make it steeper.

It was in the central building, the keep, that he exercised his greatest ingenuity. With careful measurement he selected six palms that made an oblong close to the cliff edge but leaving room enough for a 'fighting space' between their line and the stockade proper. Everything else inside this oblong he cut out. The six boles he topped. Four of them made the corners of the keep, two of them the central pillars. The trunks that he had felled were cut and set between these uprights, but only to half their height. Other trunks, specially selected, were lashed and pegged to the main pillars. On them he built a floor of wood. The whole of the lower part of the structure became an immensely strong box. Bamboos and young saplings filled the interstices between the main uprights. When it was finished it was airy, cool, and enormous. On the floor above it he built a light pavilion, strongly roofed. It stood above the stockade so that a man sitting in a great chair with a long glass in his hand could watch the lagoon, could see over the channel between Pulau Bras and Gangsa and even to the sparkle and blue of the reef.

Downie said: 'The first gale will take it away.'

Hare growled at him: 'It will go with a typhoon, not otherwise.'

The lower room was for the children. The steps, half ladder, half stair, that led from it came up through the pavilion that was Hare's own living-room.

Plandok watched its erection cynically, drifting through the work. But for the most part she played with the children; she had re-established her ascendancy over them—if, indeed, she had ever lost it.

Hare came upon her on the ocean beach one morning. Whether she had seen him coming he could not say, but she was telling them a story and they were clustered in a fan of golden nakedness in front of her. Her voice reached him, clear and gay, as he stood in the shadow of the seaward palms.

She was telling them the story of the time when the deer Plandok had been enticed into a wooden ring by the elephant in punishment for his trickeries.

'. . . for a whole week Plandok was held there and the pig was his jailer. Then on a night when he was full of anger he heard the python slithering round the ring fence.' Her arms lifted and with her invariable grace she made the motion of the great snake and hissed realistically. The children shuddered. 'And Plandok made a plan. There was a weak place in the ring fence that was too small for his body but, as the snake passed round for the tenth time, Plandok whispered: "Sir Python, what do you seek?"

'The snake said: "I seek you."

'Plandok said: "Sir Python, the pig is here with me."

'The python said: "But the pig is fast and he has sharp hooves and he is strong. You are weak."

'And Plandok said: "The pig sleeps but I am awake. If I make a hole for you so that you can come at the pig, what will you do to me?"

'The python said: "My hunger will be satisfied. Why should I do anything with you?"

' "So," said Plandok. And he made a small hole in a weak place that he knew, and the python entered and killed the pig and swallowed it.

' "Now," said the python, "I must escape before the elephant finds me and crushes me."

' "Go then!" said Plandok. And the python went to the hole, but because of the thickness of the pig in its body it could not get through it. Then Plandok said: "I will make you another hole higher." And he made another hole between two strong trunks, and he said: "Thrust through it with all your force!" And the python thrust and jammed itself where the body of the pig was, and it threshed mightily with its tail.

'The elephant heard the threshing and came in trumpeting. It remembered to shut the gates behind it before it said: "What is this threshing?"

'Plandok said: "It is the phython which has eaten the pig and is escaping through the ring fence."

'And the elephant said: "Where? Where?"

'Plandok said: "Charge it now before it wins clear! Thrust with your tusks where the white peeled logs are."

'And the elephant charged with its trunk up, trumpeting, and the tusks went on either side of the peeled logs and jammed between the great trunks next to it, and the elephant trumpeted but it could not pull loose. Plandok sprang on the body of the pig inside the python, for it made a step, and he sprang from the body of the pig on to the head of the elephant, for it made a step, and he sprang from the head of the elephant over the top.

'*Ada-nya.*' She used the ritual phrase which ends stories, and the children broke, laughing.

She left them then and turned into the palms and gave a little start at seeing Hare. The exaggeration of the start was perhaps a fraction overdone. Hare regarded her sardonically. He was sure that the story was by way of being a warning to him, sure now that she had seen him from the first moment of his arrival. But he was also sure of his own intentions: the cage was to keep the children safe, Plandok could keep herself.

He said: 'There will be no need for Sir Python here.'

She laughed at him without malice in her laughter.

Ross came when the stockade was complete and the keep two-thirds built. He came up by the normal boat passage to the anchorage and turned in towards Pulau Bras, with Davie Knight sounding over the bows with the blunt end of a boat-hook. Hare greeted him on the lagoon beach with his gun cradled in his arm.

Ross said: 'You can put that away, Alexander Hare. I have come to ask why you have moved down towards us.'

Hare answered, quietly for him: 'I have come here because I can hold this island against your murdering blackguards. I have put up a palisade that even they'll not scale and I have made a house inside it that even they'll not break into, and there will be a gun at every corner of it and it will be loaded with ball, John Ross.'

Ross said reasonably: 'We have kept clear of you since we moved to New Selma. The girls have come to us of their own accord.'

'The black one two weeks ago?'

The Zulu girl had disappeared almost unnoticed in the turmoil of the building.

'The black one too. There is nothing that I can do if the girls are willing—you know that. Do you mean to take Selma?'

'What would I do with Selma?' asked Hare sourly. 'I have enough to do to keep them at work on Direction with that fool Downie. You keep to your end of the lagoon. I'll keep to mine.'

There was sense in what Hare said, Ross saw that. 'I will do my best to keep clear,' he answered. 'I chain my boats at night now.'

'You should have done that long ago!'

Ross was hurt, for he had come in peace. 'I will go, then.'

'Before you go,' said Hare grimly, 'come and look at what I have done and tell your bastard young men. From my chair I can watch everything that moves on the lagoon, I can watch the sea reef, and there is no place that they can break through. There is a double fence at the gate. It would take a regiment to come in against my guns. Tell them that! But see for yourself.' He turned, still nursing the gun, and stalked up the path that they had made through the gully.

Davie, standing at the boat—the rowers were strange Malays that Ross had brought back from Singapore—waited till they were out of earshot and then called quietly: 'Plandok!'

The girl came, as he had expected, out of the shade of the palms. He could hear the giggling of children behind her.

'Will you come wi' us?'

'He would not let me,' said Plandok softly, 'and he has a gun.'

Davie walked into the cool of the palm shadows. The children fell back before him. He put his arm round Plandok's shoulders, and she momentarily yielded to him. 'Come awa' wi' me, Plandok,' he urged.

'No, I must stay here. Your island is full of women now.'

For the first time he realized the implications of that fact. He had heard everything that the other girls had said of Plandok. He knew the measure of their jealousies and their fears. 'Aye, there's the other women,' he agreed.

They sat silent.

After a long interval she said: 'If I come the quarrel between them and me would begin from the beginning again. It is best I stay.'

'In there?' He jerked his head up at the stockade.

'I go where I will,' she answered with an echo of her old arrogant independence.

He considered this for a while before he said: 'It was hot worrk comin' up the lagoon. Ha' ye a well yet on the island?'

Plandok called: 'Sharu'll!' and clapped her hands.

The eldest of the young girls who remained to Hare came through the tree screen to the water's edge. She stood in front of them, her eyes downcast, her face expressionless.

Plandok said: 'Take the Tuan Davee'—she gave him the title naturally—'and give him drink.'

She watched them as they disappeared between the palms. Davie was staring down at the child's slender body. Plandok allowed herself a little laugh of total wickedness.

The stockade was completed. The thatching of the keep—the house—was finished, and its ending made the occasion for a celebration. The people came down from Direction. There was a feast, there was drink. There was dancing and gamelan music.

Hare wished to make clear the security that he had constructed for himself. It looked raw on the crest of the hummock of Pulau Bras, the still-new thatch richly golden, the grey boles sinister. Little by little, however, the sun scorched and the rain worked at it and the winds, and it took on something of the aspect of the islands. Vines grew through the trunks where Hare had planted them. The green within the stockade spread and covered it as with wings. And in the great room that took the whole of the top half of the keep Hare had his being. He hardly ventured out of it now. He sat there with the telescope on a stand that they had made for it. He could command the whole of the lagoon. He could watch the sea in every direction. The place was an eyrie. He achieved the patient watchfulness of a sea eagle.

The boys had a hutment between the keep and the gate, the girls had the enormous chamber of the under part of the house. There was no door to the chamber, only the stair that led through Hare's room. Plandok slept where she chose: sometimes outside the stockade in the huts of the two families that Hare had brought down from Direction to cook for him and to keep the stockade clean; sometimes in a small shelter inside the stockade—its doors were barred and padlocked after sunset.

The young men came up from the south from time to time—Hare knew that. They had canoes now, three of them; he saw them out fishing with the New Selma boats.

He did not know that with patient ingenuity they had built a fourth at the same time as the three that Ross had ordered, interchanging it night after night so that the work proceeded in an orderly fashion. He did not know that it was kept hidden in a deep pool in the middle section of the south island after the manner of the hiding of the first canoe on the west island.

He spoke of them occasionally to Downie when the overseer came down to get his orders. He called them the hosts of Midian: 'They prowl and prowl around'. He had a little triumphant song in his heart. They could prowl and be damned to them!

Perhaps because of his inherent contempt for women he underrated Mrs. Ross. To Mrs. Ross the existence of the stockade was an offence and a stinking. Ross had told her before of Hare's practices but she had not absorbed the realities of them, for he had never been explicit. He had a harem. She had the accepted Western notion of a harem, not exploring it in her own mind. But this thing, this building that she could see crowning the hill of Pulau Bras when she went out occasionally with the boats, was an outrage to the moralities, for it was a prison of children, it was a brothel prison—it was unspeakable.

Had the boats gone closer in to Pulau Bras she would have seen the children playing naked and happy on the beach. They were fond of the keep, it had a romantic and improbable air. They were wholly unconcerned by Hare. This also was the adat.

From time to time, therefore, she harassed Ross about it. 'We cannot leave them there. Think of them—children with that man! I lie awake at night.'

Ross answered bluntly: 'They're used to it. He's quiet. These devils of ours can't get at him, there's peace at last.'

'It is too high a price to pay for peace.'

The whaler came in towards the end of the seventh month from the day that Hare moved into the stockade. Hare sent for the rest of the women from Direction Island. He held them in the stockade while the stench of the trying-out flooded across the lagoon and fouled the clean sea air. The men came ashore to look for drink and found none. Even Plandok stayed in the stockade these nights. The whaler went after ten days, her water-barrels filled. Ross had been much aboard her but nothing came of it. Hare saw to the priming of his guns and watched the boats move in and out.

Two months later the *Borneo* came back, and Ross went with her east to Singapore.

Before he went Mrs. Ross pleaded with him again. 'Rescue the children!'

And again he said: 'We have peace. Leave the sleeping dog.'

Ross, like many masterful men, underrated the determinations of his wife. She left Leisk alone. Instead she made her first approach to Dougal' Shepherd. She had no success: Shepherd was still busy discovering the not too elaborately hidden possibilities of the Zulu girl. He was neither physically nor mentally alert. She tried Hugh Johnson next, but Hugh Johnson was still wholly satisfied with Kam Ho, still the envy of the rest of the young men.

She tried them one after the other, sounding them delicately, until she came to Davie Knight. She came to him reluctantly, for in a measure Davie Knight was already a part of this thing and she was not sure of her own attitudes towards him. She spoke to him indirectly of the meanings of chivalry. She kept him at story-telling time with her children. She talked of knights errant and princesses in towers and damsels in distress. In its own way it was subtle enough, but it did not require subtlety. Davie was ready at the first hint to see a princess in Hare's tower.

It was Davie, therefore, who made the plan. Dougal' Shepherd was the actual leader because it was customary for him to be the leader, but he was also the led. Davie worked out the plan in his own mind lying through days on Pulau Gangsa, watching the stockade through a glass that Mrs. Ross had lent him. It took a fortnight to polish the details. It needed the third quarter of the moon for perfection and all the boats that New Selma had.

The arrival of the *Windhover* could have wrecked the plan. The *Windhover* was a brig. She was bound for Straits of Sunda with piece goods. Her master had heard of the new settlement on the Cocos—as by now everyone in the ports had heard of it throughout the East. Davie altered his plan to take in her presence in the anchorage.

He engendered an immense enthusiasm amongst the other young men —those who had not yet snatched women from Direction. He had the support of Mrs. Ross. There were times, as he worked at the planning, when he allowed himself to think that if after this last attempt Plandok would not come to him, there was still the child Sharu'l. Gradually the memory of her small body acquired solidity.

On the night that he had planned, the New Selma boats went up the channel singing. From very far off Hare recognized the tune. He picked them out with his long glass almost at once. The night was quiet, though it was not wholly windless. They came one astern of the other, and he thought at first that they were from the *Windhover* returning to the ship. Then he remembered that her boats had gone in long before and that nothing else had gone down to New Selma throughout the day.

He looked to the guns methodically one after the other, though he was almost certain that this was not a threat to him: Ross's young men were going up to the *Windhover* for some drunken reason of their own—she was to sail on the morrow. He watched the boats, none the less, as they came across the moonlight, black and crawling like water beetles.

It was not until they turned out of the boat channel towards the islet that he knew abruptly that it would, after all, be necessary to fight. For months he had dismissed the possibility, but now he went swiftly to the gate and shouted, and behind him he heard the stockade awake and the shrill chatter of voices and the quick crescendo of excitement. He ordered one of the two Malays to take the light boat to Direction to find Downie and bring help; and, as soon as his back was turned, both men went. They took their women and their own children with them. He returned and barred the heavy gate and as he ran back he wondered where Plandok was. He found her immediately at the firing platform on the south-west angle of the stockade. She was standing quite still, peering intently down to the moonlit water.

The singing was reaching them very clearly now:

> 'Four and twenty ladies
> Went to Kirriemuir.
> Only ane cam' hame again
> An' she was nae sae pure.'

The blustering, ribald song came up to him like a challenge, like a bawdy battle hymn. There was laughter with it and excitement, fellowship, and threat.

But Hare listened intently, and after he had listened said: 'They would not come singing like this if this were all.' And he turned away from them to watch the shallows of the reef. There were three canoes, the three canoes that Ross had built. Like Ross, Hare did not know about the fourth. He watched them grimly for a while and then he took the gun and, sighting carefully on the lead canoe, fired. 'That'll let 'em know we're aware of them,' he said, more to himself than Plandok, and, turning, he fired down at the leading boat.

A splash of water well to the right of it showed in a sudden brightness in the moonlight. From the boats a roar answered him.

He did not know of the fourth canoe as it came, drifting and silent, across the narrow channel between Pulau Gangsa and the islet. There were many things that he did not know: of the deep hole, for example, that had been dug in the floor of the children's room and the weakened lashings of the stockade on the north face. Plandok had cut the lashings herself. Sharu'l had ordered the digging of the hole; the children had done it with their bare hands, using no more than a knife to loosen the soil; it went under the footing of the palm trunks.

Davie had asked Plandok to do these things, waiting for an opportunity to speak to her on Pulau Gangsa. She stood beside Hare now, remembering the plan of the attack as Davie had told it to her.

By the time Hare was ready to fire again the boats were in the shallows, their people were splashing ashore. There were too many targets. But coolly and deliberately he put two balls into the bottom of the first boat to hamper their return. Once again there was a roar as he fired, followed by laughter and shouting and threats. Behind him in the great room the children were in a fury of excitement. There was a beginning of hysteria. The boys were running in a small compact, agitated group round the keep. The night was furious with sound, and the birds, woken out of the palm tops, were threshing through the leaves and rising clear and shrieking and wheeling to shriek again. It was a demented parody of battle. All through the trash below the trees he could hear sounds, as if the young men were making noise deliberately, trying to intimidate him with noise. They were shouting their views on him into the rustle of the night air. They were calling for Plandok. They were threatening him with unimaginable indignities.

He turned and fired again at the last of the three canoes. The first were already in the shelter of the seaward palms.

Once he said to Plandok: 'I should have cut *all* the trees,' but knew, as he said it, that the heat would have been intolerable. He fired down into them now, not aiming his shot but using it for warning.

All the time Davie and Hugh Johnson were freeing the lashings on the north face and moving the saplings and the bamboo aside.

Hare's own mood matched the crescendo of the sound. He went to the north firing platform, took up the guns there and fired them blind into the green below him. He reloaded and fired again. The shouting and the taunts and the laughter came closer and closer, but he saw nothing now; there was only noise to shoot at—and noise was not enough.

In the keep the children were screaming. He bellowed at Plandok, still standing quite still on the southern firing platform: 'Go in and quiet them!'

She said: 'If it is your wish,' and went.

The escape was going to be easier even than it had promised to be. They would not need the hole that they had dug now. She went up the outer stair to Hare's pavilion and opened the hatch that led below. The hysteria had become real. She dealt with it firmly and effectively, slapping faces, shaking, pushing. She forced order on them and then, when they were subdued enough and had overcome the outbreaks which had followed each successive shot that Hare fired, she led them to the hole in the wall. The boys joined them; in three minutes they were gone.

Around them the noise of the attackers beat on against the palisade: the thresh of fronds, the snap of breaking branches, the bellowing of the young, hilarious voices.

Still Hare could not see them, could not see enough to aim at. The light of the moon was deceptive, its shadows concealing. He was surrounded by laughter and shouted words and threats that seemed to have no meaning and insults that had no purpose. The moment seemed to have come when there was no point in attempting to defend the stockade itself. No reinforcement had reached him from Direction. He withdrew to join Plandok in the keep—at least it would be easy to defend the keep.

She stood at the hatch that led down into the children's quarters. The hatch itself was closed again.

He said hurriedly: 'They are quiet now.'

She answered: 'Yes, they are quiet.'

He began to reload all four guns, placing one at each corner as he did so.

The shouting was continuous around the fence of the stockade. They were beating at it, hammering at it, attempting to break it down.

He thought he saw movement beyond the hut of the boys and fired at it. He fired at a shadow at the main gate. He ran from corner to corner, firing, reloading, firing. The room filled with powder smoke that drifted slowly with the night wind, the smell of it pungent in the nostrils.

He developed a method. There was a ramrod for each gun, a powder-horn for each gun, balls for each gun; and he fired and fired and fired. He ran from one to the other. He was no longer attempting to persuade them that the place was defended by a force. The important thing was to fire the guns. He also had progressed into hysteria.

He set fire to the keep himself, knocking over the whale-oil lamp as he rushed from one corner to another. There was a powder-horn close to it and it flared, and the flame leapt to the hangings and from there to the roof, and at once the place was ablaze. From the roof it leapt to the trash under the palm crests. The trees themselves burnt like dry torches in the wind and the laughter died as the flames rose.

He stood appalled, still for the first time since the sighting of the boats. The sweat was running from him, his eyes were distraught. Then he shouted: 'The children! The children!' and scrabbled for the bolt of the hatch.

Beside it Plandok said calmly: 'There are no children.' And when, on his knees, he looked up at her, stricken, she said: 'They have gone. It is time for us to go.'

Without question he turned and followed her down the stair. She led the way towards the gate, but halfway there he staggered, caught himself, stood propped with his arm against a trunk, and then moved slowly round to face the burning keep. It was eerily beautiful through the slender columns of the palms.

She thought, watching him and watching the flames, that everything that she had done, everything that was of significance since she came to him, had been marked with fire: the fire in his cabin on the first day, the fire that burnt the body of the Kling woman, the fire under the head, and the fire that brought the birds, the fire that ended the power of the head, the fire that burnt the canoe, and now the splendour of this transcendent flame.

Her eyes went back to Hare. He stood awkwardly, leaning his weight against a tree. There was in his face an expression of bewilderment and of pain—physical pain. She said at last: 'The fire comes this way. We must go.' But he made no attempt to go.

The heat of the flames reached them now and she half turned to go by herself. Still Hare made no move. Finally she went to him and took his arm. He came without protest, but slowly, walking with a heavy, uncertain tread. At the fourth step he staggered and put his arm across her shoulder. It was obvious even to the girl that it was done without other intent, simply to save himself. The strength had gone out of him. They followed the curve of the path to the head of the gully that led to the beach, and again he stumbled. His right foot dragged. He did not speak at all.

In the gully they lost the light of the flames. She groped in the darkness. Increasingly she was aware that she was leading him, that he had lost his mastership. When they came to the clearing just before the beach the flames in a new uprush lit them again, and she turned to look at his face and found it out of drawing, contorted on the right side, but she was too ignorant to read any significance into it. She only knew that he was exhausted to the point of physical collapse.

She said: 'Sit here and wait. The boats from Direction will come.'

He spoke for the first time—thickly, the words hesitant. 'Don't leave me!' Very heavily he lowered himself to the ground, sat for a moment in almost childish obedience, and then lay slowly back.

She stood looking down on him. He was in shadow now. She could see only his shape on the ground. It looked collapsed, shrunken, in a sense pitiful. She herself stood free and strong. This was the climax of all her plots and her scheming, the moment that she had worked for, the moment when their roles were reversed. Strangely, it had no savour.

Still she stood, waiting some sign that would guide her, but no sign came.

The young men had come away from the fire. They were shouting to one another through the darkness of the palms.

She could hear Shepherd's voice. 'There wasna a sign o' the bastard. He musta got clean awa'.'

Another voice called: 'We searched the place. There was light enough. We'd 'a' seen him if he'd bin there.'

A third voice asked: 'And the girl?'

Shepherd's voice said: 'I wasna worrit aboot the wee de'il. She'd win clear o' the Day o' Judgement. Come awa' tae the boats!'

The shouting went on, and she heard the thud of oars and the splashing in the water, but she did not change her position.

At last, when the noise had diminished imperceptibly into silence, she dropped to her knees beside him. She said: 'Do you want me?' and in the four words surrendered her victory.

Hare's voice answered thickly: 'Come!'

When he made no move she loosed her sarong and, with a gesture that was almost of desperation, freed the silk binding of the kris and dropped it on the sand. Then she lowered herself to his arms.

He tried to clasp her, but his right arm fell away useless. He muttered: 'I don't know,' his words so slurred that she could hardly distinguish them. He made another effort. His left arm came round her and he pulled her awkwardly against him with it and then, because the effort exhausted him, lay still, panting.

Mockingly over the water came the words of the young men's song:

'When the ba' was over
They a' went hame tae rest.
They said they liked th' music
But . . .'

As if he had heard it, Hare made a fresh effort. It was horrible. He moved convulsively, like an animal dying. Even his fingers had the splayed and aimless groping of the approach of death. Yet he was trying desperately to do what he had done triumphantly all his life.

The girl drew away from him, and he fought with his left hand to hold her and somehow that increased the horror of the moment so that when she jerked herself finally from him she was repulsed and sickened. She had no knowledge of the mechanics of a cerebral haemorrhage. She knew only that he was by some sudden change destroyed. Her quick explorations had told her that he was sexless. She remembered the terrible word for impotence, the dark cloud that hangs always above a harem.

Her nerve broke suddenly and she struggled free and ran, silent and terrified, to the sea. At its edge she sank down, half sitting, half kneeling, one hand on the sand. For a minute she breathed heavily as if she had run a race. After that she sat utterly immobile, only her mind swirled in a series of distorted images.

# Twenty-six

DAVIE WATCHED her from the margin of the trees. The moon was setting. She was not against the path of its light, but she was silhouetted against the lesser darkness of the water.

Far down the lagoon the young men were still singing at the oars. It was no longer possible to hear the words and the ancient, bawdy song was transmuted by the alchemy of distance into something martial and pompous.

His own mind was moving swiftly. He had been shocked into honesty. He was aware at last that he had never ceased to need Plandok, that he had given up the hope of possessing her only because of a weakness in his own composition. It was true that by the end of the planning of the attack he had all but persuaded himself that he was freeing Sharu'l, but he knew now that Sharu'l had never held any importance in his mind. He had attempted to transfer his need for Plandok to her because he had been overwhelmed by the strength and purpose of Hare, and now Hare was broken. He knew that Hare was not wounded—the young men had fired no shot all through the night—he was not burnt; but by some intervention the power had been taken from him. Davie had heard the brief murmured words of the passage between him and Plandok, he had seen dimly the brief, abortive embrace; and he knew that Hare's reign was over for ever.

On that thought he walked down the beach, silent on the sand.

Standing behind Plandok, he said softly: 'Now we must love each other again.' And she turned in one quick movement like a leopard and flung herself sobbing against him.

A long while after she said: 'We must go now.'

'Where? Tae New Selma?'

She answered bitterly: 'The other women reign there. They would not suffer me.'

He knew this to be true. 'Tae the west island, then?'

She paused for a moment, remembering its first innocent episodes. 'It is too late for that also,' she said sadly.

That too he knew. 'Where, then?'

'Long ago I made a plan.' She nodded out towards the riding light of the brig in the anchorage. 'She sails at dawn to the east—'

He broke in quickly. 'She wadna tak' us. Hare has warned her captain —Leisk also. They dinna want desairtions.'

'Hare'—she spoke now with the ruthlessness of the very young—'does not matter any more.'

'But they dinna know that—and there's aye Downie. And Leisk will be oot before she sails in th' morning.'

'That is not in my plan,' said Plandok quietly. 'It is my plan that we sail out through the reef before the dawn. You know the ways of the English ships. She sails for the east. With this wind you know the course that she will take. We too will sail on that course, and when she comes up with us far out at sea she will take us on board.'

She put it simply and plainly, as if there were no alternative. Anyone who knew her less intimately than Davie might have thought that she believed that there was no alternative. Davie knew that she had weighed the possibilities carefully and exactly, putting into the other balance of the scale the impossibility of beating back to the shelter of the islands against the monsoon wind and the current at this time of the year.

'Well?' she said, and when he hesitated: 'We must not be afraid.'

He answered her at once: 'I am not afraid.' He held her to him, all the old magic of her body in his hands more potent than ever before. At long last he asked: 'And Hare? What do we do about Hare?'

'He does not matter now,' she replied indifferently.

'We canna leave him tae dee!' in his emotion his accent broadened.

'He will die when it is written,' she said indifferently, then with the inconsequence of women: 'My sarong is with him.'

Davie said: 'Wait!' and strode back to the clearing.

Hare still lay where he had lowered himself. Davie bent over him and heard his laboured words: 'Where's Plandok? Tell her I need her.'

Davie disregarded the command. 'Plandok has gone. We will tell Downie of ye. Th' boats will come as quickly as they may. It is time for me tae go.'

He groped and found the sarong. His fingers missed in the darkness the exquisite ivory of the hilt of the kris. He picked up the sarong and walked back to the beach and held it out to the girl.

'Th' canoe is at th' south end,' he said. 'It is time we went tae it.'

The voices were uncertain and querulous in the night. One was Downie's, the other Davie identified as that of the second mate of the

*Windhover*. They could see her boat lying off the edge of the beach, a man holding her at the bows.

Downie was answering in the agitated falsetto in which his voice cast itself in moments of crisis. They could not distinguish his words at once but after a while they heard whole sentences. 'I could not go with all the shooting. He would have fired on me. You must see that, mister! And the men from Ross's island—they'd have sunk the boat if they'd seen me. You would not have gone yourself, mister. Now would yer?'

The second mate, stubbornly pursuing a line of argument, answered: 'You said yourself his men told you he needed you.'

'Before the firing!' Downie protested. 'Before the firing it was he told them. After it I could *not* go. It would have been as much as my life's worth—from him or from Ross's men. You got to see that, mister.'

The second mate was silent, baffled.

Davie's voice disembodied from the outer water, cut sharply across the silence: 'Tak' th' boat straight, Downie. Ye'll find Hare in the clearing by th' landing place. He's hurt.'

There was a moment of shocked silence.

Then Downie's voice croaked: 'Who are you?'

Davie disregarded the question. 'Get the boat doon there fast! He's by his lane.'

The second mate of the *Windhover* said: 'D'ye hear that? He's alone and he's hurt. God damn it, man! You got no guts in you at all?'

Downie mumbled, but even his mumbling came across the water: 'How do I know he's alone? How do I know it's not a trap?'

Davie asked wearily: 'Dae we need a trap tae get ye?' He put the paddle into the water again, driving the canoe up to the north past the landing place of the village. 'Get doon tae him!' he called back warningly, in a sudden disgust at the man's cowardice.

Again Downie shouted despairingly: 'Who are you? But who are you?' as if it were more important for him to know the identity of the voice than to serve his master.

The last words they heard were in the voice of the second mate of the *Windhover:* 'For Chris' sake get on with it, ye cowardly bastard!'

They paddled steadily towards the gap in the reef. Plandok had said no word in all this time. Slowly, very slowly, the old splendour began to return to them. Their paddles moved in a green fire of phosphorescence. Fish streaked below them in arrows of brightness. The bourdon of the reef enveloped them, eliminating all man-made sound. Their backs were towards the riding light of the *Windhover* and the intermittent upward lickings of flame on Pulau Bras. Ahead of them the night held only stars.

They passed through the reef before the dawn, the broken gleam of the surf on either side and the thunder of it constant in their ears, and rapidly, the current and the wind carrying them, they moved into the emptiness of the outer sea.

At dawn the islands had sunk behind them, the palms were diminished to a bar of weathered copper on the sea rim. At sun-up they had lost even the palm tops.

They were not watching astern, they were waiting silently for the first brilliance of the sun itself over the horizon a little off the starboard bow to assure themselves that they were on the *Windhover*'s course for Sunda Strait. Plandok marked the first flash of it with a gasp of pure pleasure. She was still staring at it, shading her eyes with her fingers, when Davie turned to search for sign of the *Windhover*'s topsails.

The horizon astern of them was empty.

Turning from the sun, Plandok said: 'Today there are no gulls.'

'They dinna fly to leeward,' answered Davie, almost roughly. 'If they did they couldna get back against th' wind wi' full crops.'

'But we'—she spoke almost mockingly—'we fly to windward.'

'Aye,' he said quietly, and for the second time the realization of what she had proposed flooded in on him. He sat silent, staring at the sea's rim to the westward.

The monsoon sea ran with them, breaking in small crests—easy, measured, and regular. The noise of the white caps was like the breathing of the sea.

'It is enough,' said Plandok at last. 'Now we must wait.' She brought the canoe round in a wide sweep into the eye of the wind.

Davie cast off the halliard and smothered the sail as it came down. When he had put a lashing on it he stood up, holding to the mast with one hand. The canoe swung up and down in the lift of the sea. To the west the horizon was still empty, a perfect line of dark blue against the fading blue of the night. He said: 'There's no' a glimmer o' sail yet.'

In the steering place Plandok lifted the paddle and stowed it carefully along the bottom. When it was done to her satisfaction she said with a grave confidence: 'She will come.'

Against his will the doubts that had fleeted through Davie's mind forced him to ask: 'An' if she doesna stop?'

'She will stop,' Plandok answered. There was no place for any doubt in her as she crept forward to Davie's arms.